Endangered
Species

Stuart Anderson

Published in 2011 by New Generation Publishing

First Edition

The first part of a probable Trilogy of books by
Stuart Anderson following the delusional
adventures of Darwin Litton.

All the characters are fictional … except for
Darwin. You know who you are.

The next installment is centered largely in Brazil
where the author is based, and is called Survival.
Available shortly in paperback and at a cinema
near you.

for Ems X

CHAPTER ONE

It was a dreary misty evening in Bangor's dull and sleepy suburbs. Darwin edged his car to a crawl and slipped forward, straining on his belt harness to focus in closer on the entrance to Klienan Park. He had noticed a car parked suspiciously on the corner – it was a light blue Ford Escort, registration number BAZ 2333. There was possibly a small dent on the rear left wing and a dark red or maybe purple "go-faster" stripe running down the side. It was a limited edition Razor model, with a 1.6 Litre engine. Darwin noted all the details meticulously in his little burgundy book. He brought his car to a jerky hand-break halt, and awkwardly unbuckled his belt to get an even closer look. The driver side window of his silver Mercedes slipped quietly down into its door and Darwin's face emerged and engaged with his target. He couldn't work out whether there where 2 people or just 1 in the car. He could see the driver quite clearly, but he couldn't decide whether the passenger side was a person's head or a head-rest.

This wasn't good enough. If the case went to court, then the barrister would be sure to catch him out on this point… "I'll ask you once again Mr Litton. Can you stand before this court today and say that there was definitely only one man in the car?" Darwin would wince and twitch and bubble something "Um, well not exactly but I'm almost certain…". The root-faced barrister would smile and drop his steely eyes to the floor, "Thank you Mr Litton, no further questions."

He knew simple mistakes like that could ruin a man's reputation and career. Darwin would have to be 100% sure of the facts or forget the whole damn thing. There was definitely no middle ground on something as important as this. He let his car roll forward a few feet more to give him a clearer look through the passenger side window of the Escort.

He could see better now. Definately one person, early forties, with short (almost shaven) hair. He seemed to be wearing a darkish suit, a light coloured shirt and a stripy tie, no facial hair, a bit podgy, and *the look of a gay* – as his mother would say. There were no lights coming from the car, no-one else in the street, and not another car to be seen for miles. Darwin was certain his suspect was up to no good; murder or a gang rape – or possibly both. The story was sure to be on TV and radio the following day. The police would make an urgent appeal for anyone who saw a blue saloon car in the vicinity of Klienan Park or Klienan Road at approximately 8 o'clock on Thursday evening. Darwin would be the star witness; he would have all the facts straight by the time he got home. In fact by the time he reached the bottom of the road he would have the police statement drafted and his court script written.

However, as in every other case, a different car would be parked suspiciously somewhere else along his way home, or a strange looking woman would be walking along the pavement with a funny look on her face, and so yet another mini-drama would take over, and a new case and a new adventure would begin for Darwin Litton – The Intrepid Adventurer.

There never was a murder or a gang rape in Klienan Park nor Klienan Road. The 'murderer' in the blue Ford Escort was waiting to pick his mother up from her weekly Bridge match, and had arrived 10 minutes early. He also wasn't gay, just bi-curious.

Darwin had completely forgotten about the blue escort by the time he reached home. As he pulled up outside the house he felt his stomach curdling and the weirdest lump of nothingness worked its way swiftly from his bladder, through his stomach, and right up to his heart. Just then, the driveway was flooded. A car with full beams on aimed and fired its enormous lasers straight into his squinting eyes, and lighting up the whole garden in an instance. It had been raining earlier and everything glistened excitedly like diamonds and silver in a cheap jewelry shop. The little mist that was left clung on to the light and swarmed along the beams as if it had a purpose in life; following the lasers, caressing around their ankles and neck. It almost made a whooshing noise, but not quite.

Darwin didn't flinch, he knew this was the moment of reckoning; the years of planning were finally coming to a head, his head in fact. An attack on him and his home was almost certainly underway. There were two choices open to him. The first involved a handgun, which he clearly didn't have. The second involved approaching the car like an adult and finding out who they were.

He walked alongside the Maroon Rover, probably an old 820 model, looked like a Vitesse, so obviously more than a few years old. He couldn't quite see the full registration but there were definitely two 4's and an 'A' at the start. Having left his little burgundy book in his glove compartment, he took a mental note of the details.

"Hi", he said confidently.

In the light Darwin's silhouette created a fine body of a man, early thirties, sharp grey suit, handsome jaw-line, with dark wavy hair. He was at least 6ft tall, slightly athletic, slightly brave, but mostly slightly shitting himself. He'd puffed himself up with broad shoulders, expanded chest, narrow waist, and a hard face. Darwin did a marvelous job at looking tough - he contorted his body into the shape of a warrior, relentless in his bravery, not once daring to expose the true blouse that lay underneath. If he was going down, he was going down like a man, standing up straight, solemn and expanded. He'd practiced this look for most of his life, frequently spending hours in front of a mirror, often naked, sometimes in his underpants, but always with grit determination.

He had read somewhere once that in the animal world most confrontations between same-species are really just a battle of wits – the one that looked the toughest and the puffiest would win just by looking toughier and puffier, and that the other one would back down. Apparently it was something to do with animals wanting to preserve their own race, battling for animal territory and sex and drugs, but not actually harming one another because it would weaken their own species and that would go against their instinct. He thought it might also be something to do with DNA but his mind had started drifting by that stage of his reading and words had stopped penetrating passed his eyes. This happened quite a lot. His eyes would dart across the page, digesting every letter, word, and sentence with a desperate hunger, but somewhere between the eyes and brain, the little letters would jumble themselves up, go all soft around the edges, and drift away like angels. He consoled himself with the fact that his subconscious was probably absorbing them and that some day when he actually needed the information; his internal secretary would go and fetch the facts he needed.

As he got closer to the car window, he could see that there were at least 4 people in the vehicle; two of them had peeky hats, like chauffeur's ones. "Delta Charlie, two-forty-niner" rung out from the gap in the passenger side window. He struggled to think quickly … is that a taxi or the police? He hoped for the police but either way he'd decided that his life was probably not going to end tonight and it certainly made him feel better about going into his dark house alone.

Whoever they were, he'd make up some lame excuse for them to stay for a few minutes while he got in to the house, turned the lights on, and checked under all the beds for bogey men. His hard-man face relaxed and a little smile crept onto his left lip. He looked a bit like Elvis Presley…for a moment. "Good evening officers, how can I help you?"

'At last' he thought. All his investigative work would now surely pay off. Whatever their problem was, he was sure that he could add that elusive bit of detail they needed to solve their case. An exact location of a car, a registration number, a precise time, or a telltale piece of evidence that would make all the other bits of their case fall into place. "Good evening sir, would you know a … Mr…Darwin…Litton?" The policeman checked his notes to confirm the name.

Darwin liked easy questions. "Yes indeed I do, he lives here and you're looking right at him officer."
He immediately began to worry that he'd been too smug or sarcastic in that reply, he genuinely hadn't meant to, but it just came out that way. He had meant to be polite and helpful and had ended up looking like Elvis on crack. However Darwin was confident that

he could rectify matters, and reinstate their faith in him as a pillar of society and a potential source of reliable investigative skills and knowledge.

"*Dick-head*"… thought the cop.
"I'm afraid we have some bad news for you Mr Litton, may we come in?" said the cop.

"*Oh Shit*" … thought Darwin.
"Yes, of course you can, I'm sorry, I'll just open the door, I've only just arrived back from work - a bit late today, let me show you the way, um .. well, sure it is – that's for definite officer", said Darwin for no apparent reason.

All thoughts of being of assistance to the police investigation quickly left and a pounding headache descended on Darwin's crown. This was worse than he thought; he had prepared all his life for being questioned and being attacked - all for no good reason, and all to no avail. But he hadn't prepared for this; hadn't prepared for bad news that had to be delivered by cops. That's very bad news indeed. He decided it must have been a car accident; why else would cops come out to the house? If someone in the family had just dropped dead or something, then the hospital or a relative would have rung. He also decided that it must involve death, because serious injury, maiming, or even loss of limbs could be notified by a telephone call - he knew that much. Yes, someone had died in a car accident, but who? His sister didn't drive so that was unlikely, but of course she could have been a passenger. His brother was away in ....

"Mr Litton, please take a seat" Two of the cops had come into the house.

One was the boss, or the sergeant - he was the bad-news breaker, and the other was the young constable, obviously brought along for moral support and to make the tea and serve the biscuits. There was of course the possibility that this could be a scam; when was the last time you saw cops in a maroon Rover 820 Vitesse? Just in case, Darwin carefully inspected them. The uniforms seemed real enough. The boss was a man in his late 50s with short grey hair, whiskey aged face, yellow teeth and certainly smelt like a cop. He looked tired, very tired. Either he'd been working very, very hard, or alternatively maybe this was very, very bad news.

The other was quite a bit younger – mid twenties, swarthy, dark hair, white teeth and smelt like a chemist. He had very nearly grown into his uniform. Young cops always seemed to look like that. Darwin was sure that the cop-tailors specifically only designed uniforms for older men, and he wondered what the difference in shape was. Perhaps it was the hips or stomach that changes when you get older – whatever it was, he looked uncomfortable and out of shape in his shiny new uniform. Maybe his own one was in the cleaners, and he'd just borrowed this uniform from an old friend.

Darwin eventually did as he was told, and sat down on the edge of the settee. His migraine was now having a firework display behind his left eye, so he took a few tablets from his inside breast pocket and gulped them down without a drink. He always carried tablets, and he always swallowed them without a drink.

The cops sat down too – boss choose the beige leather swivel chair with brown piping located opposite Darwin, and the young one went for the blue velour settee next to Darwin, presumably close enough to offer his sincere condolences and maybe even hold his hand and say 'there, there' when the bad news was broken. "Can I just confirm that you are Darwin Litton?", said boss quietly.
"Yes", Darwin retorted. He was sure they'd been through this before.

"Mr Litton, I'm afraid we have some bad news for you. It's about your fiancée, Mrs Suzie Marlin, she was found with a fatal gunshot wound at her home this morning. We had been trying to reach you all day, but we couldn't get an answer on your telephone and …"

The great lump of nothingness suddenly re-appeared and followed its usual predictable path, thumping recklessly into his heart. Reality had snuck up behind him and dug her nails through his back and ripped out his guts. Tragedies never happened to Darwin. He had never lost anyone; no-one important had ever died in his life. All around him people led exciting, disease-infested, death-ridden lives, but not him.

As a kid he used to make up very unlikely things – he told his teacher that a wolf had eaten his dog. He very nearly started to believe it himself, and huffed about the house for weeks on end. "Poor Darwin, poor wee thing – just look at him, he loved that dog", he imagined everyone was saying. They weren't of course, as there were a few flaws in the story – primarily that he didn't have a dog - that in itself would have been far too interesting. And of course there was no wolf, and even if there was, it probably wouldn't eat dogs, especially not ones that didn't exist.

No, Darwin definitely did not have an eventful life. For that very reason it would make this situation more gut-wrenching than usual – he had no preparation for bad news, no skills picked up through his life, no experiences to draw on.

He remembered watching spitefully as little Johnny Mossbank was publicly removed from Mrs Black's classroom in Primary School because a runaway tractor had trampled his Mum and little sister. Johnny's sister, June, had died instantly and his mum was critical – she lost an arm and 2 toes and would probably spend the rest of her days in a wheelchair. Johnny – the lucky bastard, nothing exciting like that ever happened to Darwin.

And, true to form, today would be no exception.

"Suzie Marlin?", quizzed Darwin disappointingly, "I haven't seen her in 4 years, we used to go out together, sure … but only for about 6 months… and that was years ago." He tried to get a picture of Suzie in his mind, he nearly got it, apart from the nose – just couldn't quite picture that bit. He remembered her bum though, and her tits, he'd never forget detail like that. Darwin slumped back; relief and disappointment fought a gloves-off battle in his head.

Boss jiggered uncomfortably and squeaked loudly against the leather. "There um … "
"… seems to be a misunderstanding", constable finished it off for him. Darwin caught boss looking over at his colleague for support. They couldn't decide whether to feel embarrassed or whether that made Darwin their chief suspect - was Darwin telling the truth? Maybe he had killed her. If so, he certainly wouldn't break down and confess on the first meeting with the police. Chances are that he would say he hasn't seen her in years. They decided instead to keep their options open and said they had to go back to the car and check some facts.

Darwin remembered Suzie was a bit of a loner, she had no family, was dragged up in a children's home and had very few friends. Surely however she must have picked up at least 1 friend in the last few years - maybe someone she worked with or met in the supermarket. Surely to goodness he wasn't her closest living relative ... he wasn't even a relative. He was a brief ex-boyfriend. What was going on?

By this stage relief had passed, and lost its moment. Disappointment had grabbed the opportunity and was now teasing him. Excitement then jumped into the arena. Excitement!! Yes, he was now part of something really exciting, a real investigation. Why was Suzie being traced to him? How did the cops find him? Was there some clue that drove them to him? Oh yes, and the question of who killed Suzie?, but that was relatively far down his list as it didn't directly involve him.

After a few minutes, the cops arrived back, eyes to the floor, never looking up, "There appears to be some confusion Mr Litton, we hope we didn't shock you too much and I'm very sorry to have disturbed you. We'll let ourselves out"

"You're sorry? You silly fuckers, you almost gave me a heart attack, and besides how did you get my name? What made you think she was my fiancée?, how in hell could you have made a mistake like that? You shit-for-brains pair of twats" ... he thought.

"That's no problem, I'll see you out", he said instead.

He reckoned that he'd have plenty of time to sort out the rest of the details. Right now he needed to think. He needed to examine every possibility and mull over every scenario. This was his moment…the one he'd been waiting for all his life, and he certainly wasn't going to share any of his strategies with the cops. He walked quickly and purposefully to the door, "well, there you go, anyone can make a mistake, easily done, yes indeed, never mind eh?", and practically shoved them down the steps towards the maroon Rover 820 Vitesse, registration AGJ 440N – he noted the number, just in case.

The mist had nearly gone now and was totally disinterested in the beams of light that it once flirted with. So the lights dipped their farewells and the Rover withdrew a long reverse out of the driveway, swung left, then screeched right down the road, taking it's lights with it, but the mist didn't care any more.

Darwin waved goodbye. He had no idea why, it just seemed polite to wave the boys off and stay on the step until they got safely down the road. His mother had always reminded him that there is no excuse for bad manners. Then he sprinted back to the kitchen. He turned on the lights and the room shook itself alive in an instant. The chrome kitchen sparkled like new, which is only natural because it was just a few months old, cost him over a hundred grand, and was cleaned daily by a team of maids from a local agency. Every time he turned on the lights it seemed to surprise him just how bright it was, and he squinted briefly as he ran to the fridge to get a Budweiser.

He didn't care about the big bad men hiding in the cupboards waiting to kill him anymore. That wasn't interesting enough today. For now he had Suzie to think about, and this was a real drama. He just had to phone someone and tell them, but then he decided not to. Exaggerating, then phoning and telling; that's what he did with SMDs (small to medium-sized dramas), and the usual ones he had made up. This one was a biggy, extra large, and real! He was going to nurture this one alone for a bit longer. He liked it.

CHAPTER TWO

At the station the next morning, Sergeant Middlemoss - the boss who delivered the news to Darwin the night before - was not very happy. "What the fuck were you doing Simpson?" he screamed.

Everyone looked around suspiciously, each knowing that there was no one in the station called Simpson, and therefore he could in fact have been talking to any of them. Boss had just joined them a few months earlier and obviously still hadn't managed to learn many of their names. Today wasn't the right time to correct him and the Simpsons knew it. A couple of people apologized "sorry Serg." Boss knew that there wasn't anyone called Simpson. It saved him having to shout at 3 or 4 people individually. The ones who deserved to be shouted at normally owned up en mass.

"How could you be so stupid?"

The Simpson's bowed their heads, "sorry Serg."

"What in God's name where we doing at that man's house last night. We nearly gave the guy a fucking heart attack, and in case you hadn't noticed, we've also got a murderer on the loose. Thompson, I'm going into my office for 5 minutes to let you and the Simpsons make up a really good excuse, so you better get scheming, and it better be very, very good because I'm fuck'n pissed off at the moment, okay?" There was a Thompson in the room so he said "okay, boss".

The police had arrived at Suzie's house at about 9am because a neighbour heard something peculiar. Eventually they spotted her body remains through the window and broke down the door, Sweeny style. They spoke to several of the neighbours who all confirmed that Suzie lived alone and had no family, but had a regular boyfriend that called around sometimes. They said that she was quiet, pretty, very pleasant, but kept herself to herself, always said 'hello' and smiled shyly but never really stopped for any prolonged chitchat or gossip.

Whilst going through her personal things in her bedroom DC Thompson stumbled on a shiny tin box, where he found an old life policy and a blood donor form, both of which named Darwin Litton as the person to contact in the event of an accident, or her death, loss of limb, or any major organ. Along with it they found a few soppy love letters from Darwin and one of his old business cards. The next door neighbour confirmed that Suzie had indeed got a boyfriend, and said his name was Darwin, she remembers being introduced once.

That all seemed conclusive enough to DC Thompson, and so the Boss and his assistant were called in to break the bad news to Darwin.

However, after the well-publicized escapade at Darwin's house the previous night, Thompson thought it might be a good idea to go back to the scene of the murder and to talk to some of the neighbours again, before the boss got back to the station. Two of the other neighbours said that they were sure the boyfriend was in fact an older man with gray hair, and certainly nothing like Darwin's description.

Mrs Johnston - the women next door who told Thompson that the boyfriend was called Darwin - was still adamant about her statement. In fact even more so now, she distinctly remembered Suzie introducing Darwin, and the reason that she remembered so clearly was that the Second World War ended and Sir Edmond Hilary landed on the moon the same day that they were introduced. Thompson resisted the sudden urge to punch the silly old senile nut repeatedly in the face until she stopped breathing. He even resisted stealing her pension book or tying her up in her fucking 'scullery', and so instead smiled politely and reversed his fat ass out the door.

When he went back to Suzie's bedroom, he started to notice a few more signs, for example the life policy and the donor forms were all several years old, and the letters from Darwin, although undated, had actually turned yellow and obviously weren't written within the past year or so. Things weren't looking good for Thompson, and the Boss was looking for a scalp for his new trophy cabinet.

"I'm really sorry serg., it was a genuine mistake, you see what happened was ....", and so he recounted the story, adding a few extra details in about other sightings of a man called Darwin, so that he didn't look like a complete prick. It didn't work. "You're a complete prick aren't you Thompson", the boss said glumly. Thompson realized that his disguise had failed miserably and he humbly nodded in agreement.

The Boss quickly wiped the slate clean and marched purposefully back into the main office. "Anyway, what's done is done, and we've a murder case to solve, so lets get mov'n – Martin, you take a few uniforms and go round the neighbours again, probably best not to disturb Mrs Johnston today. Paul, get me details of all calls made into and out of the victims house for the past 6 months. Simon, Brian, find out where she works, go see her colleagues, talk to as many people as possible. Sam you come with me, we're going to find her real boyfriend." Everyone scuttled around frantically ... except Thompson.

He was doing his little-boy-lost impersonation, and huffed in the corner, kicking the wall lightly and pushing his hands hard into his deep pockets. Boss spotted Thompson in the corner. "Thompson, you go and see that nice Mr Litton man and apologise for being a complete prick and see if he knows any more about our victim." It was a crappy job, but Thompson was glad to be given any job to do, in fact he was just relieved to be acknowledged and allowed to move out of the corner for a bit.

CHAPTER THREE

That nice Mr Litton wouldn't be at home today though; he had much more important things to do. He called in to work first to explain that he'd be away for a few days on important business and that he would be on his mobile if anyone needed him urgently. A few people grunted disapprovingly but he didn't really give a toss. He owned the business and he was paying their wages, and besides, he was happy and this really was urgent business. He toppled out of the office, turned off his mobile and took off at great speed, clearly a man with a purpose and a goal, a man with a mission, a man with a real grown-up adventure! Of course that didn't last very long. He reached the bottom of the street and then realized that he had no idea where he was going, or why, so he went home to think and re-group.

When Darwin approached the driveway, he could see a stranger walking away from his door in the direction of a stranger car, looking a bit scruffy, probably trying to sell something, he guessed. His curly black hair was too long and kept blowing into strange shapes in the wind. He also had an enormous fat arse, which stuck out from under his jacket. When he turned around he seemed to have a friendly enough face, quite fat and jolly so he decided to give him a chance. Darwin pulled up beside him in his car and pretended to be looking for something in his glove compartment while he stared sideways across at the stranger, just long enough to be able to produce a photo-fit, should it be required down at the station later – which it never would be.

"Hi, can I help you?", Darwin finally moved away from the car. "Yes, are you Darwin Litton?" probed the stranger formally. "I am", Darwin made his way past him. "My name's Detective Constable Harry Thompson, I was wondering if I could have a few minutes of your time please?" Darwin stopped and smiled inwardly. "Sure, come on in"

This was the break Darwin was looking for. An opportunity to fill in some gaps - a lot of gaps, as he knew practically nothing about what had happened. Darwin popped the chrome kettle on and offered Harry a seat at the chrome breakfast bar. "It was kind of my fault... ", began Harry. "What was?" interrupted Darwin. Harry continued nervously "That incident last night when the sergeant came round to break the bad news to you. It was my fault you see, I made a mistake at the scene." He could see that Harry was feeling guilty and subdued, so Darwin knew this was his chance to drain as much information as possible from him. "Well actually I was just down at my solicitors there and ….", Darwin quickly responded. "Aw shit sir, please don't make a complaint, I'll be out on my ear. I've already got one written warning on my file" interrupted Harry desperately.

Darwin knew people - he knew how to play them like Tommy Cooper knew how to play a white rabbit. He'd taken a shot from the hip and landed right between Harry's eyes. Darwin knew the rest would be simple. "It nearly gave me a heart attack you know, I can't go to work I'm so wound up, and I never slept a wink last night", Darwin was going to milk this for all it was worth. He may not be able to put a key in a door or open a tin of beans, but he could manipulate a confused mind with little effort.

"So tell me what happened?", Darwin snapped.
"It was a legitimate mistake you see what happened was ... ", and Harry re-told the story he'd made up for the boss, lies and all. Darwin knew which parts of it were lies, so he was able to work out the true story from amongst the guff. Darwin had been telling stories like this for years. Harry just about stopped short of telling him that Suzie had been eaten by a wolf. But that didn't matter; Darwin had plenty of stuff to be getting on with. "Well it seems like a genuine mistake"

"It really was, Mr Litton. If it wasn't for that silly moose next door, we wouldn't have bothered you."
"Yeah, Mrs Johnston" said Darwin, "...I knew I should have killed her too". He stared steely-eyed over his glasses into Harry's eyes. He was enjoying this. Harry pretended to be shocked and then burst out laughing to make sure Darwin new that he was in on

the joke, so Darwin laughed too and decided he liked Harry after all. They shared a few cups of coffee together and Harry confided all his worries and problems down at the station. Darwin listened intently and laughed and agreed in all the right places. Harry liked Darwin too, but then again Darwin knew he would. By the time Harry was ready to leave, they had practically exchanged bodily fluids and were definitely on each other's Christmas card list for next year.

Harry had also achieved what he wanted – Mr. Litton probably wouldn't be putting in a complaint about him. Harry had also been asking a few questions about Suzie throughout the conversation and knew a bit more about her now. He knew she had nice tits, but unfortunately she had no nose. That was something to be going on with.

Darwin on the other hand knew quite a lot more. Susie had been found at about 9 o'clock in the morning with a single bullet through her head, fired at close range. No one had heard any shots, and nobody was seen leaving or entering the house that day. Suzie had a boyfriend who visited sometimes - he was mature, graying hair, tall, and wasn't called Darwin.

Darwin also knew quite a lot of other things about Suzie that the cops didn't know. When they were together, he had persuaded her to try and find her natural parents, and they subsequently traced her father with the help of a private investigation agency run by an old school friend of Darwin. Suzie was over the moon that she had finally found her father. Unfortunately daddy didn't quite feel the same way about her, and wrote a very polite letter back to Suzie telling her to fuck away off and annoy someone else. In fact he was even kind enough to provide someone for her to fuck away off and annoy instead. He told her about a sister that she didn't know she had. This sister had ended up in a children's home in Wales. Suzie always promised she would find and visit her sister, but never actually got around to it when she was with Darwin.

Darwin sat quietly in the kitchen on his own. He always enjoyed being on his own, but for some reason he suddenly felt lonely. This was actually quite unusual as his paranoia normally kept him company. He took out a chrome box from the utility room and hunted through 20 or 30 pictures until he found one of him and Suzie. For a moment he thought he couldn't even remember her, then one after another the memories came flooding back – the fabulous nights they'd spent together, the holiday, the restaurants, the walks in the park, the cinema, the bowling. He had no idea how much he had missed her; they had crammed a life full of experiences into just 6 months.

A wave of remorse or fear or maybe just paranoia washed right over him. He felt it run through his veins and soak into his skin - the deepest emotion he'd ever felt in his life. Utter hopelessness and joy and sadness all at once. He missed Suzie so much, yet he hadn't seen her in years. He couldn't explain that.

If only he hadn't shagged her boss in the toilets at her office Christmas party, then the two of them could still be together now.

CHAPTER FOUR

Port Sinton was a small working fishing village on the South West coast of Wales. A quiet and picturesque little spot with about 100 houses, 2 shops, 2 pubs, a garage, and a video rental shop. One of the shops doubled up as a bakery and the other as a tobacconist / newsagent. One of the pubs did food during lunch and early evenings - the other one sold nuts, and had a pile of betting dockets under the bar. The garage practically sold everything that you needed to survive outside of normal shop opening hours, but the video store sold nothing. There wasn't much in the way of industry in Port Sinton, except for a small clothing factory at the back of the garage which employed 11 people.

English people who came down at weekends and during the school holidays owned about a third of the houses. The locals hated them, but put up with them because they brought some new money into the area.

From Monday to Thursday the locals would sit in one or other of the pubs and slag off the English visitors. They talked cheerfully about the days when they used to burn the bastards out of their houses and murder their children. On the weekends they gracefully accepted drinks from their visitors and talked grudgingly about how close they had become to their new English friends.

From Monday to Thursday the English visitors would sit at home in England and talk about the dozy Welsh bastards who didn't have a brain between them. On the weekends they would buy them drinks and talk about how close they had become to their new Welsh friends.

And so life went on in Port Sinton; two sets of two-faced bastards co-existing. Like most good partnerships, they hated each other so much that they fell in love, and they had so little in common that they were practically clones.

Sally liked Flans bar the best – it was the one that sold nuts. Nobody knew who or what 'Flan' was, yet every weekend there'd be a different drunken story about it and they'd solve the riddle, then wake up the next morning and forget all about it. Flans just fell short of having sawdust on the floor. It was the preferred watering hole of the more mature section of the community, along with a select group of younger kids in long black coats who went there to soak up true old atmosphere and spirit. The beer was apparently better in Flans; which was most likely something to do with the fact that Dave had never cleaned the pipes and that gave it a richer blend. In Flans, beauty board and formica were making a strong comeback accompanied by browns, burgundies and golds.

Having said all of that, it was quite a cozy pub, where the locals could go and order a half and sit quietly in the corner, read their paper, and watch the racing in black and white whilst eating their nuts. It was one of those pubs where, when a stranger came in, they would all stop and stare until the stranger either left or said hello. When the stranger left they would all snigger and shake their heads in time together. If the stranger said hello, they'd grunt back disapprovingly, and return to their paper or the TV.

Sally arrived at about 4 o'clock and asked Dave for the time. "Its Four o'clock", he said without even looking at his watch. He didn't need to; he always knew the time.

"Half of Tonins please, Dave" chirped Sally. Dave picked a glass, filled it, and delivered it without once taking his eye off the 3:50 at Chepstow. He didn't have any money on it himself - he was the bookie. He just wanted the un-backed horses to win. His dad owned the pub and didn't really approve of Dave's bookie sideline.

Dave was somewhere between 25 and 50, and had pretty much given up on life generally. He had already completed the customary pilgrimage to the bright lights of London when he was 20 and arrived back shell-shocked 1 month later, so he had resigned himself to living in Port Sinton until he finally dropped dead, or another war started. His lack of anything positive showed clearly in his face, where half his muscles couldn't be bothered their arse moving when he spoke, and even his hair couldn't be bothered getting into a shade. How his heart kept pumping, nobody ever quite knew.

Sally put a pound on the bar and strolled over to a table beside Dick. "How are you today Dick?"
"I'm good thanks Sally, what about yourself? – you're looking great today. In fact I was just saying to Martha in the shop earlier, isn't Sally looking great today". A clump of cheesy spit cleverly hung on to each corner of his mouth as he spoke. "Thanks, Dick!", said Sally with just a hint of sarcasm.

Dick always had a fondness for Sally and never missed an opportunity to tell her how great she was. Unfortunately he was at least 30 years older than her, and he was grey, unshaven and smelt of cheese, which never really appealed to Sally too much. Especially after the night when one of the English weekend visitors got pissed and re-christened him "Cheesy-Dick" all weekend. That created a picture in Sally's mind that would pursue her to the grave, so she kept her distance.

Sally on the other hand did look really great, although a little drab. Everything was plain about her. Blonde hair swept into a ponytail and no makeup. It must have been her eyes that made her look great. They glistened brightly and they were full of hope. Sally had only lived in Port Sinton for 12 years, so obviously the sense of hopelessness hadn't quite had time to work on her completely yet. But some day she knew that she too would look like Dave.

"Have you any money on this?" asked Sally, motioning her head in the direction of the racing on TV. "I've a few quid on Toby's Luck, she's second at the moment, just about to make her move, I can tell by the sweat on Dave's brow – he knows I'm just about to clean him out, again!" Sally glanced over at Dave. Toby's Luck did actually look as if she was about to make a move, but Dave wasn't really sweating outwardly. The little beads of sweat were probably there okay, but they simply couldn't be persuaded to come to the surface of his skin.

Toby's Luck was making a strong move towards the front. Dick had £5 on it at 4 to 1 and had now moved to the edge of his seat where he was bopping up and down in time with his horse. Within a matter of seconds, Dick's horse was 2 lengths clear, smiling victoriously and galloping towards the winning post. Dave was unimpressed and took out his black drink tab book, opened it on Dick's page and wrote '-£5' and '+£25'.

Dick cheered and scooped his cheesy spit bits back into his mouth. Sally almost retched. Dave re-totaled Dick's tab behind the bar. Dick cheered again and shouted across to Dave "So Dave, how much have I left on my tab now?"

"Fuck off... Dick!" said Dave.

Dick was relentless "Come on Dave, tell me what my tab's at, you miserable shit"

Dave huffed his way back to the little black book. One hundred and eighty-five thousand, five hundred and twenty pounds, and four pence ... satisfied... Dick!" Dick and the rest of the bar laughed, a lot, as usual. They loved it when Dick made him say it out loud, which he did most days when he had an audience. "Drinks are on me then", he shouted across the bar and everyone cheered ... except Dave.

Dave normally pays the winnings out in cash to his customers ... except Dick.

Seven years ago, Dave accepted a 50p accumulator bet from Dick who had selected a horse from every race at 3 different meetings, a total of 23 horses. It was such a wild shot that Dave never even bothered adding up the payout, so he accepted the docket and dropped the 50p into his pocket. By the 22nd race of the day, Dave had started to get a little bit worried, and when Cheddar Gorge romped home in the final race at Lingfield, Dave's life was all but over, before it had even begun.

The lads in the pub calculated the total for him - £266,865.04. Dave refused to pay out on the grounds of not actually being a licensed bookie and at one stage claimed insanity. Dick got his new English solicitor friend on the case and proceedings were issued. Then everybody, including the visitors, boycotted the pub.

Eventually Dave's dad, who normally took very little to do with running the pub, asked another English solicitor friend to meet with Dick's solicitor. Between them they agreed a compromise, and Dick was given a credit of £266,865.04 on his bar tab, and contracts were drawn up and signed.

That very same day, a brass sign was erected below the TV...

"Please note that any single bet or wager placed on these premises will carry a maximum payout of £100, irrespective of the actual calculated payout total.

Without prejudice to the foregoing, these premises are not licensed to accept bets or wagers of any nature whatsoever as defined in the Gaming and Lottery Act 1989 (amended 1992).

Thank you, The Management"

Dave reckoned that should do the trick.

It was certainly a good talking point for the visitors. At least once every weekend, some visitor would ask what the sign meant and the locals would revel in telling the story. Dick never actually told the story himself - people said that it was maybe a clause in the contract that he wasn't allowed to discuss it. He never did, he just laughed a lot when someone else told the story. When he was asked if it was true, he'd pull out a random scrap of paper from his pocket and pretend to read from it. "I can neither confirm nor deny that" ...and then laugh even more. Seven years later and it was still as much a source of entertainment as the very first day.

"You're a wicked man Dick", Sally laughed along with him, "I'll have a glass of champagne since you're buying", they both laughed until Dave arrived to the table with Sally's cheap fizzy wine and Dick's large brandy. They had stopped serving real champagne six years ago when Dick started to become partial to it. "Cheers!" they said together and started laughing again. Sally liked Dick, he was always a good laugh and she loved the flattery but she was always careful never to flirt and never to get too close.

After 2 hours of gabbling and laughing and taking the piss out of Dave and a few visitors, Sally headed off up the road home, which was a pretty terrace house by the edge of the harbour. Two-up, two-down, and two-round-the-back. Sally worked from home a lot, so she had converted the two-round-the-back into an office and a small workshop. She giggled to herself thinking about Dick as she walked through the kitchen, into the courtyard, and opened her office door. Pieces of fabrics and patterns where stuck all over the walls and a computer and printer sat on her desk beside a pile of papers and at least 30 pens of all different shapes and sizes and colours.

The answering machine was flashing enthusiastically in the corner. She tried to ignore it, but it was so persistent that she eventually threw a piece of paper over it so she couldn't see it any more, then turned to her computer. The paper seemed to make matters worse as she could see the small light flashing even harder underneath it. She removed the paper and slapped the play button. The first message was from Dick at 3:15pm that day, he was laughing as usual. "It's me, Dick! I'm down in Flans, come on down for a drink. Martha in the shop told me you were looking great today; I wanted to see it for myself. Don't worry - I'm buying!" and he laughed even more. Sally laughed too and skipped on to the next message from 5:34pm.

"Hi, you don't me, my name's Darwin Litton; I'm a friend of your sister. I'm not sure if you even knew that you had a sister. Anyway, it's important and I need to talk to you. I have some very bad news. My number's 01675 876876, please give me a call when you can, thank you"

Sally stopped smiling and slammed down hard on the answering machine stop button. She was very confused. Why should she not know that she had a sister? Suzie had got in touch years ago, and they spoke every week, in fact Suzie had been down to see her just 2 months ago. She vaguely recognized Darwin's name - Suzie mentioned it to her a few years earlier.

Sally called Flans and asked Dave to get Dick on the phone. She told him she needed to see him, and before she even finished the sentence, he was running out the door and on his way up the road. Sally didn't have a phone in the house, so Dick knew she must be in the office. He came through the back gate and charged through the door. "What is it Sally?"

Sally never replied. She played the message again.
"Hi, you don't me, my name's Darwin Litton; I'm a friend of your sister. I'm not sure if you even knew that you had a sister. Anyway, it's important and I need to talk to you. I have some very bad news. My number's 01675 876876, please give me a call when you can, thank you"

They both stared at one another for a few seconds, and Dick sighed. "Who the fuck is he?" Dick eventually broke the silence. "I don't really know, I sort of recognize the name but...", said Sally, genuinely confused and shaking her head slowly. "Must be a crank, I'll ring him back and tell him to fuck away off" said Dick. Because Sally kind of knew the name, she knew it wasn't a crank, but nevertheless she didn't really want to talk to this person, whoever he was, and happily let Dick manage the situation. Dick dialed the number and got Darwin's answering machine. He listened patiently to Darwin's long and informative message and then jotted down the mobile number that Darwin read out at the end of his recording. Dick didn't speak, and quickly hung up and started dialing the mobile number. Darwin's mobile was switched off, so it diverted back to the home number and Dick had to listen to the message again, which pissed him off even more.

Dick smiled unreassuringly at Sally. This time he spoke after the tone "Hello there, whoever you are, my name's Dick and I'm a friend of Sally's. I don't know what you're playing at, but don't ring here again, okay?…ah… thank you, goodbye" Sally tutted disapprovingly at the dick, and snatched the phone from him. She called Suzie and held on until a lady said "The person you are calling has not answered", three times. Then she hung up.

"Strange" she said quietly to Dick, "She's normally home from work by now". Sally thanked Dick for coming over, and explained that she had work to do which had to be finished by the morning. Dick understood as usual, and pottered back up the road to Flans. He plonked himself into his normal seat and stared at the unusually empty table. He squeezed his mobile from his inside pocket, dialed a number, and listened. He hung up without speaking, and returned the mobile to his pocket.

"What do you want to drink?, Dick!, Pink Lady?, Shirley Bassey?, Wine Spritzer perhaps?", Dave had temporarily developed a personality and was trying desperately to be funny and get his revenge on Dick in front of the crowd of 8. Dick was in no mood for Dave's attempt at humour. "No, I don't want anything thanks Dave, but I'm sure the rest of the lads would like a drink on me, in fact, the drinks are on me for the whole the night! Just put those on my tab please Dave." Everyone cheered ... except Dave. If there was one thing that pissed Dave off more than anything - it was Dick buying drinks for his other customers. Dave couldn't understand why it hadn't been written into the contract. Apart from the fact that it was stopping money going into the till, it also meant that Dick's liver was not being attacked even further. For 7 years now, Dave and his dad had been relying on Dick's liver packing in, which would mean that the slate would be wiped clean and they'd be able to start making money again, buy a colour TV, and go on foreign holidays just like the good old days.

Dick felt uncomfortable with so many happy people in one room. He asked Dave for 4 bottles of whiskey; he smiled at Dave as he poured three of them down the sink at the side of the bar and took the last one home with him. Dave would think twice before taking the piss out of Dick again.

Home was only a few doors away up a hill, and he settled down on his favourite comfy chair and cracked open the whiskey. He sipped straight from the bottle and sighed emotionless in thought.

Sally sat in her office and tried over and over again to ring Suzie, but she couldn't get any reply. She was starting to really worry now. She slumped back, put her feet on the table, and sighed.

CHAPTER FIVE

Darwin sat at the bar of the The Wine Bar, an ingeniously named establishment less than a mile from his house. He was sitting with a different dick - a private one called Stephen McCracken, the investigator that Darwin had hired to find Suzie's parents four years ago. Darwin and Stephen had gone to school together. Darwin had called him earlier and asked him to dig out Suzie's file and fax him over the contact details of her sister Sally. Stephen had traced her to a town in Wales and had even managed to find a telephone number that had matched her name.

Stephen was the meticulous type, and Darwin knew he would have kept a copy of all correspondence pertaining to the case. That was the type of him. Darwin didn't realize four years ago that he would ever need Stephen's help again and so had queried his invoice, eventually agreeing to pay 50% of it. He now regretted doing that as now he needed Stephen's help again. When he called Stephen, Darwin never mentioned the invoice and, luckily, either Stephen had forgot about it, or decided not to mention it either.

By way of reconciliation, Darwin had invited Stephen out for a drink with phrases like "it's been ages since we last went out", and "I haven't seen you for years, we really must get out some night and catch up on old times". Stephen was curious about why Darwin wanted the information again so suggested meeting at The Wine Bar for a beer and a chat. And so the two lonely souls found themselves together, drinking beer and talking about old times back at the ranch.

Stephen eventually decided that neither of them really wanted to continue talking about their old Geology teacher who was doing 7 years for sexually assaulting most of the other members of their class. Darwin was confused at the time why he didn't get abused and even considering flirting with the teacher.

"So what's the interest in Suzie's old file then, did you persuade her to finally contact her sister or something?", quizzed Stephen.

"No, nothing like that, it's a bit more serious. Actually, I haven't seen her in years", replied Darwin. Stephen sighed feebly "Sorry to hear that, you guys break up or something?"

"Yeah, it didn't really work out in the end"

"That's a pity, you made a great couple"

"Yeah, I suppose we did"

Stephen quickly realized that there was a really juicy story in here somewhere. "Look, are you going to fucking tell me, or not?"

"Tell you what?" said Darwin very unconvincingly. He really wanted to tell Stephen about what had happened, but just wasn't sure if it was time to share his story yet. They both sat quietly…for 6 seconds, staring at their bottles of beer and reading the labels, again. It really is hard to believe that Budweiser started brewing in 1860. It was obviously intriguing both of them.

"Suzie was murdered", Darwin suddenly decided that it was probably time now to drip-feed him a bit of detail. "Shit, was she the girl found shot yesterday?" Stephen didn't miss much and had been told of the shooting incident by one of his reporter mates earlier in the day.

"Yep, that was her, single shot to the head apparently. The poor girl couldn't have had any enemies, she didn't know anyone." Darwin thought about that for the first time. He hadn't really considered trying to solve the murder before. How could finding the killer possibly contribute positively to his life or wealth or experiences? Now he seemed genuinely intrigued. Maybe it was because he was sitting close to a private investigator; it must be rubbing off on him, he liked it, so he moved closer.

"Well she obviously had at least one enemy.", said Stephen, master of the cliché and of stating the blindingly obvious. Darwin was starting to get bored with Stephen already and was scouting around the bar for anyone else he knew so that he could catch an eye and maybe subconsciously beckon them over and join his company. But Darwin didn't know anyone, and even if he did, no one would be desperate enough for company to want to join him.

He decided therefore that his best ploy would be to catch the eye of a relatively average, possibly even ugly, single female. He was tired and couldn't be bothered turning on any of the charm, so he wanted an easy catch. A girl that would be grateful or at least flattered by his attentions. Stephen realised that Darwin was starting to loose interest already, so he decided to play the game too and get the rest of the details another time. He needed to know more. It wasn't because he was nosey or even remotely interested, he just desperately needed some work and he knew Darwin had a few quid. He found that out before he took on the original Suzie case.

Stephen decided to break the ice "Look, maybe we can talk about this another time, I can see that you're not on form right now, and besides, those 2 birds over there have been looking over here for the past 20 minutes."

Darwin looked over there, at the 2 birds. He'd noticed them earlier but decided that at least one of them was too pretty. He turned back and looked at Stephen intently. He was a good-looking bloke, 6'3, dark hair, well built, and nice white teeth. Pretty bad pock marks on his cheeks, but it was quite dark and the girls probably wouldn't notice. Darwin decided that Stephen could tackle the pretty one, Darwin was quite happy with the average mate. Darwin Presley smiled, "sounds good, let's go for it". Stephen ordered a few more beers and put his arm over Darwin's shoulder, "I

45

don't like the look of the one you're getting", and laughed out loud.

Darwin knew that "cliché-man" would come up with something fucking stupid like that so it wasn't a surprise really. Darwin smiled politely. Not because he thought Stephen was funny or entertaining, but only because the girls were still looking over and Darwin learnt a long time ago that girls like to see blokes smiling, and laughing and generally bonding well in company.

When the beers arrived, Stephen grabbed his new bottle in his left hand and drained the old one with the right hand. He then hopped off his stool and John-Wayned his way over to the 2 birds in the corner. Darwin followed behind, holding his two beers and knocking into the stools as he tried to trace Stephen's steps, except without the swagger. Stephen went straight to the good-looking one as Darwin had predicted.

Darwin was thinking what Stephen's chat up line would be. He was just bound to have one. Perhaps "Get your coats girls, you've pulled", it would be something corny like that, he just knew it. Stephen smiled at the blonde pretty one "Hello, I'm Stephen, this is Darwin, do you mind if we join you for a drink?" Darwin was impressed, what a smile, what charm! Excellent, he'd definitely get the ugly bird now. The blonde bird spoke, "Hello Stephen, hello

Darwin, I'm Jenny, this is Bob, and yes, please join us, I'll have a cider and Bob will have a pint of lager thanks, oh and get me one of those tubs of hot nuts as well, I'm starving". Stephen kept his smile perfectly intact, "Of course Jenny, and anything else I can do for you?" Darwin picked up on the sarcasm but unfortunately it seemed to be wasted on Barbie. "Well actually I could do with some nice juice as well ... I'm feeling a bit dry"

Stephen kept his smile intact again, "Of course Jenny, I'll be right back" and he minced off to the bar, still smiling. Barbie was actually not as stupid as she looked and when Stephen was just out of sight, she turned to the ugly one, "Well he did ask didn't he?", and they both giggled. Bob and Jenny were sizing up Darwin, literally. They started giggling again. "So what do you do then Mr Darwin?", asked Bob politely and formally.

Darwin was starting to get a bit pissed off with the giggling, but decided he needed a shag more than he needed a night in on his own in front of the mirror, so he agreed to play along. "I'm Stephen's bodyguard, he's a record producer, and I look after him – make sure he doesn't get into any trouble." said Darwin, straight-faced and serious, "So what about you two, what do you do for a living?", he skillfully volleyed the question back before they had time to react properly or doubt his story. The girls looked a bit shocked but decided just to answer rather than pursue the issue any further, "I'm in PR", said Jenny, "and she's in advertising", said Jenny, before Bob got a chance to speak. As Darwin owned a PR Company and an Advertising agency, he smiled brightly at them. He was going to enjoy tonight, "so what does that involve then, you'll have to excuse me, I don't know much about these things?", and so the girls dribbled on about their exciting lives as account executives at his competitors. By the time Stephen came back, Darwin had found out which clients each of their company's had and specifically which clients weren't happy at the moment. That would be very useful information tomorrow.

"Cheers Steve", said Darwin as Stephen approached with a bottle of champagne and 4 iced wine glasses - no lager, no cider, no nuts, and no juice. The girls didn't care and, coincidently, it fitted perfectly with Darwin's story of Stephen being a flash record producer.

Stephen caught on after 10 minutes or so that Darwin had made up some stupid story as he listened to him telling the girls how life as a bodyguard was a dangerous pastime. Stephen had to guess what Darwin had told the girls about him, then he could join in with the joke too. In the meantime he just had to look stupid. Eventually the penny dropped when Bob asked him if he had signed any famous bands recently. Stephen wasn't quite as good as Darwin at telling impressive lies, but he struggled through and by the third bottle of champagne, he was pretending to make calls on his mobile to Scary Spice, "Yo Bitch, what's up".

The girls didn't believe any of the shite the boys were talking, but they were having a laugh so they joined in and made up a few stories of their own. Darwin was having a ball, a collection of people sharing his world for a whole night. A world of harmless lies, exaggeration, and fantasy. Everybody was enjoying it and none of them wanted it to end. By 2am they were all tired of laughing so much, and Darwin suggested going back to his house for a shag, only he didn't quite put it that way, he called it 'coffee' instead.

They all agreed that would be lovely, so they ordered a cab. Stephen took his shag black. Jenny, Darwin and Bob all took milk in their shag, and Bob took sugar in hers too. Darwin didn't notice the answer machine flashing as he bumbled around the kitchen trying to locate the sugar. Stephen did, he never missed a trick, but he was so pissed he forgot within a few seconds.

They all slumped down on Darwin's settee and floor and laughed some more, about nothing in particular. Sleepiness and love filled the dark air, as the room fell silent and warm. Bob put a pillow on Darwin's lap, then slipped her hand under it and undid his buttons. Darwin could feel himself rising to the occasion but was a bit worried about the fact that Stephen was sitting in front of them. Stephen wasn't too interested in what they were doing, he was too busy trying to stay awake sitting up, but it was a useless battle and eventually he toppled over and started a light snore. Jenny didn't care either, she used Stephen's legs as a cushion and snuggled up to sleep on the floor beside him.

Bob had turned into a super-model. This transformation happened after the second bottle of champagne. Her long brown hair fitted her face perfectly and her beautiful dark, soft skin and brown eyes finished off a lovely picture for Darwin. She looked up at him, glanced down at the other two on the floor and they both started giggling.

Bob had an incredible body; she cleverly developed that after the third bottle of champagne. She lay across the settee and started kissing Darwin's stomach, he laid his head back on the settee and closed his eyes and grinned. Bob ran her tongue down his stomach and kissed around his belly button. She cleverly removed his trousers from under his bum and slipped them down just below his knee and undid his shirt. Darwin was really going to enjoy this, he could feel himself getting harder and he could feel her tongue getting softer and closer and warmer. This was going to be best ever. He rubbed his hands gently through her hair. What beautiful hair, what a beautiful mouth.

Then, at exactly the same instant, they both drifted away in their fantasies and fell asleep.

At about 8 o'clock Stephen woke first, stumbling to his hands and knees before opening his eyes, which were now approximately 6 inches away from Darwin's left testicle. His right one had obviously got squashed underneath, or maybe he only had one. Stephen remembered someone in his class at school only had one ball, but he didn't think it was Darwin, but maybe it was.

He was momentarily tempted to investigate further; it was his job after all. Eventually he decided that his facial position in relation to Darwin's genitals was potentially compromising, so he doggy reversed for a few feet and stood up. He looked around and noticed the two birds lying on the floor. Bob was lying face down and had obviously fallen off the settee in the middle of the night and was still lying exactly where she fell. Jenny was now curled up in a ball under the leather chair. He went around the back of the settee to a safe sexual position and slapped Darwin on the head. "Hey Womble, wake up!". This was a test, he remembered that Womble was the nickname of the guy at school with a testicle shortage.

Darwin woke quickly and snapped his head up off the settee, "Womble?", he questioned. Stephen realized it must have been someone else in the class, so he retreated and wandered off to the kitchen.

Darwin slowly realized his predicament - he shyly, but swiftly, rearranged the billiard table and pulled up his trousers. He couldn't remember how the evening finished so he bent over Bob and tried to smell her sleepy breath for any salty clues, but he couldn't really pick up much apart from the smell of champagne, smoke and garlic.

He sighed sadly and went in to join Stephen in the kitchen, who was drinking a pint of water and trying to get Darwin's answering machine to work. "You've got a message", he said, when he realized he'd been caught on. Darwin pushed the right button to save Stephen any more embarrassment and went to get a glass of water himself.

"Hello there, whoever you are, my name's Dick and I'm a friend of Sally's. I don't know what you're playing at, but don't ring here again, okay?...ah... thank you, goodbye" Darwin was quite used to being spoken to like that, so didn't really take it personally. He sat pensively at the chrome breakfast bar, and expertly deflected the looks that Stephen was machine-gunning across at him.

Stephen walked up beside him, "Look, I don't know what the fuck is going on Darwin, but you need my help, and I need the work. I'll agree 50% of my normal daily rate, plus expenses, and I can start straight away."

"I'll agree 100% of your normal rate, no expenses, and we'll start the clock tomorrow." replied Darwin quickly. Stephen thought for about a second, "Deal", and they shook hands. They both knew that Darwin only paid half his bill last time, so they both felt relatively happy, but confused as to who got the best deal. They seemed to have double-bluffed each other and themselves. "Come on then, lets go", said a determined Darwin. "Where?" asked Stephen. "To Wales, where else?" replied Darwin.

Bob wandered into the kitchen and instinctively furrowed her way to the water. She had been reincarnated from a goddess to an average looking bird miraculously during the night, but Darwin wasn't too disappointed, he'd had worse. Darwin said "good morning" cheerfully just as she was walking past him. She smiled gently and muffled "good morning" back. He smelt her breath again, still nothing. "Listen, we have to go to Wales, I'm really sorry about this but it's an emergency – Tom Jones has died and Stephen has to go and take him to hospital … and I have to go with him." said Darwin, almost believing himself. Bob just gave that same gentle smile again and wandered back to the living room with her water.

Darwin followed closely behind, "I'm sorry about this, but we really do have to go, and it really is an emergency. We had a great time last night and I'd love to meet up with you again. If you feel the same, leave your number on the blackboard in the kitchen. You can let yourselves out when you're ready, okay?"

Bob collapsed on the settee and closed her eyes. "Okay Darwin. Pass on my condolences to Mrs Jones." She was totally disinterested and needed more sleep. Darwin was impressed; she had remembered his name. Barbie never moved. Darwin and Stephen grabbed their bits and pieces and sneaked quietly out the door. Stephen stopped and stared suspiciously at Darwin, "I thought you said I wasn't starting until tomorrow"

"Did you?", said Darwin innocently, "... I didn't say you weren't starting until tomorrow, I said you could start charging tomorrow. Today's free – that's what we agreed. Anyway where is Wales from here?" Stephen looked slowly up at the sun, which was just peeking out over the houses opposite, he licked his finger and held it up to wind, "420 miles, South-South-East". Darwin started the car, indicated east, and turned west. They disappeared into the sunrise...in search of Wales. They stopped a few hundred yards up the road at a garage, filled up with petrol, 8 cans of Red Bull, 2 bottles of water, a large box of chocolate Celebrations, and a bag of Jelly Babies. This could be a long journey. They scoffed the whole lot down in 20 minutes, which was just as well as the airport was only 21 minutes away. They marched purposefully to the ticket sales office and then marched even more purposefully back to the car and drove home.

Flights from Belfast to Wales aren't too common, and the next one wasn't until 7 o'clock that night, which was nearly 10 hours away. "Stupid Fucker", Stephen eventually broke the silence. Darwin replied quickly, "Me?, oh that's rich – you're meant to be the fucking investigator, the least you could have done was investigate what time the planes fly, stupid fucker."

"I kind of presumed you had a plan, stupid fucker", replied Stephen. "Stupid fucker", replied Darwin.
The Red Bull, chocolate and artificial additives were clearly starting to kick in now.

21 minutes later the stupid fuckers arrived back at Darwin's house. They quietly sneaked in, and went back to the kitchen to listen to the message again, and again. Ten hours was a long time to fill. Bob woke again and wandered back into the kitchen, looking Darwin and Stephen slowly in the face, one by one. "What are you doing here?" she asked. Darwin was first off the mark, "I live here, and he's a stupid fucker". Bob didn't try to understand; "I thought you had gone off to take the body of Tom Jones to the hospital or something?"

"You must have been dreaming Bob, what are you talking about? Tom Jones?"
Bob resigned herself to the fact that they had a good point. Tom Jones? What was she talking about? She couldn't think of a suitable reply so she closed her eyes again and wandered back off in the direction of

the living room. The stupid fuckers shrugged at each other insincerely and returned to the answering machine, "Strange girl".

CHAPTER SIX

Sergeant Middlemouse stood in front of a white board, which had some scrawled writing on it;

Suzie
Girl
31
Female
Alone
No Family
Boyfriend
Other Bloke
Phones
Neighbours
Work
Shot
Dead
In
The
Head

etc.

Along with a photo of Suzie, a photo of Mrs Johnston, and a photo of Darwin.

He tapped the word 'Boyfriend' with his pen, and then looked intensely at the photo of Darwin, then ripped the photo of Mrs Johnston off the wall, and threw it at

Thompson. The Simpsons and Thompson sat quietly and obediently in a formal circle facing the boss.

"Okay, listen up", said the boss. The audience didn't move a muscle; they were already listening up. "We've got a number here for a place in Wales which Suzie called a lot, and I've also got a mobile number registered to a Mister Stanley Watkins, who, for the moment, we'll assume is boyfriend Stan. Unfortunately the address registered with the mobile company is Suzie's address and so we're no further on with finding 'Stan the Man'." Boss stopped and looked hard at a female detective sitting to his left. He raised one finger as if he was about to speak, then he paused and dropped it to his side. "I'm sorry love, but for the life of me, I can't remember your name", he eventually spurted out.

"Jill Boot", she replied quickly, "...Detective Constable, Sir"

"Yeah, anyway, have you anything back from forensics yet", Boss turned away as he said it. "No guv, nothing as yet, they promised me by 9 this morning, then said it would be 4 this afternoon before they'd have anything worth knowing.", Jill efficiently reported back. Boot was only 23 and a miserable looking cow. Straight black hair in a bob, and tight burgundy lips. She was probably quite pretty, but her sullen tones fought back any possibility of attractiveness sneaking out from under her fringe. She looked as if her mother had told her off as a child and she just never got over it. "Okay" said boss, he had switched off after the "No, guv, nothing as yet…" bit. "We've a couple of things to be getting on with until we get forensics back. The boyfriend, and the calls to Wales. Thompson and … um, Boot, I want you on a plane to Wales as soon as possible. Check with Paul, and he'll give you the details of the address. Simon, any luck with her work colleagues?"

"Nope, small solicitor's office, she was a quiet girl, kept herself to herself, polite, hardworking etc. Nobody there bothered with her much. She always arrived on time and left on time and worked very hard. They didn't know anything about her friends or boyfriends and nobody had ever met Stan. The receptionist Marge, who was friendliest with her, was off sick; I tried her at home but no answer."

"Shite", said boss. "The only thing we seem to know about Suzie is Fuck All. Come on everyone, I need some digging and I need some answers. We'll meet back again at 6 to see if we're any further on. Brian, could you get on to forensics please and tell them I need some information by this afternoon, latest. Thompson make sure you call in before 6 and let us know how you're getting on. Okay, that's it everyone."

CHAPTER SEVEN

After about 10 minutes of listening to the telephone message over and over again, Stephen and Darwin got bored with each other's ugly faces and decided to part company and meet at the airport at 6 o'clock that night. Stephen had kindly offered to relieve Darwin of Barbie, but insisted that Bob could make her own way home – she wasn't pretty enough to warrant wasting any petrol on. So Darwin sat quietly on his own in the kitchen while Bob snored quietly in the living room.

Darwin jotted down the list of clients that Bob and Jenny had mentioned the night before, then wrote "we need to contact these companies now, not happy with their agency, thanks, Darwin. PS I'm off to see a new client in Wales, back in a few days, call on mobile if you need me", then he slipped it on to the answering machine / fax machine combo, pressed 'office', and pressed 'go'. He was getting to grips with technology. The fax noise was in danger of wakening Bob so he watched it and the kitchen door intently until it had passed through the little fax wheels and came out the other side. He snatched it quickly from the back tray, crumpled it up and skillfully sent it flying 20 feet towards the silver bin on the other side of the kitchen. Then he walked over and picked it up of the floor, 3 feet left of the target, and placed it carefully in the bin.

He played the message again. "He seems pretty pissed off", said Bob, as she slowly traced her way back to the watering hole. "Yeah, he does, doesn't he", replied Darwin, not once breaking his long, hard stare at the answering machine. "Who is he?, who's Sally?, what did you do to upset them?", asked Bob quietly between gulps. "Sally is the lead singer with ....", began Darwin. "Fuck off", said Bob, "...last night is over. It was a great laugh, I had a good night, but don't treat me like a fucking idiot. You're Darwin Litton, you're not a bodyguard, you own Litton Advertising and Communications, I'm Bob Page, and I certainly don't work for an Advertising agency, I own a clothes shop, and Jenny is an accountant. It's a small town. Now, if you're going to get on like a twat for the rest of your life, then can I please borrow your phone to call a taxi?" Bob's face hardened slightly and she quickly marched out of the kitchen back to the living room. Darwin was almost certainly going to be a twat for the rest of his life, so maybe he should just call her a taxi.

Darwin quickly grabbed another piece of paper from the combo in-tray. "Disregard last message, except the bit about Wales, sorry about that, thanks, Darwin", and quickly sent it express-fax to the office, and walked swiftly after Bob. "Look, sorry about that Bob, I've a lot on my plate at the moment, and I didn't mean to get on like a twat. You're a very nice person and I was being stupid. I wasn't thinking straight. I am a male after all." Darwin smiled shyly at Bob, and flicked his eyes from the ground, up to her eyes and back to the ground again. "Sorry", he added. He knew it would work, it always did.

"Me too", said Bob, "I shouldn't have been so rude – a bit hung over and a bit pissed off with men talking shite. I just split up with Brian-the-lying-bastard boyfriend recently. He works in an advertising agency, in fact that's how I got all the juicy inside information on all their clients. He was always talking about work. I just can't handle any bullshit, that's all. I'm sorry for being nasty and I'm sorry for all the lying too, it just seemed like good fun to go along with it at the time."

Darwin had turned the argument masterfully around, now she was apologizing to him. "Hey, no problem Bob, I understand", said Darwin cheerfully. He ran back into the kitchen, grabbed a blank sheet and scribbled, "Revert to original fax, sorry about confusion, thanks, Darwin" and sent it on its way. "Fancy a coffee?" Darwin shouted from the kitchen. "Yeah, love one thanks", replied Bob.

So Darwin and Bob spent the rest of the day together, drinking fresh coffee and sharing their life stories. Darwin liked her so much he even threw in quite a few bits of truth, just to keep it real. Bob pretty much knew the score, she had worked out that underneath it all he was probably a nice honest guy and she didn't let him away with much. "Wolves don't eat dogs", she remarked wisely. *Damn*, thought Darwin, *she's a smart cookie*.

Slowly throughout the day, Bob started to get beautiful again for Darwin, and miraculously without the power of champagne. Either the coffee was very strong or perhaps she was actually quite pretty after all. Darwin was confused.

CHAPTER EIGHT

The airport was almost empty. "Darwin, what the fuck is she doing here?", whispered Stephen loudly, jerking his head towards Bob. "She's my friend." said Darwin "What's your excuse for being here? Oh yes Stephen I forgot, I'm paying you to be here – yes, much more honorable. Stupid Fucker." Bob, Darwin and Stephen sipped quietly at their coffee in the departure lounge. Stephen suddenly recognized a few familiar faces. "Don't look now, but there are 2 cops in the corner behind me, one male, one female…." Darwin looked. Stephen buried his head in his hands "For fuck sake Darwin, I told you not to look"

"Harry!!" yelled Darwin, bouncing off his seat and making his way over to the very suspicious looking cops in the corner. "Darwin!!" replied Harry in exactly the same tone and volume, "… how the hell are you man?" They hugged. They had missed each other.

Harry politely introduced Jill, the miserable cow, and Darwin excitedly brought his long lost happy friend over to meet Stephen and Bob. Stephen was mesmerized as he grinned slowly and shook hands formally. The subject of why they were all going to Wales just never came up in conversation. Harry of course knew why, and Darwin knew that Harry knew. Jill didn't know much really, Stephen hadn't a clue what was going on, and Bob liked Darwin, she was pretty sure she did anyway.

When they touched down in Cardiff, they went through the motions of saying their goodbyes and farewells, then accidently met up again 10 minutes later at the train station. There was only one way to get to Port Sinton, so they shared a carriage.

Darwin and Harry discussed last year's holiday in Cypress. It turned out that they were both staying in the same village, in adjacent hotels, at roughly about the same time, so they compared notes and stories about the local bars and restaurants and the day-trips and the weather.

Stephen and Jill sat quietly on opposing sides, each trying to find an elusive square of wall that they could stare at which meant they wouldn't have to look at each other, or anyone else. Bob sat relaxed, legs crossed, slurping at a carton of Ribena, nibbling at a Dime Bar, looking over at Darwin, deciding whether she really liked him or not. Darwin would catch her eye every now and then, and smile pathetically back at her. Harry asked Bob what she did for a living, and suddenly Bob was part of the gang too. Harry's wife regularly went into Bob's shop; in fact he'd been dragged in himself a few times, and even thought that he'd recognized Bob.

Stephen and Jill eventually found their piece of empty wall and stared hard at it. They both had their own one-man gangs, and no one else was allowed to join without the secret password.

When they reached Tarnlough, the nearest train stop to Port Sinton, Darwin, Harry and Bob all jumped in the same taxi, "The Quays Hotel please", said Darwin ".... What about you Harry, can I drop you off somewhere?" There only was 1 hotel anywhere near Port Sinton, so Harry was staying there too.

Stephen and Jill followed in a taxi behind. Neither of them had been told where they were going, so Stephen instructed the driver to "follow that cab", trying hard not to make it sound like in the movies, but it was no use, he was born a private investigator. Jill sat quietly and sternly in the back. She hadn't worked out yet whether she was undercover or not, and who these other people were. She decided to play it safe and subconsciously slipped into being undercover anyway, cleverly disguised as a tax inspector with hemorrhoids.

The Quays was a typical seaside hotel. It had somehow scraped 3 stars but was little more than a glorified Bed and Breakfast. Originally it would have been a double-fronted Victorian stately home, where Lord and Lady Crinkleface would have sat in front of their large open fire and stroked each others puppies. If they wanted a cup of tea or coffee they certainly would not have been tempted to put the kettle on, but instead would ring a bell from beside the fireplace in the front room and one of the maids would quickly be there, waiting for her instructions.

It now offered a friendly welcome, a pleasant reception, a cozy bar, a bright and sunny day room, a separate dining room with views over the bay, 11 double bedrooms of which 9 were ensuite and 4 had sea views ... according to the brochure. The Quays was clean, and for most of the regular guests, that seemed to be quite important and excused it from all the rest of its inadequacies. The carpets were threadbare and the paintwork consisted of many hundreds of randomly flaked and faded coats – much of it probably caused by all the cleaning.

By the time Stephen and Jill had arrived at the hotel, the other gang were already in the cozy bar, waiting for their first pints of Guinness to settle, and guffawing loudly at each others' impersonations of the spotty attitude-ridden bar boy who was serving them. Three Guinness' later, the laughing slowly deteriorated into polite smiles and titters.

"How much do you know about why you are in Wales?" asked Darwin, suddenly dragging the cheerful conversation to an abrupt end. "Not much, to tell you truth Darwin, we really don't have a lot at the moment. All we know is that Suzie made a lot of calls to an address in Port Sinton, to someone called Sally

Burton. I have an address and that's all. The guys are working on other contacts she had - work, boyfriend, family, and we're still waiting on forensics."

Darwin stared sideways at the dartboard. He had no idea why, but he had to look as if he was thinking very seriously about something, which he wasn't. "Ok", Darwin, finally re-engaged, "I know what the connection is between Suzie and Sally. Right now you know nothing that I don't know, but that'll change. I'll swap you that information for a copy of the forensic report when you get it."

"Fuck off", said Harry. He winked at Bob and the two of them smiled knowingly at one another, "you know I can't do that." Darwin didn't know that he couldn't do that, but pretended he did and looked back over at the dartboard for inspiration. Bob looked at the dartboard too. "I'll tell you what", Bob reinstated the negotiations and swung round to Harry. "We'll tell you about Sally and Suzie, and you let us ask you ....10 questions about the forensic report when you get it."

"Deal", said Harry, low-fiving Bob. "Deal", said Darwin suspiciously, and clumsily avoided the low-five. Darwin pondered for a few moments and wondered how Bob knew he was looking at the number 10 on the dartboard. He eventually re-engaged with Harry. "Sally and Suzie are sisters."

"Suzie doesn't have any family", said Harry quickly. "She does", continued Bob, "Darwin hired Stephen to find her family a few years ago. She has a father who doesn't want anything to do with her, and an estranged sister called Sally Burton who lives near here."

"Hmmmm", said Harry detectivingly. Jill and Stephen appeared mysteriously from behind the bar, cleverly taking a shortcut from reception to the lounge. The gang all raised their eyebrows as Jill approached the table. Her face shone with a passionate glow. Her body was bouncing as if she'd just had a bath in Silverkrin. She walked sharply and her hips and shoulders swung beautifully in time with one another. Her breasts perted themselves towards the audience, looking at each person one by one. She exuded a level of confidence that even made Bob feel uneasy.

Just as everyone was trying to work out where she got her happy pills from, Stephen appeared from her shadow, pretended to pull up his zip, and smiled and winked at Darwin. He shook his head slowly back at Stephen but couldn't help but let go of a little smile that only Stephen could have seen - The dirty bastard had just shagged miss grumpy drawers. Harry dropped his head and avoided the glances of everyone, especially Jill who was trying to tell him that he'd forgotten to phone the station for the update.

Bob looked at Jill and pretended to be interested in what she was saying and pretended not to see Darwin smiling at Stephen. Spotty-bar-boy looked at Jill's legs and followed the ladder right up to the top of her thigh.

When the looks had finally settled down, Harry explained that he had to call the Station, and then disappeared sheepishly upstairs with half a pint of his Guinness and a local newspaper that he'd found at the bar.

"We need to talk later", Darwin said to Stephen. Then he motioned to Bob to follow him, and they made their way outside, silently following the path down to the shore. "Listen, sorry to drag you into all this crap Bob, I'm sure you've got better things to be doing than sitting here with a sad bunch of very amateur detectives, drinking beer and talking shite". Bob didn't reply, but instead took his hand and swayed it high up in the air in time to Onward Christian Soldiers.

Bob had a great skill of getting things into perspective and, more importantly, of giving Darwin a sense of *her* perspective. The only moment that was relevant to Bob was the very moment that she was living. What had just happened had passed, and therefore wasn't significant any longer. Sure she still thought about things, but not to any degree that would stop a new moment arriving, so the doors were always open, and the entrance was always free.

Although Bob had always considered that she had come from a stable and happy home, she sometimes let her memories drift back to her days with her natural mum. She had died when Bob was just 7 and every year that passed made it more and more difficult to recapture her face in Bob's mind. Sometimes Bob wasn't really sure if she could actually remember her at all, or was just remembering having remembered her. A subtle difference that forced Bob to never look at old photos of her mum, therefore disciplining her to hold those thoughts and memories sacred only in her mind. She could sometimes remember school the next day after her mum died. Her teacher had been told about the killing but Bob begged her not to tell the rest of the class; after all she had a math's test that day and she didn't want anyone thinking that she had been trying to get out of it because of a family death.

Darwin walked like an awkward teenager, not quite in time with the marching, pretending to be confident in himself but secretly worrying about their first real snog. Just to complete the metaphor, he slowly slipped into a huff. He decided to break the cycle before his spots started re-appearing. "So who's you favourite band?" he chirped "…mine's Talking Heads" he added victoriously before Bob could reply. He could feel a juicy whitehead appearing on his chin.

"My favourite band?" replied Bob softly, somewhat inquisitively. "Um, well I suppose it would be Nine Inch Nails at the moment." Onward Christian Soldiers had stopped playing, so they marked time on the spot.

"You're soooo un-cool".
Bob retaliated immediately "Excuse me? So you're saying that Talking Heads are cool and Nine Inch Nails aren't? Get with the new Millennium, dinosaur-Darwin."
"Well God help us all if those Nine Nailer Inch-twats represent the new Millennium"
Bob stopped marking time. "I can't believe that I thought I might actually like you, I mean, just for a moment I thought that you might be okay. Of course you're a twat, but I knew that before I met you. I just thought that underneath you might be ... I don't know ... that maybe underneath you might be a 'nice' bloke." Darwin poked his stiffy further down into his pants via his pockets.

"You're frigid", spat Darwin, and he walked off along the sea wall. "Is that right pimple-dick? Well why don't you ask Stephen whether I'm frigid or not, I had to rely on him to 'give me a hand', well ...most of it anyway, after you fell asleep the other night."
"slut" whispered Darwin just loud enough for Bob to hear. "What did you call me?" They marched back towards the hotel in time to Onward Christian Soldiers again.

Darwin stormed into the bar where Stephen was waiting patiently alone. "You guys okay?" asked Stephen, sensing a bit of tension in the air. "Yeah, we're grand thanks" replied Darwin "...just getting our first argument out of the way"

Stephen was somewhat confused, "...so what did you want to see me about?, and how do you know Harry? Two questions, then I'm off to bed." Darwin signaled to the bar-boy to bring him a drink by cupping his hand as if he was holding a glass. "You want another one Steve?"

Stephen and the bar-boy both, simultaneously, completely ignored Darwin – Stephen ignored him because he thought he had made it perfectly clear that he was heading off to bed and didn't want another drink, and the bar-boy ignored Darwin because he was an ignorant little shit with a serious attitude.

"For fuck sake. Can I have a Pint of Guinness, please?"
Bar-boy started pouring slowly. Even the beer seemed to fill the glass with resentment.
"Did you fiddle with Bob back at my house after I fell asleep the other night?"
"No, well not that I can remember", said Stephen quickly and honestly, looking Darwin hard in the eye. Darwin held his gaze for a moment as a test – Stephen appeared to have passed. "Good. Anyway, Harry is going to allow us to ask 10 questions about the forensic report when he gets it tomorrow, and I've

73

traded that for telling him about Suzie's sister, which he didn't know about. They're only here because they've traced some calls back to Port Sinton, which means that Suzie must have made contact with Sally."

The bar-boy arrived with the Guinness, which was dribbling over the edge of the glass and hadn't settled properly. "Thank you very much indeed young man", said Darwin politely, "and take one for yourself for being so helpful and polite." Darwin liked confusing people. He turned back to Stephen "…and the reason I know Harry, is that he was the cop who made the dubious connection to me at Suzie's house when they found the body, and was then sent around to apologise and make sure I didn't make a formal complaint. We kind of just hit it off; he's actually quite a nice guy."

"Do I have to take a Guinness, or can I have something else, or actually would it be okay if I just took the money instead?" the bar-boy was still standing at the table. "You must have a Guinness…" replied Darwin in his best teacher's voice "…That's the rule."

"Oh…okay…thanks" and the bar-boy shuffled back to his station.

"Ten questions?" probed Stephen. "Have you decided what your questions are going to be?"

Darwin thought about that for the first time "No, well actually I've never even seen a forensic report before, so I wouldn't have a clue what to ask, but I suppose we'll think of something. Have you seen one before?"

"Yes Darwin, apparently I'm a detective, I was a cop for 6 years, and I've seen dozens of them. Would you like me to put the questions together? I might just be slightly better at it than you." Stephen said quietly and sarcastically. "Fair point" admitted Darwin "I'll tell you what I'll do, you can have 9 questions and I'll have 1, okay?"

Stephen hated negotiating with children, mainly because he always lost. This pattern normally resulted in him having to take his estranged son Benjamin to McDonalds for a kid's meal on alternate Saturdays. This time it just meant losing a question. He thought about it for a moment, and then agreed and tried to change the subject quickly. In fact he considered it an overwhelming victory bearing in mind that it was Darwin he was dealing with. Darwin realized this immediately. "Actually" said Darwin "you had better make that 8, Bob will want one too, she'll go ape-shit if she doesn't get a question as well." Stephen puffed in defeat, ordered a Big Mac and a Happy Meal, and sat back in his chair. "8 it is then. Listen, I'm knackered, I'm going to have to get some sleep"

Darwin had removed what little energy Stephen had left. "Okay mate, I'll see you in the morning" said Darwin brightly. A few seconds after he left, Darwin sneaked behind the banister to get a secret view of which way Stephen turned when he reached the top of the stairs to make sure he went to his own room, and not to Bob's, by mistake.

"So what's you name?" he shouted over at bar-boy.
"Bryn" he mumbled back.
"...and what do you do Bryn, apart from working in here?"
"I'm a student; I just started a degree in Music." Bryn suddenly perked up.
"Excellent, you like it?"
Three hours and 8 pints later, Darwin and Bryn finally finished re-writing the words to every Police song they knew and decided it was time to call it a day. Bryn was too pissed to drive home, so Darwin said he could sleep on his floor ...as long as he didn't sing all night long or fart. So the duo stumbled their way into Darwin's room, where the light was already on.

Bob jumped out of the bed, naked and swearing, grabbed a blanket off the floor and scampered out the door, and down the corridor towards her room. The 2 boys watched her from the entrance. Darwin watched to make sure she went back to her room, and not to Stephen's, my mistake. Bryn watched to see if any bits of flesh were still visible.

"Nice tits" said Bryn scratching at himself through his pockets. They started singing in unison, "Every little thing she does is magic, every little thing just turns me on..." They decided Sting's words were better than the ones they'd made up earlier.

CHAPTER NINE

Port Sinton awoke.

A small stalky woman screamed in desperate, lonely horror, and sprinted uncontrollably down the Main Street, out of number 6 and into number 12. Someone else suddenly shouted from the other side of the street. Sirens whizzed quietly in the background.

Sally sat up rigid in her bed.

The sun peeked relentlessly through stubborn black clouds. The sea sat quietly watching, hardly daring to wave at the sea wall. Seagulls stared at each other in silence.

Curtains twitched.

Dick lay slumped in his favourite chair, with an almost empty bottle of whiskey down by his side. He didn't seem to be noticing the commotion.

Lights began appearing in upstairs windows. A dog started to bark, then suddenly seemed to change its mind. The street lamps reluctantly clicked off, and dawn resumed the lighting duties.

The butt of Dick's shotgun rested between his foot and the bottle. A dark red hole stared motionless from his face where his mouth and nose used to be. The back of the chair lay matted with fragments of bone and hair joined by sticky life-juice and clear slime. The ceiling speckled like chicken pox. The wall behind his chair displayed an almost perfect circle of red pebbledash, and lines of congealed blood stretched lazily down to the carpet. A sealed brown envelope managed to avoid any of the mess and "Sally" was carefully written in pencil and underlined twice.

The top of Dick's head had settled like a crater, and crimson lava had solidified down the valleys of his suit jacket. He sat alone. Just as he had sat alone every morning; waiting for someone to pop in for a cuppa and a chat. The front door lay wide open, and banged gently against the telephone table in the hall in time with the tender gusts.

Two new screams bellowed from the High Street in chorus.

CHAPTER TEN

The taxi ride to Port Sinton only took about 10 minutes, and Stephen was armed with Sally's address and a small faxed photo, retrieved from his original investigation file. He sat in the front of the taxi because he was officially an investigator. Bob and Darwin sat in the back. Darwin popped a few headache tablets and Bob tutted in mock disagreement. Neither had mentioned the night before, and seemed to have put the event behind them. They pulled up outside Sally's house and Darwin instructed Stephen to pay the bill. Stephen began to ask for a receipt but then remembered that he wasn't getting paid expenses. Darwin on the other hand didn't forget details like that and he smiled victoriously at Stephen.

They all absorbed the mysterious atmosphere that hung in the air. Stephen finally knocked the door several times, then peered through a gap in the curtains. "Hmmmm, no-one in", he muttered half to himself.

Port Sinton seemed very quiet - a dull grayness shared the atmosphere with a fine drizzle. "Look, there's no point in all of us dragging around together", said Stephen. "We're not exactly inconspicuous as a group, and I need to sniff around, and find out some details. Where she works, who she knows etc." Bob and Darwin both stared silently at the ground. It wasn't fair - they wanted to play investigators too.

"There's a pub at the top of the street, I'll meet you there in a few hours, okay?" Offered Stephen impatiently as he headed off along the promenade. Although Stephen didn't have that much experience with children, he knew that sometimes you just have to be strict with them, tell them the truth sternly, then move on.

Bob and Darwin supped the head off their first pint and thanked Dave very much indeed. Darwin read the sign under the TV but refused to give any opinion. There was no one else in the Bar. "It's very quiet here" Bob commented to Dave. He almost smiled back but resisted using up any valuable facial energy. "Yeah, one of the locals was found shot dead this morning. Left here last night with a bottle of whiskey, drank it, then appears to have stuck a shot-gun in his face and blew half his head off...allegedly. They're still cleaning bits of him up now. Poor bugger."

Darwin picked up a slight sense of insincerity in Dave's summary of events. "That's terrible" said Bob "Did you know him well?"

"Yep" said Dave, and returned to cheerfully washing up last night's dirty glasses and ashtrays. Bob turned back to Darwin as she was clearly getting nowhere with Dave. "God, who would have thought it, something like that happening in a place like this."

Darwin was equally unresponsive, and was concentrating on scribbling down example questions for the forensic report questionnaire.

What signs were there of a forced entry?
Whose fingerprints were found at the scene?
Do they know what type of gun was used?
Did the killer know his/her victim?

Darwin tried hard to pull on his Sunday night resources – when the family would all sit attentively in the living room, watching Quincy. He recalled one episode in particular, a body found shot and abandoned on the floor. The woman had few friends and no enemies. There must have been a scene when they were discussing the forensic report … What was Quincy's first name?, he mulled – he had never heard him called anything apart from Quincy. That would be a good question for a pub quiz. He suddenly remembered that he was in a pub. "Bob, what was Quincy's first name?"

Bob ignored him and returned reluctantly to Dave instead. "What was he called? …The guy that was found dead?"

"Dick!", snapped Dave "…an appropriate name for a man of great standing like him."

Bob had no idea what he was talking about "Do you know a woman called Sally? She lives just down the road."

"I do"

"Really?"

"Yes" Dave tried to end the conversation by turning his back.

"Cool" finished Bob.

"Darwin - the barman knows Sally, and there was a man found dead this morning." she whispered. Darwin stopped writing; he approved of Bob's new investigative skills. However, as neither of them knew how to interrogate, they decided it would be best to simply keep an eye on their witness, and wait for Stephen to arrive and get the rest of the information. They were sure that he would have all the requisite skills to make their new hostage sing.

"Sorry about last night by the way", whispered Darwin. "Obviously if I had known that you were in my room I wouldn't have invited Bryn back. I was going to chuck him out but you had run off before I could do anything."

"It's okay Darwin. Besides Bryn was quite cute, you made a lovely couple" Darwin smiled sarcastically. "Look, presumably we'll be staying here another night, so why don't we just have a quiet evening in. I'll get a nice bottle of wine and come round to your room. We can sit and watch TV, have a chat and relax. What do you think?" Bob thought for a moment "I think we've both got a bit of thinking to do, don't you?" Darwin didn't need to think about anything. "Yeah, I suppose we have" He decided that he wanted to be complicated as well, and didn't want to appear too shallow.

It didn't last for very long. "Was there something in particular you need to think about? Maybe we could talk it over and we could help each other?"

Bob smiled brightly and her knowing eyes shone and glistened. "Thanks Darwin, you're so sweet." She gave him a quick mummy-kiss on the nose "Such a wee sweety" and returned to watching Dave. Darwin was suitably confused but joined the stakeout, as he really didn't know what else to say. Bob was still trying to like Darwin a bit more than she did. She hated that he was generally a manipulative, lying little toad; but on the other hand, she liked that she was learning how to turn that back on him, and take advantage of him. Her ex-boyfriend Brian was a liar too, but he lied about more important stuff; like which hotel he had stayed when he went to Barcelona on business last month. That's a different sort of lie, but maybe a liar is a liar.

At about 12:04 an Express Post delivery man arrived with a large box for Dave. He suddenly lit up with excitement and scraped wildly at the tape that wedged it closed. He enjoyed a long and loving stare at the contents, then eventually removed an instruction booklet, and retired behind the bar to read it in peace. Darwin took a note of the incident just in case, although he couldn't quite see what was in the box, and so left a medium sized space in his notes so that he could fill it in later.

At 12:28 an old man with an old suit and an even older face toddled in and made his way on autopilot towards the loo. He stopped at the entrance "Terrible about Dick, isn't it?" he shouted back to Dave. Dave *hmmm'd* in apparent agreement without looking up from his instruction booklet.

"Is there any bog-roll in the shit-house?" the old man persisted in trying to get a response from Dave, but he ignored him, and kept turning the pages. The old man lifted one of yesterday's newspapers off the floor and slammed the door behind him.

Bob watched intently, listening for clues. Darwin however was trying to work out whether the newspaper was for reading, or whether it was a Plan B in case there was no bog-roll.

"Dick" whispered Bob half to herself. "Dick, the guy who was shot was called Dick" she raised her whisper. "The voice on the answering machine" replied Darwin quickly, pretending he had already worked that out. Being investigators was thirsty work, so Bob shouted over to Dave "Excuse me". Dave thought for a moment about ignoring her but then remembered that paying customers were now his future. "How can I help you? Same again?" he smiled awkwardly.

The old man never, ever returned from the toilet.

Bob and Darwin sipped their new drinks in investigative silence, watching Dave disconnect the old black and white Redifusion TV and replace it carefully with the contents of the box delivered earlier. A new shiny silver Sony 38 Inch Plasma stared victoriously down from the shelf. It dominated the entire bar, and made everything else look small, filthy and old. It was going to take more than a few days for this diamond to blend into its surroundings. Finally Dave stood back into the middle of the bar in appreciation. "She's a beauty isn't she?" Bob and Darwin agreed. It truly was a fine looking TV. "Ready?" prompted Dave "Three – Two – One …" and he flicked the switch. The bar shone with colour. Wonderful, miraculous colour. The browns became golds, the golds became yellows, and the purples became pinks.

From about 1 o'clock onwards, people started arriving one by one. Each one going through the drill of saying "Did you hear about Dick?" and then followed by "…Oh, nice TV!" and then looking disapprovingly at Bob and Darwin - just for being there. Darwin noted all the arrivals, along with times and brief descriptions. Finally at 2:05pm Stephen appeared at the door and Darwin made his final note for the day. "Drink?" said Bob. "Yeah, Diet Coke please"
"Two pints and a Diet Coke please" Bob shouted across to Dave.
"So what did you find out?" quizzed Darwin.

"Well, let's just say that a lot has been happening in sleepy Port Sinton in the last 24 hours. A local guy by the name of..." he consulted his notes "...Richard Williams died from fatal gunshot wounds this morning. I made a contact with a local cop and I even managed to get into the house where it happened – not a pretty site. Also, one of the neighbour's said there was a letter found at the scene from Williams to Sally, but I can't get a hold of that at the moment. Sally was at the police station this morning, and she's identifying the body later on tonight. Apparently she's in a bit of a state over this, and they had to prescribe tranquilizers for her. Sally and Mr. Williams were apparently close mates, so probably not the best time for us to tell her about Suzie as well"

"Is that it?" interjected Darwin "Is that all you know? How much am I paying you?"
"What are you talking about? Is that not enough fucking excitement for one day? I've traced Sally and made a connection between her and another freshly dead body. And whatever you're paying me, its not enough to ..."
Bob started first and stopped Stephen in his ranting tracks "So let's go through this slowly Sherlock ...the dead man's name was..."
Stephen consulted his notes again "Richard Williams" Darwin joined in next "...and people called Richard are sometimes known as..." Stephen was getting severely pissed off now. "What? Um, Richie, Rick,

Rich, Ricky fucking Ricardo, what's this got to do with anything."

"Dick!" said Darwin painfully." Ring any bells?"
"Answering Machine?" helped Bob.

"Here's your drinks" shouted Dave. His newly acquired customer services skills hadn't stretched yet to providing waiter service. Stephen took the opportunity to get out of the current situation by retrieving the drinks from the bar and paying for the round. "...Yes, Yes, your new TV's lovely..." Stephen extracted himself from Dave's enthralling dialogue about LCD technology and returned to the table. "Fucking weirdo that barman" He took a long swig of his Diet Coke and cleverly avoided all eye contact with Bob or Darwin. "You know, I think you might just be right – it's possible that our Mr Williams could in fact be Dick."

CHAPTER ELEVEN

Harry and Jill sat quietly in Port Sinton Police station. They weren't impressed - In Northern Ireland it wouldn't have qualified as a police station. It didn't have barbed wire or security entrance gates, there were no guns lying around, it didn't have cameras everywhere, and it definitely hadn't been bombed in the last 20 years. In fact it was a pathetic little terrace cottage with "roses around the door" charm as the estate agents would have described it, had it been for sale.

It was originally a small house, and the good room at the front had been converted into a reception area, sporting 6 orange plastic chairs and the original floral carpets. The walls were a combination of public warnings and public notices. Warnings about wearing your seat belt and keeping your doors locked at night, mixed awkwardly with advertisements for a local fair 4 years ago, and a promotion for Willy the Window Cleaner who would clean all your windows for 4 Pounds and 50 Pence. If you had tried the rest and would now like to try the best, then Willy was the man to call. He even had a 24-hour emergency answering service should you need your windows cleaned urgently in the middle of the night.

A hole in the wall had 2 reinforced glass panels that led through to an office in the back – the nerve center of Port Sinton intelligence services. Although just between the hours of 9am and 2pm Mondays to Thursdays, and 9am to 11am Fridays and Saturdays. Closed Bank Holidays and Sundays. Outside of these hours, the port was vulnerable and open to undefended attack. Perhaps if Dick had just managed to hold on until 9am then things might have been different.

Ewan, the local Port Sinton cop, arrived at the hole in the wall. "Hello folks, Constable Ewan Barber, how can I be of service today."

"Hello Constable Barber. I'm DC Harry Thompson, and this is WPC Jill Boot, I believe someone has spoken to your sergeant about us coming in to see you today?"

"No, no, well...maybe, I don't know to be honest, I haven't seen him in 3 weeks, he's based up in Tarnlough, which is a bit of a way away, so we don't get to meet much nowadays."
"Right, well perhaps you could call him?"
"I cant – he's playing golf this morning, but I'll send him a text message and I'm sure he'll get back to me later this afternoon. Maybe you would like to pop back tomorrow. I'm a bit busy at the moment so if you don't mind, I need to get on and ..."

"We're investigating a possible murder", shouted Harry, "we're from Northern Ireland, and we've come here to follow up a specific lead. We are also Police Officers, Constable Barber, so I would appreciate a bit of assistance. Okay?" Ewan was now very suspicious. "Do you have any ID?"

Jill flashed her card and badge in a second; she was obviously already holding it open in her pocket. Harry joined her a bit later with his which was buried in papers in his jacket pocket

"… you should have been told that we would be coming."

"Boy, you guys in Ireland work fast", said Ewan. Harry and Jill took the complement honourably. "Thanks… anyway about this murder, can we ask you some questions please?"

"You can, but just for the record we haven't confirmed that it was murder, as Tim the ambulance man thinks it was suicide, but anyway…ask away!" Harry and Jill were suitably confused. "I'm confused" said Harry, "…how could it possibly be a suicide, there was a bullet hole in the face and head and no gun found at the scene, so how in God's name can that be suicide?"

"Well…", started Ewan, "…there was indeed a gun found. I know we shouldn't take anything for granted these days, and I have an open mind regarding this, but the facts are clear as they stand at the moment. I attended the scene almost straight after the discovery, and there was a gun there all right. Of that I'm sure.

Anyway, what's the connection with you Irish boys, what has it got to do with you lot!"

"How in God's name did you attend the scene straight afterwards Constable Barber", said Harry, "...have you got a frigg'n helicopter or something, or was it just a case of being in the right place at the right time, in which case what were you doing at the right place, when you should have been here in this God-forsaken shit hole of a wrong-place, at ...at... the wrong time".

"Well, there's no need for that sort of attitude" said Ewan "I can assure you I don't have a helicopter, but since it was only 300 yards down the road, I don't think it would be necessary. In fact, I'd say it would be a bit of 'overkill' – if you'll excuse the pun." Ewan, reversed his head triumphantly back from the hole and in a second appeared through the door to join them in the waiting room. He was dressed impeccably in his new well-pressed uniform, and looked larger and more in charge than the face that had been confusing them from the window. It was like Mr Ben exiting from the changing room.

Harry and Jill suddenly realized that Ewan was possibly talking about another death, and Jill worked out that the only solution would be for everyone to be right. "Lets start again shall we", she began politely, "We're from the PSNI - the Police Service of Northern Ireland, and we are investigating a murder that happened 2 days ago in Belfast, in Northern Ireland, for which we have a reason to believe there may be a connection to one of your residents here in Port Sinton. That's why we are here, and we are not investigating any other case that you may be working on at the moment. Our sergeant phoned your sergeant last night to make sure you knew we would be coming. Perhaps that might help to clear things up."

"It sure does Constable Boot", Ewan replied politely. Whilst throwing Harry a sly side-glance. "I can assure you that you'll get all the assistance you need from the Stalag DPF …that's Sinton, Tarnlough and Leighbridge area Glens, District Police Force… in your investigations, and I stand before you now as the proud representative of the afore-mentioned. To help further clarify the situation WPC Boot, we were saddened ourselves today that in this very village where you stand, there was a terrible death this morning, when one of our finest residents, Richard Williams, or Dick as he was affectionately known, was found only this morning with most of his head distributed on to his walls and ceiling, and a gun and the remains of last night's whiskey at his side"

Jill and Harry stood a little shocked for a moment – somehow Ewan had managed to get the upper hand, but they weren't quite sure how. "I'm very sorry to hear that", consoled Harry unconvincingly.

"Anyway, is there any information that you can give us in relation to a …a Ms Sally Burton from Port Sinton. We now understand that she is the sister of

OUR murder victim, who is a Ms Suzie Qua..., I mean Suzie ... a... Marlin, ...I believe." Harry looked sheepishly at Jill, by way of confessing that he did indeed nearly call her Suzie Quatro. Ewan didn't catch on. He was a die-hard Shirley Bassey fan, and had never heard of Suzie Quatro. He had, however, heard of Suzie Marlin. "I'm sorry" he said quietly. "This is indeed a very traumatic day for all of us". Harry and Jill didn't feel particularly traumatized so they found it strange that Ewan should take the news of their murder victim so badly.

"That lovely Irish girl, Suzie was her name", muttered Ewan. "That's right," jumped in Harry "you know her?" he bubbled excitedly.

"Sort of, yes" replied Ewan, "...I've met her a few times when she was here visiting Sally. God it's such a cruel world we live in."
"It sure is." Finally Jill and Ewan had something to agree upon. "It's made worse by the fact that Sally was the closest friend to OUR death, Dick – the body we found this morning - in fact they had to give Sally some tranquilizers just to get her through the day, and she has to identify the body later. As if life couldn't get any worse for her, the poor child's sister is now dead", Ewan slumped helplessly in his plastic chair.

Harry looked at Jill for signs that she too was thinking that Ewan is just a dumb, emotional welsh wreck, but instead Jill was also making her way down to the seat beside Ewan, and was wiping a tear away from her left eye. "The poor girl" It was becoming contagious and even Harry felt a little sad at the thought of poor Sally having to deal with such trauma. He tried to imagine how dreadful it must be to loose your closest friend and your only known relative at the same time, mainly so that he could feel really sad and appear more caring.

CHAPTER TWELVE

Sally sat subdued at the bottom of a bed in the Tarnlough Dental Research and Maternity Hospital, the closest medical facility to Port Sinton. She had been given a few tablets to settle her nerves, and was quietly slipping from complete consciousness to semi-consciousness and back again.

Complete consciousness brought with it the horrific reality that was hers alone for today. Just last night she had sat with Dick and talked and laughed and earlier had been taking the piss out of Dave at Flans. Sally just didn't have any answers. She didn't even know what the questions were. She was lost in complete confusion and panic. The whole situation was just too profound to apply any logic or understanding to it. She just wept and shook in hopeless agony and frustrated anger.

Her periods of semi-consciousness were induced by heavy doses of Diazepam which seemed to kick in and out of effect, and brought at least some light relief. During these periods, Sally's mind was allowing her to think that just maybe, perhaps, it is a dream or something other than reality. A weird and cruel play on her mind. The facts were still the same to her, but during these times it really seemed like a play. Nothing was real, not really real. She remembered back to her drama lessons as a child in

Hopen's Children Home. "Its okay", her drama teacher would assure her. "Its okay, it's only a play, its make believe. When it's real you'll know."

Sally had drifted into a period of consciousness when she heard Ewan's voice outside the door of the hospital. "Doctor, I appreciate you don't have the correct facilities or resources here but I need you to help me for the moment. Sally is going to need professional support and probably additional sedation, so anything you can do for me would be very helpful."

Sally felt shivery and weepy as Ewan and a nurse approached the side of the bed. "It's time isn't it?" sally muttered through a mouth of saliva and snot.
"Time?" questioned Ewan.
"Yes, its time to identify … to identify…Dick's body?"
"Ah, no Sally that won't be necessary for the moment. We'll make some other arrangements. You don't worry yourself about that". Ewan sat beside Sally and put his arm around her shoulder. His ginger hair looked transparent under the hospital lights, and his pink, pale face looked stark against the white, clean and crisp hospital pillows.

"Are you sure?" said Sally rather confused. "I'm stronger than I look". Sally felt safer in Ewan's grasp, and allowed her shuddering to slow down a bit, as she regained her grip on the tranquilizers.

"Sally, I've got some more bad news for you. I'm afraid there is just no easy way to say it, so I'm just going to take a deep breath, and say what I have to say. I'm not going to move, and we're just going to sit here for as long as it takes afterwards"

Sally loved the drama class at Hopen's; it was her only real escape from the torture from her room 'mates' in her children's 'home' where she spent much of her youth. The class was held every Tuesday morning from 10am to 1.30pm, and Sally spent the entire rest of the week wishing each day away, so that Tuesday would come round again.

"Two policemen arrived at my station today from Northern Ireland, with some news."

She loved taking on the part of someone else. Even just having a different name for a few minutes allowed her to make her brief escape. Sally loved playing the Princess. In one play she successfully auditioned to be the beautiful Princess Tasmin, the most beautiful Princess in the world, who met the most handsome Prince in the world - Prince Graf Castell, who was played by Tommy Speak. Tommy was one of the few people she liked from the home. Originally Prince Graf Castell fell in love with Tasmin's cousin, Princess Christina who was played by the retched monster Rachel T 'Rat' from her dorm room. Prince Graf and the Princess Christina were engaged to be married.

"They are here because they are investigating a murder back in Belfast, where a young woman was found dead from a gunshot wound."

Prince Graf Castell met Princess Tasmin at a family wedding, and they looked into each other's eyes just once and fell immediately in love. One of the servants saw Graf and Tasmin cuddling together and told the King about it. The King insisted that Princess Tasmin be sent to France, to live with an aunt, as a mark of the shame she had brought on the royal family. Prince Graf's father (then King of Iberia) told his son that he would be disinherited from the family and removed from his succession to the throne unless he stopped seeing Princess Tasmin, and instead agreed to marry Princess 'Rat' Christina.

"From the initial investigations, the police believe that the body is that of your sister, Suzie."

But Prince Graf Castell no longer loved Princess Christina and could not stay away from the beautiful Princess Tasmin, and set sail immediately to find her and ask for her hand in marriage. The Rat Christina was very angry and persuaded king daddy that he must have Prince Graf killed before he reached the beautiful Tasmin. A group of 8 men were recruited from the King's special guards and they set off to follow the Prince and intercept him on his way to France.

They caught up with him just 30 miles from reaching the Princess, and a bloody fight ensued. Tommy loved sword fights, and he wielded his weapon and butchered 4 of the Kings guards in one swipe. The remaining 4 pretended to make a deal with the Prince, only to get him to put down his sword and spare their lives. The Prince was fooled by the trick and was overpowered by 3 of the guards, whilst the fourth killed the handsome Prince with his own sword, and returned with his head to the King, where he was later rewarded with the Rats hand in marriage.

No matter how many times they performed, Sally would always run over to Tommy afterwards to make sure he wasn't hurt in the sword fight. "Its okay", her drama teacher would assure her. "Its okay, it's only a play, its make believe. When it's real you'll know."

"It was a single gunshot wound to the head, and she would not have suffered any pain. I know there is nothing I can say Sally to make things better, so I'll not even try."

CHAPTER THIRTEEN

"Have you decided what your question is yet?" asked Darwin. "Well…" Bob was as excited as Darwin was. "…I was thinking about asking whether there were any other fingerprints found at the scene. That way we would know whether someone else could be placed there at the time."

Darwin tutted. "Nah, already thought of that one. Think about it, of course there was someone else there – its pretty obvious, so the only answer you're going to get is 'yes', or I suppose 'no' if the murderer was wearing gloves. It doesn't really get you anywhere does it?" Bob retaliated "Yes, but then if the answers 'yes', then you could use your question to ask if they know who the prints belong to."
"Bob, why don't you just ask … 'whose fingerprints were found at the scene?' That way you get the complete answer, or not, in 1 question." Bob reluctantly agreed. "Smarty pants, so anyway what's your question going to be?" Darwin checked his notepad. "I have a shortlist, but probably my favourite at the moment is …um… 'what signs were there of forced entry?'. That way we should know whether she knew her attacker or not."

Bob acknowledged in semi-approval and gave the impression that she could see a flaw in the question, but wasn't prepared to discuss it. "I wonder if we should be asking about whether there was any evidence of theft or something, that way we could work on a motive" Darwin returned the semi-approval-saw-the-flaw look. "Hmmm, we should probably also ask about whether Sally was defending herself ... you know, stuff under the fingernails or whatever, to see if she was attacked or shot in a struggle, or even shot from a distance."

"Oh, Hi Harry" chirped Darwin, "...what's with the long face?
"Hi Darwin, we're fine, we just didn't have the most positive of days today" replied Harry. Darwin realized Harry was being a bit serious so he stopped smiling momentarily "Sorry Harry ... you want to talk about it?" Harry took a long breath "No, not really". Darwin moved the chair around beside him and motioned Harry to sit down "Come on Harry sit down and tell uncle Darwin – A problem halved is best shared, or something like that. Come on Harold, take a seat. You too Jill, come on have a seat and get things off your mind"

Harry realized that Darwin was not going to let up. "We met with the local Port Sinton constabulary today. There was a death in the Port and the man that died was Sally's closest friend, so the poor girl had to deal with the news that her friend and sister had died in the same day. Makes you think. Poor girl." Darwin and Bob decided that it would be best to just pretend that they didn't know all that information already, so instead they joined Harry and Jill in looking glum. Darwin counted slowly from 1 to 60. He predicted that 1 minute's silence was more than enough respect to pay for Sally's bad news and Dick and Suzie's untimely death. Princess Diana didn't get much more than that. "Poor girl" Darwin broke the silence "Makes you think" he continued wisely. "How was she after she heard the news?"

"No idea Darwin, the local guy Ewan told her. I'll be speaking to him tomorrow again, so I'll find out. Probably suffice to say that we won't be interviewing her for a day or so. Anyway, how was your day?"

"Not too bad I suppose" replied Bob, "We spoke to a few locals, got a bit of gossip, but we're not really much further on. That man who died, Dick, seems to have been a very popular bloke. Everyone seems to know Sally as well, and a few of them even remember meeting Suzie a few times, so Suzie and Sally had definitely spent time together here."

The subdued and relaxed atmosphere was suddenly blown apart by Stephen who burst through the double doors. "Darwin!!, you wont believe what …", then he realized that Harry and Jill were also there. "Sorry folks, I didn't realize…, anyway, Darwin can I have a word with you please – privately?"

Darwin looked around the other faces for some sense of approval, but didn't get it. However he decided that Stephen's news was definitely more exciting than sharing glum stories amongst the gang, so he avoided their eyes and speed-walked into the bar, near the window. Stephen vaulted in with a very smug look. "Who's the best detective in the world?"

"You are" responded Darwin quickly. He decided a surprise tactic of flattery would get him the information quicker. "That's why I hired you rather than Poirot or Holmes. You're the best Stephen, better than all the rest." said Darwin sincerely, even though he could hear Tina Turner finishing off his sentence. His tactic worked. "Um ... thanks" Stephen replied suspiciously, before moving swiftly on to telling his exciting story. "Suzie and Sally's father George R Harman – the one we traced for her" Darwin said nothing. Silence would speed up the story. "Well, I went back over my files and asked a few of my old contacts to do a bit of digging for me, just to fill in a few gaps. Anyway, I just got a call about 20 minutes ago from some friends in America to say that our father-of-the-year is actually THEE Rod Harman." Darwin was hoping that Stephen was going to elaborate as he didn't have a clue who Thee Rod was. It didn't work, and Stephen stopped talking.

"Keep going Stephen..."

"Oh, well, it turns out that when Harman left politics after all the scandals, he got involved in some dodgy import-export business from Ireland to America. Eventually the FBI picked him up from a sting operation in Vegas. Of course in true Harman style he blamed everyone else, and agreed to testify against his partners and clients, who each went on to get between 16 and 40 years in jail. Harman got charged with a few minor offences, done a few months in solitary confinement, then walked free as part of a deal with the Feds"

"Wow" Darwin was still keeping words to a minimum, and prompted Stephen to keep going by raising his eyebrows. He searched and searched inside his head for any recollection of any Harman he had ever heard of in his life.

Stephen thankfully obliged, "Needless to say his locked-up partners are not very happy with Harman. He had been living in Scotland for a while, and apparently there where 3 contracts out on his head at one stage. Intelligence officers in Belfast uncovered details of a plot to kill him by 2 of the leading names in the IRA, who actually had his full address in Scotland. So they decided to move him again, but nobody knows where. I should have known that there was something dodgy about him." Stephen appeared to have finished the story. "Why?" snapped Darwin quickly.

"They had to move him from Scotland because…"

"No!, I mean why should you have known that there was something dodgy about Harman?"

"Well, because quite a while back, I was called by the police to say that they were making some routine enquiries about outstanding warrants or something, and that their records showed that I had been trying to contact Harman a few years back. They wanted to know why I was trying to contact him, and they also wanted contact details for Suzie and Sally. I explained the whole situation to them, and they seemed happy enough. I never heard any more about it and didn't really think it was that significant."

"Outstanding Warrants?, doesn't sound right Stephen. Was the cop that called an old work colleague?" Stephen was confused to where the conversation was now going. "No, I had never spoken to him before, he just called up out of the blue."

"And you just gave him the information did you?" Darwin was starting to get frustrated.

"Um, yeah. I speak to the cops all the time – I didn't really think to question them."

"Stephen, let me get this straight. Someone phoned you a while back, said that he is a policeman and asked you about some very confidential information, and you just tell him, without even verifying who he is." Darwin was finally getting through to Stephen.

"Oh shit, this is my entire fault isn't it – I probably gave Suzie and Sally's details to Suzie's murderer." Stephen slumped over in the chair and cupped his head in his hands. "I'm such a stupid fucker. But Darwin I didn't know all this then, I just thought Harman was some dickhead who had dumped his kids, I didn't realize who he was or why anyone would want to get at him."

Darwin refused to give Stephen any sympathy, and left for the dining room. Bob was sitting alone. "Where did Harry and Jill go?" Bob was slightly taken aback with Darwin's sharpness. "They went up to get packed. They've been summonsed back to base, but Harry reckons he'll be back over again in a few days to interview Sally when she has recovered a bit. Why?"

Darwin's plan had been to drag Harry and Jill into the bar and make Stephen tell the story again, so that real qualified police investigators could hear what had happened and take the case over. This was all getting a bit too serious for Darwin now, and he just wanted someone else to take the responsibility. However as Harry and Jill weren't there, it gave him a few seconds to perhaps re-think the strategy. Harry only needed to know enough information for him to take the situation seriously. Darwin re-connected with Bob, "Bob, can you go and sit with Stephen in the bar. Ask him to tell you what he just told me. I need to speak to Harry."

Harry was standing in the upstairs corridor talking on his mobile phone. "yes, yes ... um yes, yep, yeah. Yes boss" and with that he ended the call.

"Playing hard to get Harry?"

"What?"

"Never mind. Listen we need to speak urgently. Stephen has uncovered something which is kind of important. Suzie and Sally's absent father is Rod Harmon."

"What?"

"Their estranged father – the one Stephen managed to trace a few years ago is actually Rod Harmon. We didn't realize at the time as it was just a name ... George R Harmon in fact. No reason for us to assume that it was actually Rod Harmon."

"Thee Rod Harman?" quizzed Harry "...the one with half the Mafia chasing him?"

"Yes" confirmed Darwin thankfully, as he just realized that it would be very embarrassing if Harry had said 'Rod who?', as Darwin still had no recollection of the name before today.

"Anyway, we now think that the people after him got both Suzie and Sally's details from Stephen a while back, which means that Sally is probably in similar danger as Suzie. We're going to have to do something, urgently." Harry agreed. "I'll call Ewan".

"Ewan, hello its Harry here from the PSNI. Listen, there has been a development. We believe that the people who killed Suzie Marlin in Belfast may well be after Sally now, and that they know where she lives. We need to make sure she's safe and get her into protection urgently."

Ewan and Harry agreed to meet at the hospital in Tarnlough were Sally was still being sedated. On the way, Ewan called his sergeant who in turn called Leighbridge police station. Leighbridge had 2 armed response officers, who were quickly mobilized and on their way to Tarnlough. Under a new Government initiative, every resident of the United Kingdom must be within a minimum of 1 hour's response time of an armed unit. In practical terms this meant that even some small police outposts had to send 2 personnel on the GPP Armed Response course, and in addition the 2 officers also needed to do a monthly top-up of 100 rounds at the police firing range in Swansea, as well as a quarterly training weekend at a secret army training location in England – believed by many to be the graduation school for the SAS.

The unlikely armed recruits packed their weapons and live ammunition in a special black foamed boot compartment in an unmarked Vectra and sped in the direction of Tarnlough. They went through every red light and pedestrian crossing along the way, and somehow arrived safely at the Tarnlough hospital with over 8 minutes to spare. Harry and Ewan were already standing guard at Sally's door. They had checked to make sure she was okay a few minutes earlier, and thankfully she was fast asleep and totally unaware of all the commotion.

The Armed Response Unit approached with guns drawn. One stood astride the door, whilst the other opened it slightly to make sure only Sally was in residence. One gun was trained down the corridor, the other pointed in the room. They reversed back and closed the door. One gun remained trained up the corridor. The second gun went back into its shoulder grab, as its owner beckoned over a nurse from the next corridor "Can you take me to each of the entrances and exits of this facility please?"

Hard to believe that even in the arse-end of nowhere you can still witness such a polished maneuver.

Sure in the knowledge that Sally was being protected, Harry and Ewan stood down their watch.

CHAPTER FOURTEEN

Bob and Darwin were helping Stephen to get over himself, and his guilt trip. "We know you didn't do it on purpose Stephen" twittered Darwin "...our only concern is that Sally is protected now, and I think we all agree on that ... I mean Suzie is dead – there's not much any of us can do about that now. What's happened has happened and nobody blames you. It's not as if you pulled the trigger Stephen."

As usual Bob knew exactly what he was doing. It wouldn't be right to keep giving Stephen a hard time, so Darwin was giving him a bit of sympathy, but then mingling in a bit of blame in disguise every now and then – just in case Stephen could ever forget that it was totally his stupid fault. On hearing the 'pulling the trigger' analogy, Stephen once again buried his head in his hands and moaned pathetically. Darwin sat quietly with his salty finger in the open wound, waiting for Stephen to recover enough to take another attack.

"What I can't understand..." Said Bob, hoping to drag the attention away from Stephen's pain "...is why someone would want to kill Harman's kids, I mean what did they ever do wrong?"
"It's just a way of hurting Harman – I don't suppose his enemies really care who they kill to get back at him." Bob wasn't convinced "No, think about it –

there's only one person they want and that's Harman – they don't give a toss about Suzie or Sally. In my opinion, they just want to bring him out of hiding, bring him out into the open where they can get him. They think that if they kill one of his daughters, then he will come out of hiding to protect the other one. That's what I would do … if I was after Harman"

Darwin liked her train of thought. "Yeah, you could be right Bob. I mean, if they killed both his daughters then he would have no reason to appear, and they wouldn't get him. Any father … maybe even an absent one… would try and protect his only daughter. They are sitting waiting for him, in fact they're probably at the hospital now watching for him to appear."

"…If I was after Harman…" Bob continued with her thought process, "… the first thing I would do now is to let Harman know that I know who Sally is, where she lives, what she does, and that I'm serious, and that I will kill her, and that it was me who killed Suzie. That's the message I would give Harman."

"Yes, but you can't exactly call him up and say…"
"No, no, I know Darwin, but think about it…"
"I am. Just tell me what you're thinking Bob"
"Dick", said Bob triumphantly.
Stephen raised his head from his hands, just to let Bob and Darwin know that he was listening.

"…If I was after Harman…" Bob was off again. "…I would kill Sally's best friend, in the same way that I killed Suzie. That way I achieve everything – Harman knows I've found Sally, he knows I'm serious as I'm prepared to kill her friend, he knows it was me who killed Suzie as Dick was also shot in the head, and he knows I'm here, waiting for him. He knows he either has to give himself up, or I'm going to kill his only living daughter."

Darwin half-agreed "There are 2 flaws in that theory. Firstly, Dick possibly committed suicide, or at best it was maybe made to look like suicide, which doesn't make sense in your theory. Secondly, as far as I can make out, and Stephen can back me up on this, Harman didn't really give a toss about his daughters, so I'm not sure if that would bring him out, or even if he knows Suzie has been shot." Bob conceded a little "Yeah, I know it's not perfect, but I'm just saying what I would do."

"I like it" admitted Darwin, "I just think we need to think it through more" Stephen rose slowly from his crouch "I think you're both full of shite. Dick killed himself – I saw the scene myself."
Darwin responded quickly with some extra salt, "Of course he did Stephen, I mean its bad enough that you blame yourself for Suzie's murder, without putting another death on your conscience as well. Yes, that's right, Dick killed himself Bob."

"Oh my god…" slobbered Stephen, "you're right – I was probably responsible for Dick's death as well." And he returned to his usual pose of head in hands, then let out a long groan. "I'm off to my room."

"Poor Stephen" said Bob. Darwin realized that this was a fine balancing act, between making Stephen feel crap and guilty, but at the same time not turning him into a victim. He worried that Bob then might take sympathy on Stephen and maybe fancy him, rather than Darwin. "It's his own fault, stupid tosser probably caused Susie's death. We're taking it easy on him Bob. Poor Stephen my ass."

"Fancy a trip into town?…chance to get away from this miserable hole for an hour?"
"Bryn!", Darwin shouted through the bar-hole.
"Uhhh", Bryn appeared in his usual life's-a-bitch tone. Darwin didn't care "Do me a favour big lad, call us a cab … we're hitting the bright lights of Port Sinton."

Just 1 minute later a 15 year old Toyota Carina tooted outside. It was a private taxi which belonged to Bryn's uncle, although he couldn't be bothered driving it tonight, so instead his auntie was disguised as the taxi driver. She never spoke one word the whole way into town. When they reached Flans she looked down the side of the steering wheel, pretending to have a taxi meter.

"That will be eight pounds and 20 pence ... excluding gratuities." She broke the silence. "What time do you want to come back at? ... It's not so easy to get a taxi from here – not the demand really... as you can see. I'll pick you up later and get you back safely. No point in wandering around the streets looking for a taxi – not safe either, especially this time of year. Did you here what happened the other day..."

"Here, thanks...", Darwin pushed a ten pounds into her open hand. Once she started talking, there was clearly no stopping her. "Eleven o'clock would be great", and Darwin and Bob tried to make a quick departure.

"In that case...", continued Aunty Bryn, "...I'll wait here. There's no point going all the way back home. By the time I got in to the house and got undressed, it would be time to start getting ready again and start the journey back down. The last time..."

"Undressed?", quizzed Bob. "Never Mind" said Darwin. "Some things are better unexplained." And he pushed Bob in the direction of Flans front door. "See you at eleven then, bye, bye", and they both left Bryn's Aunt waiting outside the pub.

Inside, Dave was alive. The rest of the crowd however was somewhat subdued, which is fairly natural, considering one of their friends was dead. Deep down they were more depressed about the fact that they would now have to buy all their own drinks, or stay at home during the week and wait until the weekends for their English friends to buy them some. But it was still too early to be discussing that outwardly, so they all pretended that they were missing Dick's company for now.

The sparkling television still totally dominated proceedings. Its volume was turned down, but the little pictures darted around the screen shining all different shades of colour into every corner. Corners that had only ever seen darkness and the occasional sprays of spring sunlight. Their inexperience was exposed as they reflected the electric colours awkwardly. Soon they would get used to it.

Dave recognized Darwin and Bob from before. "Hello there folks, you're very welcome back to Flans international hostelry ... by the sea. I had heard rumors that we had a couple of Police Officers here at the Port – a gentleman and a lady from Ireland, but I didn't realize it was you two." pushed Dave. The rest of the bar waited for a response, but tried not to look. They didn't want to scare them off completely, as they desperately wanted to know what was happening.

"No, we're just here on holiday" Replied Bob "Two pints of your finest please". Dave winked in collusion, and started to pour the drinks – even the beer seemed to come out of the pipes quicker and with a bounce in its step. There appeared to be a lot more bubbles than there were before. The band of locals lost interest in their visitors when they realized they might not be cops.

"So any more news on Dick?", Bob started the questioning off.

"Haven't you heard?" replied Dave excitedly. Bob and Darwin perked up to the thought of getting the hottest news. They had denied being cops but hadn't really been overly convincing so they were sure that they'd get all the juicy details from the locals. Dave continued "…he's definitely dead. Not a chance of recovery apparently. In fact so much of his head was removed, that Betty at number 45, who used to be an auxiliary Nurse in Tarnlough, said that even if his heart was beating, he would still be clinilogically dead. So that's the end of him. Good and proper. Dead."

Darwin and Bob tried to ignore the fact that Dave seemed pleased that Dick was dead.

Darwin tried a new tactic. "I heard rumors that it may have been murder, did you?" he tried.

"No!" shouted Dave, "and even if it was, I have a rock solid alibi." He turned to the rest of the crowd. "Did you hear that lads – Dick was murdered! Heard it straight from the horse's mouth!"

Every conversation stopped. A lone voice from the back shouted "I hope you have an alibi Dave?", but Dave ignored him, and the rest of the bar tried not to laugh too hard, in respect of the dead.

116

"Murder?" was echoed a dozen times in the next few seconds as the village came to terms with murder in their own back yard. Murder? *But who would murder Dick?* They all thought quietly.

"But who would murder Dick?" they eventually started mumbling to one and other.

Darwin was now starting to worry about what he had started. How many people were going to loose their sleep tonight because of his wild and totally unfounded claims? Now was not a good time to show any cracks. "Oh yes" Bob confirmed, "...they say it was murder all right." The bar huffed quietly as it was confirmed. Murrrrder! Even in Wales, it sounded better in Taggart accent.

"Shall we take a seat?" Darwin pushed Bob forward as they realized that they had become the centre of attention; inadvertently some of the locals had created a semi-circle around their position at the bar. "Probably best to change the subject." Bob realized that at least one quarter of the bar were still tuned in to their conversation, and the other three quarters were waiting for the story to be relayed back to them through Chinese whispers. "Yeah, I agree Bob. So... when do you think you and I are eventually going to get it on?"

In the background Chinese whispers was failing badly. Mainly because most of the bar was half-deaf due to their age, and therefore it had evolved into a bizarre cross between shouting loudly and mouthing silently.

Bob giggled "I know, just hasn't worked out yet has it? Although I must admit it is mainly due to your sleeping habits – falling asleep at the wrong time, sleeping with the bar-boy … that sort of thing. When you get your sleeping sorted out, I'm sure it will work itself out." Darwin never realized he had a problem with his sleeping before. *"Look, shall we just have a few beers here, grab aunty-cab home early, then head back to my room for a night of passion?"* thought Darwin.

"Yeah, you're probably right" said Darwin instead.

The locals in the background had lost interest in their conversation as it didn't involve murder any longer, and they had started to talk amongst themselves again and pretended to drink their halves of beer. This could be a long night and they knew they had to make them last until closing time without Dick.

"Look" pointed Bob through a gap in the velour curtains. "…that silly old bat is really going to sit there waiting for us. Let's hope she manages to keep her clothes on". Darwin imagined her sitting outside, clothed, and then unclothed and naked. Any port in a storm, he thought. Even Sinton.

"I wonder if Harry got the forensic report yet?" pondered Darwin out loud.

"Just thinking the same thing. I suppose on a positive note, maybe Stephen won't want to ask his questions now – then we could get to ask all of them. Mind you, I'm not sure if I could think of ten questions."

"Not a problem", reassured Darwin, and he produced his 'short-list' of at least 30 questions. Darwin had been preparing for this all his life and although he had never seen a forensic report, he could sort of imagine it; however he hoped that things hadn't changed much from Quincy's days. Bob seemed impressed as she read through his list.

"Shall I give Harry a ring?" asked Darwin, although he didn't wait for a response.

"Hi Harry, Darwin here. Just a quickie to see how you are feeling now, and if things went okay tonight? …Yeah. Absolutely correct Harry. No, not at all – I mean you've done your best. It's in the hands of the experts now Harry, its over to them. Anyway, so are you guys staying for a bit longer now? … have you not? …Oh right … yes … is she? … Ha Ha Ha … in one go? … Ha Ha. Anyway, sure I'll catch up with you tomorrow. Yeah, you too. Bye."

"Well?" prompted Bob "No, he doesn't have it yet. Jill has gone on back home, and Harry is staying here for a day or two, or until he can get to interview sally. She's safely under armed guard now. He's hoping to get the forensics faxed over at some stage tomorrow. So how did you get into the clothes shop business in Belfast then?" asked Darwin apparently from nowhere

- so far from the left wing that he thought even Bob might be confused. But of course she wasn't, and she was just about to ask him where he bought his kitchen from as she was thinking of replacing hers.

"A bit by accident really. I used to manage the logistics in a large department store in Edinburgh. I came back home for an uncle's funeral. My cousins had been running his clothes shop on the Lisburn Road for years in the hope that he, and it, would make a recovery, but when he died they decided just to close it. I got chatting to them at the funeral, and agreed to take over the lease for them. I used my contacts in the purchasing department in Edinburgh to source a few new lines, and that's it ... Bobs-your-Uncle."

Darwin pretended not to catch on to the pun. "That's what the shop is called" said Bob by way of explanation. "Oh right, sorry, yes ... Bobs your Uncle, that's really good" said Darwin almost convincingly. Having worked in advertising most of his life he had grown a hatred for tacky business names – many surrounding the likes of Hairdressers such a 'Snip above the Rest', or 'Curl up and Dye'. He looked strangely at Bob for a second – 'Bobs your Uncle' was right up there with the worst he had ever heard. To think he once fancied her?

"Not really" Bob giggled, "...but it was on the short-list. It's actually called 'Bonicia', after an African art form. The ancient patterns are used in fabric designs by a few of the Houses I buy from."

He liked Bob again, and Bob liked him too, but then again he knew she would.

"Another beer?" chirped Darwin "We've only got 1 hour and 55 minutes before Aunty-Cabs will be in here looking for us."

"Yeah, why not. See if they've got any nuts or anything, I'm starving. That meal at the hotel was rare wasn't it."

On queue, Aunty-Cabs tooted outside at exactly 11 o'clock, and shortly afterwards, they made their way through reception, giggling and trying to work out why it was 8 pounds and 35 pence back. Did the old bat really believe that she had fooled them into thinking she had a proper taxi meter. She didn't even have proper brakes or lights. Darwin spotted Harry sitting alone in the bar, but he pretended not to and tried to usher Bob upstairs quickly. "Its okay Darwin, go and see Harry – make sure he's okay. We'll catch up later." Darwin was impressed that she picked up on his thoughts. "You sure?" queried Darwin just in case it was a test. "Yes, yes, yes. Go on", and she kissed him slowly and lightly on the lips ... for just a second.

"Hey Harry", said Darwin "how's it going?"

"Hi Darwin. Not too bad thanks. Sally is now safely tucked up asleep and sedated with 2 armed guards at her door. Ewan says he wasn't sure whether Sally heard him telling her about Suzie's death, but I suspect she did. Either way things aren't very positive for her are they? The Serious Crime Squad in Swansea will probably take over the case now. We'll just have to get Sally through the night.

Darwin sucked his lips "So, I take it that this Rod Harman is a nasty piece of work then?"
"Not really Darwin, he was a very senior cabinet minister back in the seventies in government as you know, ex-secretary of state - a very influential man. Then he was caught accepting favours to try and influence a few votes from some planning committees or something. Not really big league to be honest, but it caused a stir at the time, as the press was trying to give the government a hard time over sleaze…"

"…yeah, I remember" blagged Darwin, "…so what happened after that then, is that when he got involved with the import/export business?"
"Import/export? that's a new word for it."
"Is it?"
"Yeah"
"Anyway, continue on…" Darwin tried to re-gain Harry's momentum.
"You've never heard of Rod Harman have you?" probed Harry.
"Of course I have, but you know, you hear that many things, it was ages ago, it's hard to remember everything you know"

Harry was suspicious of Darwin, but decided to give him the benefit of the doubt, and continued. "Well, all went quiet for a time. Rod obviously got a proper job, or at least managed not to get caught. Then a UK haulage company that he partly owned was discovered bringing illegal immigrants into the USA from South America, then they traced the company back to a similar route operating between Ibestistan and France. Harman was way out of his depth. Of course he claimed that he knew nothing about it, but there was more evidence that linked him to another haulage group caught transporting cocaine through Guatamala. Nobody really suspected that Harman was the mastermind or even involved directly, probably just that he had supplied the lorries and customs papers without asking too many questions. This was big stuff and they were after the main guys. So the FBI probably just scared the shit out of him, and he spilled the beans – put a lot of top names behind bars of which 2 were on the FBI's top 20, so it was a really big operation. I don't suppose Mr Harman was very popular in certain quarters, so he probably went into hiding or something."

"Yeah, that's sort of the version I remember as well. Bob reckons that Dick was murdered. Sort of a warning to Harman. We've *killed one of your daughters, we've now found the other one*. So they kill her best friend, as a final warning to Harman to come out or they'll kill Sally too. Suppose it sort of stacks up."

Harry was responsive, "Yes, must admit that thought did go through my mind as well. It does seem a bit of a co-incidence. I'll check again with Ewan, make sure a full autopsy is done – if Dick was murdered, then we'll find out. Forensics these days are so accurate, they'll work it out."

"One thing I can't understand…If Stephen could find Harman easily enough, then why can't these top gangsters manage to do it – I mean Stephen's not the sharpest knife in the set?"

"Simple really, I presume he used to be a cop? … Well he would know then about the Witness Protection Program. Basically in the police we can reach anyone who is being protected on the scheme. We simply send a letter to the WPP Internal Logistics Centre in Manchester, then they filter the letters out to the various police regions, who eventually work them through to the single contact points, who bring the letters to the witnesses or not – it's really at their discretion. The program's quite effective really and nearly all the post you send - providing it's not a threat or anything sensitive, will get through to the witness. We use it all the time, although it can sometimes take weeks. Cops just do it as a matter of course if you can't find someone through the normal searches."

Darwin agreed, but something was still confusing him. "So how could someone have known that Stephen had got through to Harman? Assuming the call asking about Suzie and Sally wasn't actually from the police, then how did they know that he had managed to get a letter to Harman?"

Harry shrugged "Could be anything Darwin. He could have mentioned it innocently to someone, not really knowing what he was saying. Plus, the chances are that Stephen probably put a lot of feelers out there initially when he was doing his searches on Suzie. All the local courts and local councils, adoption agencies, children's homes and local authorities, Salvation Army, Police, Connect and a dozen other charities and registers, not to mention the internet where most searches eventually end up. It's more than likely that the people looking for Harman were probably looking in some similar places to Stephen, especially when he found Suzie's father's name. So they possibly just stumbled on Stephen and chanced their arm by phoning him up. The truth is I don't know Darwin, but it doesn't surprise me that they got his name eventually."

Darwin knew something didn't make sense. He wished Bob was here. She would know the next question to ask. "Another drink?" was the best question Darwin could some up with. Harry smirked at Darwin's line of questioning "Yeah, why not. Bryn has gone home so we'll have to serve ourselves."

CHAPTER FIFTEEN

At 7am, Bob popped her head in the open doorway of the bar on her way out for a morning jog. Darwin and Harry were asleep in identical poses. Both slumped in beige armchairs, with their heads touching in the middle. Both with their right foot up on the coffee table, and the left foot spread out straight ahead. Each had a glass of whiskey or brandy in their right hand, and both had managed to keep a hold of the drinks despite now being in very deep and noisy sleep.

As Bob looked at Darwin sleeping, she was truly struggling with how she felt. Not about Darwin's motives for not coming to bed; she already knew that he desperately wanted to, but as always, he was drawn to the moment's brightest light, like a lost fluttering moth living out its last hours. Instead, she was struggling with her own feelings – she couldn't work out how she felt about not sleeping with Darwin. On the one hand she wasn't really glad about it, and she genuinely did fancy him. But on the other hand she couldn't work out why she wasn't disappointed. She should be, but that emotion simply hadn't entered her head. She knew Darwin wanted her, and she even knew that she would happily shag him, but the fact that they hadn't didn't concern her at all. She didn't really know if she even liked Darwin most of the time, but for some reason she loved being with him and sharing his journey.

Yet with Brian ... well, that was simple for Bob. She loved Brian, and Brian loved her and they would have been at it 3 times a day. Black and white. She so wanted to fall in love with the many complicated shades of Darwin's grey, and some of the time she did, but the clarity of black and white was the only thing that was truly stimulating her. Her complete emotional ambivalence to this new relationship was surprising and disappointing her.

Bob suddenly spotted the extremely loud door bell ringer in the bar; she ran to the front door and held the button for a few seconds as the clanging filled the morning air, then took off down the road like a naughty teenager.

Darwin and Harry both bolted up straight in ringing horror.

Darwin was still nursing a mild hangover at eleven o'clock. He had persuaded Bryn to make him some breakfast, even though breakfast had officially finished at 10am and the chef had left for the day. A crisp 20 pound note was all the persuasion Bryn needed, and he done a great job in microwaving enough things from the fridge to fill a reasonably sized plate. Hangover breakfast for Darwin was purely a quantity affair, and this certainly met that criteria.

After the door-bell incident at 7 o'clock, Darwin decided to leave the bar and wandered upstairs. First he tried Bob's room to see if he still had a chance there – he worked out that if he kept the curtains closed and the hall light on then maybe Bob would think it was still the middle of the night, and welcome him into her warm and sleepy embrace. Bob's door was unlocked, but of course she wasn't in her bed as she had just gone out for a run. Darwin immediately assumed that she was with Stephen and beat himself up on Bob's bed. What an idiot he had been – he had practically driven Bob into Stephen's arms. They were probably still doing it now.

Darwin eventually plucked up the courage to do something about it. He did of course consider doing the adult thing like knocking Stephen's door, and demanding that he unhand his women, but that would be potentially confrontational and he was tired and weak, and still a bit drunk. Instead he choose an unusual path and carefully dismantled and set-off the fire alarm in Bob's room, then ran on tiptoes back to his own room, took off his shirt and shoes, then burst out of the room again shouting "What the hell is that?"

Stephen came out of his room making similar noises, so Darwin quickly checked the room for any signs of Bob – there were none. It was a mystery. The whole hotel shuddered with constant, deafening ringing that was at least double the volume it needed to be to wake even the most determined of sleepers within a two mile radius. Darwin was ready to go to bed now declaring "false alarm, false alarm…" and encouraging others to repeat it with him, whilst trying to locate the 'Off' button for the fire alarms. However the night caretaker informed everyone that it was not a drill and therefore they all had to exit immediately and gather at the rendezvous point at the front of the car park.

They all stood there quiet and well-behaved in the morning cold and waited for the Tarnlough Fire Brigade to save them. In the meantime, the role-call eventually highlighted that Bob was missing. Darwin was momentarily tempted to run through the imaginary flames and rescue her, but he was sure he could hear the fire engine in the background somewhere, and didn't want to get in the way.

Bob and the Fire Brigade arrived at the front of the hotel at exactly the same time, half an hour later.

Where the fuck have you been?" Screamed Darwin. Bob was a bit confused "I was out for a run, why? something happened?"

"No nothing really ... we were all just having a chat over breakfast and someone mentioned that its been a long time since we saw a big fucking red fire engine, so we called up the local fire station and asked if they could send one around for us, then we all got dressed in our bed clothes and we've been out here in the car park waiting for it to arrive. Isn't it lovely! You made it back just in time." Screamed Darwin, slightly quieter than before. "You sleep like that?" Bob eyed Darwin's trousers and socks "...any wonder you never get laid."

After a few minutes of rummaging through the hotel corridors and kitchen, the Tarnlough deputy Chief Fireman, Samuel Jones, declared the building safe. There was a huge feeling of relief from the owner, Gwyn, who had arrived a few minutes earlier to the thought that his pension fund was burning to the ground.

Harry was still dressed in his grey suit, but had cleverly done up all the buttons, fixed his tie, and brushed his hair enough to make it look like he was up and ready to face the day already. Darwin and Harry acknowledged each other in mutual understanding but didn't speak. Neither of them knew how the previous night had ended, so they were both keeping their options open and waiting for their memory to return later. Finally at 8 o'clock Darwin curled up alone in bed to enjoy what was left of the morning's sleep time. Just before eleven, the persistent buzzing of raging vacuum cleaners finally forced open his eyes.

There is something wrong with a microwaved sausage. Difficult to say exactly what – it seemed to taste fine. It just looked ill. Darwin vowed never to microwave another one, and dipped them into some brown sauce to take the bad look of them. Bacon and microwaves worked well together. Beans of course could be microwaved with the best of them, but the tomatoes were struggling a bit – they seemed to be far too hot compared to everything else. Bryn had even managed to make some toast, in the toaster, which helped to mop up the watery microwave juices that filled up most of the plate. All in all a relative success, and 20 pounds well spent.

Darwin cleared his throat and called Bob on her mobile. He tried not to be hungover, but his voice was at least 2 octaves lower than normal. "Hi, how are you this morning?"

"Grand thanks" and Bob walked into the dining room and sat down at the table beside Darwin. "I met Ewan this morning – you know the local cop" said Bob proudly. "…he was here to see Harry earlier, so Harry introduced me. He seems like a nice bloke. He had checked with the hospital this morning, and Sally is doing fine. Still alive, and still no attacks on her. The

Serious Crime Squad are on their way down from Swansea. Apparently they want to know how Harry made the connection to Harman. Naturally he blamed us, so they want to interview us all this afternoon. We had better tell Stephen as well."

Darwin tried relentlessly to clear his throat again "Aheeeem, huucckem, sorry – did you get to ask him about Dick's death … the murder theory?.

"No, I was going to, but Harry was already on to it. Told me that he had already raised the issue and that I wasn't to worry about it any more."

"huucckem" Darwin was recovering slightly "Did Harry get Suzie's forensic report through yet?"

"No, I asked him again this morning and he was still waiting for the fax, but he did say that he had some new information about the death but couldn't really share it with us."

"Where is he?" coughed Darwin. That had clearly insulted him. "Don't know. He was in reception a minute ago, should be around here somewhere". Darwin jolted up. Then he jolted back down again, drank some orange juice, plopped 2 more tablets down his neck, and then stood up slowly this time. He made his way past reception, where he could see Harry pacing up and down the corridor, agreeing intently at the instructions he was receiving from his mobile. "Yes, Yes I know, I agree, Yes that's right, Yep … speak later", and he hung up.

"Hi Harry"

"Hello Darwin, how are you feeling this morning?"

"Not too bad, considering"

"What about you?"

"Pretty much the same … could do with a few more hours sleep but there you go, not much I can do about that now."

Darwin was finished with the pleasantries. "Bob says that you've got some new information about Suzie's death." Harry adopted a serious and official tone. "I do, Darwin, but I can't tell you anything we find out – I'm a police officer, I'm a detective, and you're in advertising. This is what I do for a job. We've had a good laugh, but it's time that we all got on with our own jobs. This is a serious matter – at least 1 murder, possibly 2, with another in police protection, plus a crooked politician, murderers and terrorists from 3 continents, death contracts, Interpol, FBI." Harry now looked sterner and older. "Sorry mate, but you're leaving here after you've been interviewed, and you're heading back home. Your flights are booked. Your adventure is all over. We'll try and keep you up to date on Suzie's murder through your local liaison officer in Belfast."

Bob had joined Darwin in the corridor. They looked at each other in total desperation. It was over. Darwin and Bob were having the time of their lives, and suddenly it was coming to an end. Suddenly Harry was being professional and serious. Suddenly the

Serious Crime Squad was arriving from Swansea to take over the case. Everyone seemed to be closing ranks, and Darwin and Bob were of no rank. They didn't fit into anyone's team. Harry wouldn't even tell them his new discovery over Suzie's death. Darwin could feel the blood draining from his face. He felt like a hopeless school boy that had just been told that he hadn't been picked for the football team, in fact even worse. Not only was he not picked for the team, but he wasn't even being allowed to watch.

Bob realized that they had just got a little carried away. She was sharing Darwin's dream, but for her it was just a case of enjoying the train ride. With Darwin it was different – it was his train, he was the train-driver, he even owned the tracks. She felt worse for him, than herself.

"I can't believe you would do this Harry." He whimpered.

Harry's phone rang. You could see him almost mouth the words 'saved by the bell'. Harry turned his back on Darwin and Bob "Hello Ewan, how can I help."

"Bar", Darwin snapped, and pointed roughly in the right direction. "I'm sorry Darwin", Bob held his gaze as they sat down on the same 2 beige chairs that Harry and Darwin had slept on the night previously. "Never mind", perked Darwin. "It just means that we have to change strategy. Wouldn't be much of an adventure if it was predictable and plain sailing now would it?"

"Adventure?" Bob homed in on Darwin using the same word that Harry was accusing him of being. "Is Harry right? Is this just an adventure to you Darwin?"

"It's just a word Bob. To be honest it's just life, or more accurately, just my life. It's what I do. I do it in work, I do it in relationships, I even doing standing up some times. It works for me. I'm happier more often than I'm sad – which I wasn't for a long time. I have a reasonable life. I dream like everyone else Bob, the only difference is that I don't have that filter that everyone else has that stops dreams seeping through to reality. They all blend into one for me. Usually that means something stupid like going on a holiday to Iraq, or buying a red hot air balloon, or building a wacky business or something."

"...but now?" probed Bob. "Hey, now I'm here. This is today's journey." Darwin opened his palms and looked around the room. Bob responded with a small ironic smile, and surveyed the dreary uneventful room that Darwin seemed to think represented his exciting journey.

"At the moment I like this journey, this life, this fucking 'adventure'. Sure it may end this afternoon or maybe tomorrow. But the bottom line is that I like this journey, now. It's the best one I've ever had, and probably the best I ever will have. It's the adventure that I have always been working towards. It may even

be journey's end. So!..." he perked up even more. "So!!... I'm going to keep it a bit longer."
"You in?"
"I'm in – just 2 things."

Darwin encouraged her to continue. "Number 1 – how do you plan in getting us back into the adventure? Number 2 - what was that 'journey's end' shit about?" Darwin laughed. He loved it when Bob caught him on trying to be all deep and philosophical. "I have several plans Bob, and at least 1 of them is bound to work. Can you see if you can find Stephen. We need him at the moment. Bob ran out and returned with Stephen a few minutes later. "He was in his room" reported back Bob.

"Um, thanks Bob. Stephen we're being pushed out of the deal here. The Serious Crime Squad is coming down this afternoon to interview us about the Harman connection, then after that Harry has booked us all on a plane home. Seems like everyone wants us out of the equation. Harry even has some new information on Suzie, but he won't tell us, plus he's holding back on the forensic report. Bottom line is … we've been shafted – they've used us to drag out every piece of information that we know, and have given us back nothing. Now they know everything we know – we've been discarded." Stephen unintentionally started mimicking Darwin "Bastards".

"Stephen, I'm assuming that you want this advent…, I mean investigation to continue … even if it is just for the hourly rate!" Stephen did. Hourly rate seemed as good a reason as any. "Good, so we're all on board now. So what is our strategy for getting back into the mainstream investigation?" Darwin paused for just a second, in case anyone else had an idea. Even if they did, a second wasn't enough to interject, so he continued.

"Firstly, we need to get Harry back on our side and supporting us … I know how to do that one easily enough. Secondly we need to either have (or appear to have) more information so that they need us.
Thirdly. Well 2 will do to start – no point in overkill.
Stephen, can you work on the 'more information' strategy. Work out a way to make them think that we know more than we actually do. Doesn't matter what it is, but just make it big. Myself and Bob will get Harry on our side again. Then we'll be rocking. Okay gang?"
"Okay!" they mumbled in almost unison.
"Great, we'll meet back here at thirteen hundred hours. The serious crime squad will be here after lunch, so we've literally only got a few hours."

Stephen had a look of pleasure and hope. He clearly had an idea of how to make the police think that they know more. Darwin was confident Stephen would come up with something, and was delighted to see the hope back in Stephen's eye.

"Okay Bob, now for our plan ..."

CHAPTER SIXTEEN

Harry was now on his third call of the morning to the sergeant. "Yes, yes sergeant, that's right, she is, yes," Bob waited patiently for him to finish. "Fucking idiot", whispered Harry loudly at the phone – checking first of course that it was definitely off. He could feel someone nearby, and turned back to find Bob waiting formally at the side of reception. "Hi Bob", said Harry sheepishly and avoiding all eye contact.

"Harry can I have a word please, it's important and …"

"Look Bob, I'm sorry but …"

"It will only take a minute of your time."

"Yeah, of course Bob."

"Great, come and sit with me for 5 minutes in the bar, I promise it won't take any longer."

Bob stopped when she reached the door. "Oops, Darwin's in there on the phone. Wait here and I'll see if the dining room is free." Harry waited reluctantly. He could just about hear Darwin on the phone. He moved closer to the door to see if he could pick up any more.

"Michael, I don't give a fuck how much it will cost – I want a formal complaint against that tosser Harry now for what he did to me, and a civil suit issued by the end of the day. I'll tell you how serious it is Michael, I was so traumatized that I haven't been able to go back to work since! That's costing me twenty grand a week. That idiot's mistake could cost me millions by the time I've recovered."

Harry moved nervously closer to the door. "I said I don't care Michael. Look I'll transfer a hundred grand to your account today – is that enough to be getting on with? ... Oh and by the way, I presume your fee includes a few calls to your Chief Constable friends? ... ha, ha ... yeah thought it might cost a bit more! Okay, okay – 150k, but I want the full works on him okay! I want him hurt every way that you can." Harry stayed motionless and silent.

"His name and address? Shit I don't know everything Michael, but I'm sure I could find out. His name's Harold Thompson, I'll have to try and find his address ... oh can you? ... even better... yeah you too buddy ... ha, ha, ha ... yeah, maybe even more than ..."

"Harry", Bob called from up the corridor. "Come on, the dining room is free." Harry shouted "shhh" up the corridor to her, and tried to re-tune back into Darwin's call."

"ha, ha ... Bye" was all he caught, before Darwin walked straight out of the bar, and almost bumped into Harry. "Hi Harry, how are you?"

"I need to talk Darwin."

"Do you? That's good, well don't let me stop you." and pushed past him.

"Come on Bob, we've got packing to do." He pointed up the stairs. Bob pretended to be confused "Um, well

Darwin, I was just going to speak to Harry for a minute and …"

"Harry?", Darwin laughed. "There's nothing that 'has-been' can offer us any more."
"Darwin it's not my fault, I'm only obeying orders." Begged Harry as he followed Darwin to the bottom of the stairs. "Well it's a pity others weren't as obedient", spat Darwin as he stared at Bob "I said we've got packing to do! – now either you're coming or you're not, either way suits me." Bob almost cried as she looked fearfully back at Darwin. "Darwin please just give me two minutes – I promise I'll be there, and I promise I'll get the packing done in time. Please trust me on this one."

Harry frowned as he noticed the sheer petrified look on Bob's face, followed by a well of convincing tears running down her left cheek. He walked over to put his arm around her, but Darwin quickly put a stop to any attempt of comfort. "Get your hands off her." Darwin said calmly and without blinking – staring Harry hard in between the eyes. Harry lowered his arm.

"Two minutes", Darwin turned and ran quickly up the stairs, shouting back "two minutes" at least 5 or 6 times until he reached his room.

Bob let out a cry, and held her head in both hands. "Come on", said Harry and whisked her into the dining room. "What the hell is happening Bob?" Bob let out another cry. "Its Darwin, he has completely lost the plot." Harry put his arm around her. "Just talk to me Bob, I'll help in any way I can."

"It's everything, he has just completely changed. Since you told him it was all over, he has completely freaked. He just had a row with Stephen, accusing him of being in on it with you - of betraying him! Straight after the row, he phoned up one of his dodgy pals in West Belfast and told him he wanted Stephen hurt – badly hurt. Five grand he promised the guy for at least 2 broken bones. What makes it even sicker, is that he asked him to take a photo of Stephen after the attack. I just don't know who he is any more – he'll stop at nothing. I need your help Harry, Stephen is in danger and Darwin is going to make sure everyone suffers."

Harry hugged Bob tightly. "I know Bob. I just heard him in the bar telling his solicitor to start a formal proceedings against me and also a civil suit, he was even bribing someone to talk to my Chief Constable. I'm absolutely finished Bob – He's probably already got me sacked, and then he's going to bankrupt me with the civil action."

"He really will stop at nothing Harry. I reckon that's just the tip of the iceberg to what he's going to do. Anyway, Harry I have to go, otherwise God alone knows what he'll do to me. But just please promise me Harry that you'll try and help Stephen as well?"

Harry didn't really care that much about Stephen's well being, but nodded warmly.

"I'd better go, he'll be timing me to make sure the 2 minutes are not up."

"Bob, look I can't afford to loose my job, or my house and everything I've worked for. Oh, and of course I want to help Stephen. I'd like you to ask Darwin to reconsider. Tell him that it wasn't my decision, which it wasn't, and that I'll do everything within my powers to keep you guys in the loop, and also tell you everything I know, and try and keep you involved. I can't promise I'll succeed, but I can promise that I'll try my hardest. If I commit to that, will you ask him to call off his solicitors and whatever else he has planned for me ... oh and of course against Stephen as well."

Bob felt dreadful about what she was doing, and didn't really think she had it in her. She felt bullied a bit by Darwin to play out his plan, but that was no excuse – it was the adrenaline, momentum and excitement that really kept her forging on. At least now she could apply for her equity card.

Bob looked sadly back. "Harry, I think to be honest it's probably too late, but I can only try. I better run, otherwise I could be the next victim." She ran over and hugged Harry quickly, then turned and ran out of the dining room, and up the stairs. Harry could hear Darwin bellow at Bob through his door "11 seconds to spare!"

"That guys a fucking nutter" Harry whispered to himself "How could I ever have trusted him."

Five minutes later, Darwin joined Harry in the bar. "Listen Harry, none of your bullshit okay. I want to be able to ask our questions as agreed on the forensic report, I want any new information that you have, and I want your support and commitment to keep us as close to the action as possible ... i.e. here – for the moment. I don't give a fuck how you do it, I just want it sorted."
"Darwin, you know that I'll do my ..."
"Harry, drop the bullshit. The only word coming out of your mouth next will be 'Yes'"
Harry looked around like a hopeless bullied child, before finally agreeing. "Yes" he mumbled reluctantly. "Good, Harry, that's the right decision. Now, we'll put together a plan to convince the others that we know more than we do. You will play along with this, and make sure that everyone else is convinced of our ongoing value to the investigation. Okay?"

"Oh, sorry ... just one thing." Harry dared to speak. Darwin gave him permission to continue, "Stephen had nothing to do with it. He wasn't in on anything. He's a good guy and very loyal to you. I ...um...just wanted you to know that."

"Just before 1 o'clock, Darwin, Stephen, and Bob were together again in the bar. Stephen was laughing, whilst Bob and Darwin were 'shhhhing' him. "Quiet, Harry could be anywhere."

Stephen laughed more, "Poor Harry, that's just not fair! – you realize he'll never speak to you again when he finds out?" Darwin was trying not to look too smug, but it didn't work. "Anyway, Stephen – tell us your plan of how we're going to look as if we know more … or I'll have you beaten up, bad!" They all giggled again.

"Okay, well to start with, I've added a couple of bits in to Suzie's file which the Serious Crime Squad will hopefully be seizing later today. I've put in a few scrawls that would indicate that the person who called for Harman's information was called Fernandez. Then I've added bits and post-it notes to appear that I had spoken to Harman on the phone, as well as to Fernandez before I got Harman's name. None of which really makes sense, but that's exactly what we need to do."

"You certainly succeeded on that front … but I like it!" encouraged Darwin. "So go on then …"

"Well, the other tactic will be for the interviews this afternoon with the SCI's – that's the name for the Welsh Serious Crime Squad." Stephen looked around for approval, but none was forthcoming and Bob and Darwin looked blankly back at him.

Stephen continued, "Well, I've done a few interrogations in my time, and we're taught how to tell if people are lying ... we call them SOLs – That's 'Signs of Lying'" Stephen stopped again briefly for approval, and was again disappointed. "There are a few basic giveaways, so I want us all to learn some of them quickly. Then we'll apply them separately during our interview for the same questions. The most common SOLs are ...

Double-blinks, quick ones like this.

Looking away just before you answer.

Fiddling with something when you answering.

Coughing or other noise distractions.

Repeating yourself, etc.

There are dozens more, but they'll do for starters.

So the general rule is that you always tell the truth – that way you won't get confused on cross-interrogation, but on a few specific questions, we'll all use some of the techniques. So, any question that involves Suzie's murder – we all drop a SOL. Any question about how we first heard of Harman's name in relation to this investigation – we all drop a SOL. .Just those 2 things mind, we want this to be very subtle. During the questioning I'm also going to drop in Fernandez' name, then quickly correct myself and try and cover over it. It won't make any sense to them at the time, but the penny will drop when they seize my files later.

The final tactic is consistency. The interviewers will be looking for consistency between stories. So again, a very subtle inconsistency. When they ask about

Sally, Bob and I will say that we have never met her – which we haven't. But Darwin you'll say that you think we all met her in Flans a few nights ago, but you're not really sure."

Stephen stopped and sat smugly upright in his chair looking intently at Darwin's eyes.

"That's really crap" said Darwin, carefully throwing in a double-blink.

"That's the worst strategy I've ever come across" Bob followed, but looked away and started fiddling with the beer mat.

Stephen grew a great big smile, and they all laughed and high-fived in unison.

CHAPTER SEVENTEEN

At Tarnlough Police Station, Darwin and Stephen were sitting in the front foyer. It was the closest thing that they had to a waiting room. It was much more impressive that Port Sinton's pathetic excuse for a police station, and the foyer was clearly sporting signs of action, mostly of the nasal variety.

Beer, smoke, and urine always mingle well together as a group. There was only 1 poster, which encouraged all the residents to join forces and become a part of the Stalag Neighbourhood Watch. A fat middle-age woman adopted the "Your Country Needs You" pose, and pointed at you. Wherever you were located in the foyer, you could feel her point following you around the room. They sat on dark stained benches, and flicked old fag-buts across the brown tiled floor with their feet.

Stephen had been interviewed first. Everything seemed to have gone well, but they didn't know for sure, as they had agreed not to discuss the matter until it was over and they had all left the station. Stephen had been in and out in 15 minutes, and Bob had been in for 20 minutes now. Although they weren't discussing it, they were both starting to get worried as to why Bob was in for so long.

The Serious Crime Squad had taken over Interview Room 1 (the only Interview Room) for the duration of the day.

Another eight minutes later, Bob walked through the door leading to the inner station. They wanted desperately to ask how she had got on, but they made an agreement not to, and it was important that they didn't crack at this stage. Ewan followed Bob though a few minutes later. He had got the job of usher for the proceedings. "Mr Litton …" Darwin stood up and made his way towards Ewan. "*This is it!*" Darwin whispered to himself.

Only when he reached him, did Ewan decide to finish the sentence. " … could you please wait for a few minutes, as the SCI boys are having a break or something." Darwin smiled un-politely and shuffled back to his seat.

After at least 20 minutes, Ewan returned. "Mr Litton …" This time Darwin was taking no chances "Yes" he said politely, but remained seated.
"They are ready to see you now".

That great ball of nothingness once again appeared and ripped through his inners. Suddenly his adventure wasn't so much fun. This was his first police interview – his first interrogation. He had no idea how he felt. Sure he had all the usual excitement and nervous feelings, but this time it was something different. It felt as if the heat had been turned up just a little bit too much. He tried not to cry as Ewan lead him down to the gallows.

After 2 of the longest hours ever, Stephen eventually poked his head through the inner door, and motioned for Ewan to come over. "Do you have any idea how much longer they'll be?" whispered Stephen impatiently. Ewan sucked his teeth "It could be a while yet. In fact they've just sent out for coffees and sandwiches, so I'd say we could be in for a long one. I'll be taking the coffees through in a few minutes, so I'll ask them for you."

Another 25 minutes passed before Ewan came back in. "I've some bad news for you. It appears from my conversations with the interviewing team that they consider it prudent to detain Mr Litton for a while longer. They consider that the period of this detention could be significant; therefore they would advise that you should leave and call later for an update. If the questioning continues late into the night, then we will arrange for Mr Litton's return travel to the Quays Hotel."

Aunty-cabs was waiting down the street, but Stephen signaled with his fingers to ask her to wait 2 minutes. Aunty-cab pretended to start the taxi meter, and signaled back that the clock was ticking.

"That's not a good sign" confessed Stephen when they were far enough away from the station. Bob agreed nervously "I know it's not, I'm really worried for him – you know what he's like"

"I do Bob, and that's why I know he'll be fine. Whatever is happening in there, Darwin will wriggle his way out of it. He is probably having a ball – he loves all this drama and excitement. He's probably chatting to them about life in the Serious Crime Squad as we speak. He's probably tying them up in knots, and asking profound questions."

"God I hope so." Bob took 3 or 4 large gasps of fresh air into her lungs.

"He'll be fine, I promise" assured Stephen "Come on, let's get back to the hotel – I think we could both do with a drink" He put his arm around her, and they walked back towards the cab.

At 3am, an unmarked police car stopped with authority outside the Quays. "Goodnight Mr Litton". Darwin stood on the small pavement outside the hotel. His mouth said "Goodnight" but unfortunately his throat forgot to join in. The car drove off anyway. Darwin's eyes looked hollow in his head. His hair was ruffled, and he seemed to have grown 3 days worth of stubble. He thought that he could maybe hear some voices in the bar, so he tiptoed slowly and quietly up the hall, then up the stairs to his room. He closed the door gently and double locked it. He lowered himself on to the bed, then he lowered his head down to the pillow, breathing heavily and deliberately. Once or twice a squeaking noise could be heard from the air in the way in. His heart was thumping so hard that it echoed through the bed, and deep into his ears and head. He kept his eyes open, but they looked dead and could not have been effective at seeing anything other than the blackness.

CHAPTER EIGHTEEN

"What time did you get in last night?" Stephen had just arrived in the dining room, and was standing behind Darwin.

Darwin finished his mouthful of toast and marmalade. "Hey Stephen, good morning. It was gone 3am I think! … wow those boys can really interrogate cant they?"
"Can they?" replied Stephen wisely. "I'm fine" said Darwin unconvincingly, but with a smile that Stephen understood. He knew not to push it any further. Bob joined the table and sat beside Darwin. She held his arm hard with one hand and finished off his slice of toast with the other. Stephen put his hand on Darwin's shoulder and munched away on his apple. Sometimes, things are better left unsaid, and for the moment they realized that the most they could do for Darwin was to just be there for him – even if it did mean eating his breakfast.

After a few minutes, Harry humbly strode in to the dining room. He wouldn't look at Darwin for fear of getting a beating, so he addressed the 3 of them at once. "Just to let you all know that I've spoken to the investigation team and, to say the least, they are now convinced you guys know more than you're letting on. I agreed with them of course, and even made up a few stories about stuff that didn't add up. I've also spoken to my sergeant and told him that you have been instrumental in this case so far, and that I desperately need you to stay as you have an inside track to Sally. He has squared it with his Chief Constable. I've also had a chat with Ewan last night, and I've told him that Darwin and Bob are actually undercover officers, and that he must never repeat it, but must give you all the help and support you need. That should help. I've got the forensic report in my room, and also details of the new discoveries in the case. I've also had a chat with the SCI's and have some more info on Harman. So let me know when you want to go through it together. I even cancelled your flights. I can't think of anything else that I can do, but if I do, then I'll let you know."

Harry reported his update proficiently and without catching anyone's gaze. He looked up to still see Stephen and Bob obviously consoling Darwin. He shook his head – clearly Darwin had threatened them again. "I trust that is enough to call off your people Mr Litton?" Darwin really didn't want to engage with Harry but assured him that everything would be okay.

Darwin had lived in Northern Ireland all his life, in a town just 13 miles from Belfast. Every early evening as a kid, he used to sit on the arm of his father's chair and watch the events of the day play out over the news. He would tut in time with his father, as the day's toll of victims would be analysed by a few local commentators, then justified by an actor's voice talking in monotone to the mouth movements of the Sinn Fein leaders. He had 2 uncles in the police force – but both happily survived the 'troubles'. Darwin often lay in bed as a kid and wished for someone he knew to be involved in a horrific bombing, but it just never happened and he experienced no troubles. All that time, and he never once heard a gunshot or a bomb. His local town was blown up once, a 500lb bomb less than a mile from his house. It was sheer devastation – the entire Main Street had been flattened and the staff at Woolworths were giving away fire-damaged stock at the rear of the building. However, Darwin was in Spain at the time on holiday with his parents and missed the whole episode. He had always felt deprived of any troubles, but now for the first time he was seeing things in a different light.

"Ooops" said Stephen, "I suppose we're going to have to tell him at some point – the poor guy's shitting himself ... although I must admit it's certainly '*objective achieved*' so far."

"Did they come for your file on Suzie yet?" asked Bob, almost moving the subject on.

"I presume so. Put it this way, my door was unlocked and open when we came to bed last night, and the file was gone ... and nothing else was missing. That's the problem with the police nowadays – they've no manners. All they had to do was ask and I would have given it to them."

Darwin flicked from his thoughts about back home and pondered inwardly over Stephen's words. "...my door was unlocked and open when WE came to bed last night..." Who is WE, and what were WE doing at Stephen's open hotel room door? He looked over at Bob with disgust.

"Anyway, I have a few calls to make..." continued Stephen. "...I'll be around all day buddy when you feel up to talking.", and he slapped Darwin gently on the back. "See you later", and he winked at Bob. "See you later Stephen."

"I'll bet you will" thought Darwin. As if things weren't bad enough. While Darwin was being psychologically pummeled by Interrogators, those two were probably at it like rabbits. He should have noticed something suspicious when they both arrived down to breakfast at the same time. Maybe Darwin should arrange for Stephen to be beaten up after all. Darwin didn't know anyone who would do the beating, but it couldn't be that hard to find someone who was desperate for a few quid – especially in Belfast. A few hundred pound should be enough. He didn't imagine that there would be the same abundance of beater-uppers in this part of Wales however. He even considered doing it himself, until he remembered that Stephen is probably trained in some kind of Martial Art, or whatever it is that policemen are taught, and so decided that would be unwise.

"Bob … I … I … I think we should tell Harry about our little scam. I mean, he's in so deep now he cant go back – he's lied to the investigation team, and his sergeant, he's made up stories, he's even told the local police that we're undercover cops. I think its time we were all back on the same side again. What do you think?"

"God, I've been dreading this. But I agree we need to tell him – it worked too well and now it's getting out of control."

"There are a lot of things getting out of control at the moment Bob, so let's start pinning them down one by one, so that we can get on with our adventure in much more relative calm. No time like the present."

They walked down the corridor to where Harry was normally conducting his morning telephone conversations. He wasn't there, so they checked the bar. Harry was sitting alone eating his breakfast – obviously too frightened to eat in the dining room next to Darwin. "Harry, we've got a bit of a confession." Started Bob. "…that whole escapade yesterday with Darwin, and the solicitors, and Stephen, and then you agreeing to help, and well … all that stuff that happened." Bob took another deep breath. "It was all a bit of a con … like a made up story or something … it was just a plan we concocted to get back in with the investigation, after you told us that we had to go home."

Harry sat motionless. Darwin tried to help Bob. "You see, we had been having such a great time – especially getting to know you and the others, and we really believed that we could help, and anyway, we just kind of got a bit carried away … we panicked, and thought up that plan to get back in again." Darwin stopped and threw the ball to Bob. "We just wanted to say that we're sorry. You are a friend and what we did was wrong."

Harry marched out of the room without once catching Bob or Darwin's eye.

"I think that went fairly well" started Bob. "Yep, me too" finished Darwin.

Bob suggested that they should go for a good long walk, so they both grabbed their coats from reception. Their intentions were slightly better than reality, and they stopped for a rest, about 500 metres away. It was a violently windy day, and this was being exaggerated by their close position to the sea. The tide was fully in, and the water was smashing hard and fast against the sand and shingle. They each took deep breaths – trying to draw in and borrow a little of this enormous energy for themselves.

"It must have been a bit of a nightmare last night – I only had a short interview, and it scared the shit out of me … I can't imagine how you coped for over 7 hours." Bob decided not to keep avoiding the subject. Darwin let the hard wind and spray rip at his face.

"I know you don't want to talk about it, but I'm a friend, and I'm here." Bob backed off, but just for a few seconds. She knew it would help Darwin if he could talk about it a bit. "Was there some reason why they kept you for all that time – did they find something out after interviewing Stephen and me that made them keep you for longer?" Darwin finally looked down to protect himself a little from the wind pain that was being absorbed through his burning face. "No. It was my fault Bob – I was just being a smart-ass. It was my fault. I just got in too far. I deserved what I got. I just pushed it too far. If we had of stuck to the plan, it would have worked perfectly. I thought I was never going to get out – that was the longest 7 hours of my life."

"Tell me why they kept you so long."
"Look Bob, I've already told you it was my fault."
"Darwin its okay to show a little bit of weakness sometimes … it's okay to be vulnerable, or even to make mistakes!"
"I know it is. I make mistakes all the time, and I certainly made one last night."
"So what's all this shite about then? Why cant you talk about what happened. It doesn't make it any more or less real if you don't talk about it. It doesn't go away if you avoid the subject, and it certainly doesn't

get worse if you say it out loud. Trust me, I know a doctor."

Darwin didn't rise to the bait. "I've just got to move on. What has happened has happened.", and he tried to stand up to walk away, but Bob pulled hard on his arm to hold him in his position. "That's exactly my point Darwin. What has happened has happened. It's over, and it isn't coming back. Now, wind your neck in and tell me why they kept you for 7 hours, and what they done to you – because whether you like it or not, it has affected you."

Darwin puffed sadly. "You're not going to give up are you?"

"I care for you Darwin. We fit well together. I'm good at this type of stuff, you're crap at it. There are lots of things that I'm bad at, that you're good at. It's a partnership."

"Is it?" Darwin pushed is face up into the wind and spray again to cause as much pain as possible.

"I hope so"

Darwin didn't respond, but just pushed his face deeper into the pain – the more the better. Bob was not ready to give up. "Right, now open your frigg'n mouth and tell me what happened – just do it … now … go on …" Darwin held on for as long as he could, then a bit longer. "I did something stupid."

Bob stayed completely quiet – she certainly wasn't prepared to accept that as any type of explanation, and she stared back at Darwin to continue. Darwin started talking eventually "Okay, well remember the imaginary Fernandez character that Stephen was to throw into his interview?" Darwin grimaced in the wind. "Well, I thought it would be a smart idea to accidentally drop it into mine as well. The moment I did, they stopped everything and made me go back over my version. Obviously I didn't mention Fernandez' name again but it wasn't good enough. They spent 4 hours going over and over again, trying to trick me into telling them who Fernandez was. Clearly they had jumped on it with Stephen as well, but I didn't know. They said that it was impossible that Stephen and I could have both accidentally mentioned Fernandez. After 4 hours of repeating my answers maybe 50 or 60 times and completely denying that I said his name, they brought in the video and screen and played back both Stephen's and my interview – there was no mistake, needless to say." Darwin's face was now so cold he could barely keep talking.

Bob took over for a second. "You weren't to know that they were taping it, or even that they had picked up on Stephen mentioning Fernandez. It was a simple mistake Darwin – you couldn't have known."
"I shouldn't have done it – it was a seriously bad judgment call, I wasn't thinking straight. We were on a roll from Harry's scam and I just kept going."
"So what did they do after they showed you the videos?" Bob tried to get back to the full explanation.
"An hour of the same again – repeating the story another dozen times, then they told me that I was

going to be arrested, and charged with withholding evidence and perverting the course of justice – a minimum of 4 years apparently. They even called through to Leighbridge Police Station to confirm that they had a free cell for the night. A few different agents came and went, all trying different tactics. One even started to get physical – kicked the chair from under me, and threatened to beat seven shits out of me unless I told him about Fernandez."

"Poor Darwin", Bob consoled.

"Then they just left me for an hour on my own, with the interview videos playing on a loop. Then they started again, repeating the story over and over – then they sent in the 'good cop' to try and do a deal – tell them about Fernandez and I would get bail. Finally, they told me that I was now being charged, and even asked if there anyone that I wanted to contact. They handcuffed me, with instructions that I would be formally charged at Leighbridge and held overnight, then transferred to Swansea to appear in the high court tomorrow, where I would definitely not get bail. They gave me a last chance to reconsider, then suddenly they just let me go, for no reason – not even an explanation. They just winked at me, then let me go – bastards."

Bob held his hands tight "What the hell was that about?"

"I've no idea Bob – one minute I was going to prison for 4 years, the next minute I was being treated well, and then driven back to the hotel without any explanation."

"I'm not surprised you're shook up. Poor Darwin." And she put her arms around him and held him tight.

Darwin was proud of himself – he very nearly told Bob the complete truth, so he knew he must like her. Apart from being kicked off his chair, and being told he was not getting bail, and apart from the bit about being transferred to Swansea – Apart from those things being bollocks, he had actually retold the story as it happened.

"Darwin!" Stephen was shouting and running up the street. "Darwin!" he repeated a few more times. Stephen had nearly reached them now and was puffing heavily, gasping between words "You'll never guess what?" The silent guessing encouraged him to continue "The cops from Swansea have just been at the hotel requesting that I provide them with a copy of Suzie's file."

"Shit" said Darwin and Bob simultaneously. "Exactly" heaved Stephen "If it wasn't the cops who took the file, then that means that 'they' are definitely here ... who else could have taken it?"

"*They* are here all right" said Darwin thoughtfully.

"I can feel it" confirmed Bob.

"The cops aren't going to be too happy are they?" asked Darwin

"They don't care, I had a copy anyway, so they've got that now. The only problem is that I didn't get a chance to make those changes on the copy – so I'm afraid the imaginary Fernandez thing won't make any sense to the Swansea cops now."

Bob turned to Darwin, "That should hopefully help your case."

"You think so?" snapped Darwin quickly. "Think about it – it now means that 'they' as in blow-your-head-off 'they' will be looking for Mr Fucky-Fernandez as well … as if things weren't complicated enough." Stephen looked a little confused but didn't ask for an explanation. "I think its all going to really hot up now.", he said instead, then made his way back down to the hotel with a misplaced triumphant skip in his step.

Darwin said he needed a little time alone, so Bob headed off back to the hotel too. After about 10 minutes alone, Darwin got bored with himself again and so he also started back towards to the hotel. He figured 10 minutes should be enough for Bob to think that he was relatively deep and meaningful, whilst being short enough for her to think that he was tough and handling the situation like a man. He also decided that 10 minutes was enough time for Bob and Stephen to sneak up to their bedroom, and then Darwin would burst in, and catch them red-handed.

Harry was standing in reception, with his suitcase packed at his side.

"Hi", Darwin shyly tested the waters. The waters were icy cold, and he received neither words nor looks in response. "Are you heading off?" said Darwin, throwing a quick look down at Harry's suitcase. Again, nothing. Harry's mobile phone rang, and he answered it immediately without offering Darwin any courtesy. It was his Sergeant. The word (via Swansea SCI's) had just got back to him that Suzie Marlin's file had been stolen from Stephen's room. Firstly Serg was pissed off that Harry didn't even know about the file being stolen... "Sorry Serg, I was...",

then he was curious whether Harry had a brain or not... "Yes Serg, I have",

then whether Harry was still capable of doing the job... "Yes, yes sir I am"

and finally whether Harry could unpack and stay a few days longer and try and work out who took the file... "Yes, of course"

It was the only new lead that the Serg had on Suzie's murder case so Harry might as well stay in Wales and follow it up. "Fucker", shouted Harry ... he didn't bother checking whether the phone was switched off or not this time. He grabbed his suitcase, and made his way to the reception desk to check back into the hotel again. There was no-one there.

"Suzie's file was stolen from Stephen's room last night." offered Darwin by way of bartering for a civil word in return. Harry still ignored him. "I reckon that things are really going to hot up now ... it almost certainly means that 'they' are here ... you know, the ones after Harman." continued Darwin. Harry realized that Darwin wasn't going to give up. "Darwin, I don't really have anything to say to you. In fact up until a few minutes ago I was hopeful that I was about to leave here for good and would never have to speak to you miserable lot of tossers ever again in my life. Unfortunately, I've now got to stay because Stephen's file on Suzie has gone missing ... and it wouldn't surprise me if that was another one of your scams. Anyway, I would appreciate it if you could just leave me alone – it's not too much to ask."

Darwin looked sincerely back at Harry "Actually it is too much to ask. I messed up and I'm sorry, but it's not going to stop me talking to you. It's up to you whether you listen or not." Darwin followed Harry up the stairs, a few steps back just in case Harry tried to punch or kick him. "You'll never guess what happened to me last night ... The Swansea Serious Crime Squad interrogated me for 7 hours, arrested me and kind of beat me up ... it was unbelievable. They seemed to think that we knew more than we did." Harry reached his room, and slammed the door to leave Darwin standing talking alone on the corridor.

CHAPTER NINETEEN

The Swansea Serious Crime Squad was now firmly encamped in Tarnlough Police Station. They had taken over Interview Room 1, along with 2 offices upstairs, and the canteen out the back.

"We're getting quite a lot of intelligence reports from Interpol. The word is well and truly out on the street that Harman is going to surface here." said Sergeant Morrison who was leading the investigation.

Seven armed officers agreed obediently. The entire team all looked the same, and were all dressed in black. They even had exactly the same hair styles – short, dark and neat. Except for Morrison, he was in his late fifties, so a combination of aging and Grecian 2000 had given him a consistent muddy hair colour. His face was well worn and tanned, and his eyes were grey and sunk back in his head. He had probably been a fine figure of a man in his days, but now his stomach was starting to overtake his large chest, his arse had started to sag, and his legs seemed thinner than they should be to support his frame. Besides this, he looked to be in charge, and he looked genuinely tough. You wouldn't want to mess with him

"There are now 2 active Termination Contracts that we know about on Harman's head. Both of which have been doubled to two million dollars within the past 24 hours, so it's definitely likely that Harman is going to appear at some stage – somebody knows something. Witness Protection lost contact with Harman a long time ago, so we've really no way of warning him, and the only certified photograph we have was taken 12 years ago!" He stuck a photograph of a forty-something man on the board. He was wearing a smart suit, a clean and crisp white shirt, and a gold and brown tie. He was clean shaven and swarthy, with dulling green eyes. His hair was neatly parted, and the background was black-washed – normally a sign that the photograph had been taken in a studio. This made sense as the picture looked unnatural and posed.

"Our job folks is to intercept him and protect him from the nasty men that want to kill him. The B Squad will stay at the hospital, to guard Sally, and also pull Harman if he turns up there. Just to update you on those idiots we interviewed yesterday, I've had it confirmed that Litton and that girl are undercover officers from the PSNI – I don't know what the hell they're doing here, and I've no idea why that tit Ewan waited until 3am to tell us about it. Anyway, I checked with the DC staying at the Quays ... Harry someone, and he has just confirmed it. I also checked with the local Tarnlough Serg here, and he remembers being contacted by the PSNI last week to tell him that a male and a female plain-clothes would be coming here as part of the investigation into the Belfast murder, so it all seems to stack up I suppose. Pity Mr

Litton let it go on for so long, but I'm sure he had his reasons – those undercover guys have a hard job to do. I still don't know what to make of this Fernandez thing, but we'll keep an open mind for the moment. I'm also pretty sure they were all lying about a few things, so we'll have to keep an eye on them. They're obviously holding back information on Harman and Suzie.

"So guys, that's where we are now. Unless some new intelligence comes through, then I'm afraid this is just a waiting game."

CHAPTER TWENTY

Darwin, Bob, and Stephen sat quietly in the bar together, waiting patiently for Harry to forgive them. Darwin huffed loudy. "Shouldn't we be doing something – like out solving murders?" Bob agreed with Darwin and they both looked over to Stephen for approval. Stephen smiled lightly at the thought of Darwin being out solving a murder. "I think you're letting this go to your head a bit Darwin. You're not really an undercover police officer … remember. I think its time we all started to face facts before it goes too far. We're just getting in the way here. I mean, in 1 day we've managed to fuck Harry's head up, blackmail him, and turn him against us, we've lied to the SCI's, tampered with police evidence, and we've started an Interpol worldwide search warrant for someone called 'Fernandez' who doesn't exist. You and Bob have also managed to impersonate police officers as if all that wasn't enough. Lets face it, we're hardly helping the situation here – everything we have done has only served to set the investigation back further – we're certainly no closer to finding Suzie's murderer are we?"

Darwin and Bob sat quietly like 2 children being scolded. "That's certainly one way of looking at." Confessed Darwin. Bob burst out laughing, and stared wide-eyed at Darwin, with her hands over her mouth.

Darwin laughed a little in return, but only to try and calm her down. "What is it Bob?"

"Oh my God … I've just got it" pushed Bob. "That's why they let you go last night. Ewan told them that you and I were undercover cops. That's why they suddenly let you go. Harry said that he had been speaking to them, so that means he has probably verified the story. That's why they let you go."

Darwin and Bob laughed heartily, but quite nervously, together. Stephen pretended to think it was funny as he didn't want to isolate himself too much. Darwin ran through to the phone booth in the hall, and returned clutching the telephone directory. "Quickly" he shouted at Bob and threw the book at her. "Get the number for Tarnlough and Sinton Police Stations." Darwin got his phone out ready, and was soon tapping the numbers into the phone.

"Can I speak to Constable Ewan Barber please?" He had tried Sinton Station first. "Oh, hello Barber, its Inspector Litton here, PSNI Underground Management Squad."

'*Underground Management…?*', Bob and Stephen mouthed together, then looked at each other in total disbelief. Darwin obviously hadn't listened to one word Stephen had said, and was off on another journey.

"Yes, Inspector Litton, how can I be of service?"

"Listen, I know what you did last night was in good faith. I realize that you just wanted to get me out of the interrogation, but that was part of the strategy, and you really shouldn't have disclosed my identity – you could have put my life at risk."

"I'm sorry Inspector, but when I heard them arranging for a cell, I thought it was time to explain to them…"

"Anyway, it doesn't matter now Barber and we'll just have to use another strategy to find out which of the SCI's team is a spy-mole." Replied Darwin. "I'm sorry", offered Ewan again, "I just thought that I was doing the right thing… I didn't know anything about a …a spy-mole."

"It's no big deal Barber, and what's done is done, just please don't tell anyone else, it's very important – and also don't tell DC Thompson that we've had this conversation, is that clear?" Darwin was on a roll again. "As you'll be the only one who knows about us, I'll be relying on you from now on to assist us. I'll be in touch Barber, goodbye".

Darwin and Bob laughed to each other in exited yelps. Needless to say Stephen was not amused, and mumbled away to himself …

"'underground'?, surely he meant 'undercover'?.

"'Inspector'?, he made himself a feck'n 'Inspector', he probably doesn't even know what the rank means.

"A 'spy-mole', we've got a 'spy-mole' in the Serious Crime Squad. Whatever to fuck a 'spy-mole' is – haven't heard that since the Cold War ended…"

Darwin and Bob were far too excited to listen to Stephen's negative mumblings. "Come on Bob, we've got a case to solve. You coming Stephen?" Stephen snapped "No I am not going anywhere with you…" in instinctive reply, but he came anyway.

"Does that mean I out-rank Harry?"

"Probably" replied Bob, "I wouldn't imagine that he would be particularly high up the pecking order."

Within 20 minutes, Darwin and Bob had commandeered Ewan's office at Port Sinton Station. Stephen wasn't a policeman, so he had to stay in the waiting room, were he perched himself on an orange chair and looked through the window into 'Intelligence Central Office' as it had been renamed by Darwin, who was now pacing the office. "Ewan, I've been underground for a while now so can you bring me up to date with everything you know please?"

"Yes, of course sir…but what about … him", and Ewan threw a glance at Stephen, who was wedged up against the window from his position in the waiting room. "I can't exactly discuss confidential information in front of other people, especially not private detectives." Darwin had to think quickly, "Good point Ewan and it's very important that you are thinking like that. However, lets just say that our hanger-on here as a representative of our …American friends." He winked knowingly at Ewan. "Officially he's not here Ewan – you know how these things work."

Nobody in the room, including Darwin, had any idea what he was talking about. Ewan winked back "Understood...Sir. Well Sally is still in shock, they're keeping her for the moment under armed guard at Tarnlough Hospital. I heard the SCI's saying that they want to move her as soon as possible to a safe house in Glasgow. The SCI's B Squad are staying with her, but to be honest I don't think they are exactly encouraging her recovery as I believe they're using her to tease out Harman and of course the ones who are after him. There are a couple of active contracts out on Harman's head, so the SCI's think it's likely that at least half a dozen private contract assassins will be around the area here, waiting for Harman to show up. They had some intelligence reports or something that indicated that 'they' expect him to surface here shortly.

"The untimely death of our neighbour, Dicky Williams is still unsolved, although the word out on the street here is that it definitely was murder. Some locals overheard two police officers discussing it at the local pub, but that's an unconfirmed report. Forensics from Swansea are being wheeled in today to go over the evidence again, so there's obviously something they're not happy about. Nobody has a clue were Harman is, and..."

Darwin stopped him "What about back in Northern Ireland? I haven't had a chance to catch up with Harry yet."

"Not too sure, Harry says The PSNI still suspect that Suzie's mysterious boyfriend was not who he was supposed to be. They found a body lying beside some river in Belfast yesterday morning, and the fingerprints matched some of those found at Ms Marlin's house. His identity hasn't been confirmed yet, but it matches the description of her boyfriend. They also ran his prints through Interpol and they matched him to a different name, but a similar description, so there's something a bit strange there, and they are doing DNA tests and running dental records."

After a few minutes of silent thinking, Darwin realized that Ewan had stopped talking. "That's it?" he questioned Ewan sternly. "Yes sir, I'm afraid that's everything that I know, but then again I'm only the local bobby, and I just hear things being said – it's quite unlikely that the SCI's or PSNI would share their findings with me. You're probably better to speak to Morrison directly."

"Quite", confirmed Darwin. "The note that Dick Williams left for Sally. Is there any chance of getting a copy of it?"
"Note?" said Ewan, clearly confused. Stephen suddenly perked up and squeezed his head further through the gap. "Yes, I spoke to some old lady a few doors away who was apparently the first to find the body, and she said that she found an envelope with 'Sally' written across it". Ewan still looked confused.

"That was Mrs Canning. It wouldn't be like her to make a mistake like that. I'll call around later and speak to her, but as far as I know, there was no note at the scene … not by the time I got there anyway."

Darwin had started pacing like Poirot, a fellow inspector. "This is an important piece of detail Ewan."
"I know it is Sir, I'll find out what has happened immediately. Sorry Sir."
"Good man" chirped Darwin, and they all left the station to return to headquarters. They had been in Flans a few times now, so when they pushed open the doors, the locals pretty much left them alone, and one or two even nodded in semi-approval of their existence. "At least one thing's for sure" said Bob on seeing the same old faces, "…there's not much chance of missing some strangers who arrive here. I think if one of those 'hitters' decides to visit Sinton, we'll all manage to spot him."

It certainly wouldn't take a photographic memory to spot a new face in Flans. Bob, Darwin, and Stephen were all suddenly drawn to a figure sitting in the corner. "Hi Harry", ventured Bob. The response was not audible, but they made their way over to the table beside him. "Harry…" started Bob, "… we really miss you as part of the team. I can't apologise enough for the way we treated you – it was wrong, it went too far, and we weren't thinking." Harry tried not to respond but he liked Bob "Bob, I know it wasn't your idea, but you knew what you were doing. I've only got 2 days left here, so we'll just try and avoid each other, and after that we don't need to ever see or speak to each other again."

"Look, if it's only for 2 days, then can we at least be civil. As you say, after 2 days we'll all never have to see each other again, so how about just being civil for the next few days. That can't hurt anyone can it?" Darwin was impressed, Bob was learning well from him. He knew it was him that Harry was annoyed with mostly, so Darwin stayed very quiet and avoided all eye contact. Harry smiled meekly. "No, it probably can't do any harm Bob, but that's not the point. What you guys done was …"

"Can I please buy you a drink Harry?" butted in Stephen. "I'm getting in a round anyway. Darwin, Bob – the usual?" He didn't wait for a response from Harry, and instead went immediately to the bar to get four drinks in. Bob took over again "Harry, you would have pissed yourself laughing earlier. We were at the station with Ewan, and he was asking about Stephen, as Ewan didn't want to be discussing police information in front of him. Anyway, Darwin turned around, face straight, and said 'Stephen is here as a representative of our …American friends. Officially he's not here Ewan – you know how these things work.' We all just sat there in shock, then Ewan winked back and continued on – it was hilarious, wasn't it Darwin?"

Darwin and Harry stayed quiet and avoided each other's gaze. Harry was not going to respond to anything that would make Darwin look good or clever. Darwin stayed quiet for a dozen different reasons. Bob decided to stay quiet too. Together they all created a fabulously stale atmosphere that seemed to last for hours. Harry suddenly burst through the smell, "Why would Ewan be discussing police matters with you two?" Bob and Darwin remained suitably quiet.

"Oh, don't tell me you're still bring undercover cops!, holy shit, what are you guys doing? Have you any idea how serious that is? Not only that, but as if you haven't caused me enough grief, it will be my neck on the line again when your found out! I don't believe it!", and he stormed out.

Darwin thought that might happen.

Stephen handed Bob and Darwin their drinks. He set Harry's pint down on the table beside his empty seat. "So what do you reckon about this letter then?" Darwin and Bob pretended nothing had happened. "It's a strange one Stephen" said Darwin, "I just don't know what to make of it. Was there a letter in the first place? Who took it? Who could have taken it? And Why? Was the letter written by the murderer to make it look like suicide? Lots of questions, but I'm a bit short on answers. Are you sure that Canning woman saw an envelope?"

"Yeah, positive. She even described the writing on the front – she definitely saw an envelope."

"Maybe it was empty, just an envelope that he had lying around with Sally's name written on it – maybe there is no letter at all. Or alternatively maybe Dick had written a note to Sally about something else, anything, before he was murdered. Maybe the note said 'Sally can you please pick up my laundry from the dry cleaners for me'. Dick didn't know he was going to be murdered, so it could have been something as simple as that. "

Darwin and Stephen 'hmmmm'd in semi-agreement. Although Darwin didn't really think her story was plausible, he liked the way she thought. She was happy to have an explanation without necessarily having a logic. That sort of lateral thinking normally led to another twist or thought that could open up into a better idea. "It's possible I suppose" encouraged Darwin. Stephen didn't really think it was possible so he changed the subject. "Harry away to the loo?" as he looked around the bar for him.

"I think he had to go. So what is the strategy now then?" She looked equally between Darwin and Stephen. Darwin swiftly assumed the role of Chief Investigator before Stephen had a chance to respond. Besides, he was sure Stephen had never made it to the rank of Inspector during his time in the police. "I guess we'll just have to wait and see what happens with the lost letter – Ewan is going to leave no stone uncovered until he finds out what happened there. The forensics from Swansea are waiting to re-look at the Williams evidence so we'll just have to wait for that. The PSNI are still waiting for the update on Watkins, so we'll have to wait for that. If there are hitters waiting here for Harman, then we'll have to wait for them to show up. And as for Harman, we'll have to wait for him to surface."

Bob and Stephen looked blankly at one another. "So if there was one word to describe your strategy Darwin, what would you say it was?" prompted Stephen. Darwin was oblivious to his 8 'wait's in his strategy, and shrugged awkwardly. Bob and Stephen grinned secretly at each other, but of course Darwin saw it. They were definitely bonking each other. He was convinced now.

They spent the next hour implementing Darwin's strategic plan. Finally it worked and 2 new faces appeared at the bar. One was late forties, black jeans, blue and black patterned polo neck jumper. The other was probably early fifties, cream chino type trousers, brown suede casual jacket over a light shirt. Neither really looked like 'hitters' as such, although both had relatively short dark hair with grey highlights, and they were talking to each other about golf.

The waiting was maybe going to pay off. Darwin took the lead again, "Stephen, it's your round – so go to the bar and make casual conversation. See what you can find out. Bob, you check outside for … anything suspicious. I'll keep an eye on the rest of the bar." Darwin made it appear that he had got the biggest job to do.

After just five minutes, Bob came rushing back in. She approached the table sporting a quiet whistling noise for some reason. "3 at 2 o'clock", and she motioned behind her. The door opened and 3 more new faces trotted in. The groups had arrived separately, but seemed to somehow know each other. Darwin looked around at the locals who, for some strange reason, weren't even noticing this incredible buzzing of activity. Just as things seemed to be reaching chaos, another one arrived.

Darwin and Bob stood open-mouthed. They couldn't believe their luck. Ewan had mentioned that there could be half a dozen hitters coming to the area, but never in their wildest dreams did they expect them all to arrive at the same place at the same time. This was perhaps Darwin's big break. Should he stand up and shout 'stop – put down your weapons, you're all under arrest", then dispatch them one by one to the floor. He decided not, as they probably wouldn't have their weapons with them now. Perhaps instead he should disappear to the toilets and secretly phone the SCI's or Ewan, or even Harry. In the end he decided to wait. Consistency in these matters was important. He motioned for Bob to sit down beside him, and they tried to catch Stephen's eye at the bar.

Stephen was chatting casually to 2 of the hitters; however Darwin and Bob couldn't hear what they were saying. Eventually Stephen let himself be caught by Darwin's eye, and excused himself from the hitters. He approached their table with a smug look. Darwin and Bob both said "...well?" at the same time. Stephen smugged himself up even more. "Its Friday" he finally said. "...and that's relevant because..." started Bob. "Just spit it out Stephen" finished Darwin.

Stephen remained smug. "It's Friday, as in the start of the weekend. It's Friday. This area is a holiday resort, apparently. Although God only knows why anyone would want to have a holiday here. Anyway, every weekend hundreds of English holiday makers drive down here to their holiday homes. According to Brian and Jim, this place will be absolutely packed tonight. There will be dozens of English visitors here for the weekend."

"Shit" barked Darwin, "how the hell are we going to spot our hitters now – it'll be impossible. We'll have to think of another strategy. Stephen, got any bright ideas?" Stephen sparkled even more smugly than before. "Well actually I have Inspector Litton. I couldn't help but notice that Ewan had a computer terminal in his sad little office at the Police station here. I don't know for sure, but I would guess that it is connected through to the central intelligence database, which is set up so that all stations (even ones in the shit-hole of nowhere) have access to shared police files. If you can get us logged on, I'm sure I could get some more information."

Darwin had already flipped open his phone, and was waiting impatiently for Ewan to answer. "Ewan, its Inspector Litton here, where are you? ... are you?... well I suggest you make your way back to the station. I've been asked to pick up some files by Internetpol, so I need access to your computer... yes ... yep, that's fine... see you in 10 minutes then."

"Can you believe he's at home eating with his parents?" tutted Darwin, "but its okay, he's on his way back to the station now."

Darwin and Bob continued to watch the door and take a mental note of each person that came in. Finally they sipped the last of their drinks and headed back up the hill to the station. Stephen made his excuses to his new friends, and followed after them. They waited outside the station for 5 minutes before Ewan arrived. He was still in uniform. After another minute or so of fiddling around with the keys, Ewan finally managed to open the main door. He said "Wait here" while he ran forward to the security pad to turn off the alarm. Nobody waited, and they all took a note of the number Ewan tapped in. It was "999", so it didn't take much remembering.

Darwin pretended to receive a call on his mobile, "Yes, yes sir, I understand sir, yes I'm just about to have a look now, just wait for one second please sir.." and he took the phone away from his face and covered the mic with his other hand. He whispered loudly "Ewan, I need to get access urgently please – can you log in while I try and calm the super-chief down." Ewan turned and started tapping while Stephen watched over his shoulder and noted his login and password. Login Ewan34, and password Ewan999.

Darwin pretended not to be totally relieved that Ewan had agreed to log them in. "Sorry sir, I was just talking to the local officer on the ground here. Yes sir, yes, very much so sir, that won't be necessary sir – Constable Barber is being very helpful indeed. Goodbye sir".
"Are we logged in Ewan?"
"Yes Sir"
"Thank you. That will be all. You can go now, and we'll look after it from now on."

Ewan started to make a weak protest, but Darwin put a stop to it before it amounted to much. "That's an order Ewan ... a very high ranking order – in fact much higher than you might think."
Ewan agreed reluctantly "You can just pull the door after you. You'll need the code to put the alarm on..."
Darwin smiled knowingly, "Its fine Ewan, we already know the code – we're all part of the same team remember. Now go back home and relax, you've done

a great job, and we really do appreciate your assistance – it will not go unnoticed."

"Okay Stephen, do your stuff." Ordered Darwin when they heard the door click softly closed. Stephen was already at the keyboard and was typing relentlessly. "That's strange, there's nothing at all coming up on Harman except the current records over the past week or so – nothing prior to that. Must be because of the Witness Protection scheme."

"What name are you searching under?" said Darwin.

"Rod and Rodney" replied Stephen, then he suddenly remembered the full name of George Rodney Harman, so he quickly typed 'Harman' into the surname, and 'George' in the first name. "Bingo" said Stephen. "It's the Witness Protection way of securing information. They still need to keep the details of everyone on the central database, but obviously they don't want to use the new alias, so they create a new first name for the person on the system. It means the information is still accessible on the network, but wouldn't be easily found unless someone had the new first name. Anyone who legitimately needs access to his old files would know his new name."

Stephen scribbled various notes down on a piece of blank paper, then he turned to Bob and Darwin who were waiting eagerly for some more information. "We knew most of this already…" he began "…but it says here that Witness Protection lost contact with him years ago. No recent pictures, and no updates. They don't even know if he's still alive."

"What about his new identity – is it mentioned anywhere?" said Darwin. "Nope" replied Stephen, "…they don't keep stuff like that on the central computer."
"Let's try another one - Watkins, Stanley Watkins" suggested Bob, "the guy that was found in Belfast that they thought was Suzie's boyfriend."

"Well, very interesting." Said Stephen.
"…His known associates include 2 of Harman's old business partners. There are also a load of outstanding warrants for him, including 4 from America where he's wanted for attempted murder. My guess is he was drafted in by 'them' to befriend Suzie, and therefore try and get to Harman. After they realized Suzie really didn't know where Harman was, they obviously decided to kill her instead, to try and draw him out."
Darwin joined in "Yes that bit makes sense okay, but who then killed Watkins, and why?"

"Maybe he had served his purpose" said Bob "…you know, maybe he had done the job they ordered but afterwards became a liability – the police, Interpol, and the FBI were all looking for him. Forensics would link him to Suzie's murder. He certainly wouldn't be someone that I would want in my gang."
"Or…" started Stephen "…maybe Harman got to him. Maybe he heard about Suzie's murder and then came

after him. The hunted becomes the hunter!" They all agreed, either alternative could be possible.

"Okay, let's go through everyone, starting with Suzie, then Sally, then Dick. Something has to pop up." Suzie's file had only been created last week. Up until then, she hadn't done anything to justify having a place on the database, but now she had 43 pages of information. Stephen worked the down arrow key, whilst all three of them scanned each page quickly. They were all delighted to see the forensic report as well. That was a real result, although Bob and Darwin were disappointed that they wouldn't get to ask their questions.

"Holy shit" said Stephen. They were all reading the sections on the state of Suzie's body, including the mess of her face. For the first time they realized that Suzie had not just died quickly with a single shot to the head. As if the description wasn't gruesome enough, one more tap on the scrolling down key filled the entire screen with a photograph of Suzie's broken face. She was unrecognizable, even though all the blood had been cleaned away.

The entire top half of her nose had been scraped up and pushed through a hole were her left eye used to be. Her one remaining eye was closed and was shining deep purple. What was left of the bottom half of her nose was pushed in against her top lip, which was split with a v-shaped gash. Her bottom lip was adorned with 2 of her bottom teeth, which had ripped right through the skin and were still sticking out the holes. Her jaw was twisted, clearly broken, and appeared to have been turned around her mouth. Her cheeks were a sore red, and offered up a series of scrapes and cuts in every direction. Her matted hair sat like a wig. It just didn't appear to be a part of her body any more. A couple of disturbing dips and caverns in the hair line clearly indicated were the bullet had exited.

Stephen and Bob bounced back in shock. They weren't prepared for a picture, especially not that one. Stephen retched but managed to avoid heaving the contents of his stomach on to the keyboard. Bob turned away with a quiet yelp, but Darwin stayed staring at the picture. He pretended it was because he was brave and accustomed to such pictures, but really he was searching for some kind of likeness to the Suzie he remembered in his head. His looks darted from her eyes, to her mouth, to her nose, to her hair. He couldn't find one match to the image he was nurturing. Death wasn't meant to be like this, it should be a serine open coffin in the living room at home, with uncles and aunties weeping quietly into their perfectly ironed handkerchiefs, soft music in the background, floral tributes, personal notes and comforting smiles and re-assurances. Nobody had explained this scenario to him. There was certainly nothing romantic about this pulped face that was staring back at him. Darwin's self-indulgent grieving for Suzie could now never be satisfied and he was destined to never be a true victim of death. He fixed his mind instead on the funeral of Princess Diana; that seemed to work better in the circumstances.

Stephen kept tapping on the down key, trying to make the horror disappear. It took about 20 taps, but eventually it flicked up and a new page of text was finally displayed. They composed themselves relatively quickly and resumed their reading positions.

Two swabs of different saliva were found on Suzie's face. One was her own. The other had now been confirmed as Watkins. Fingerprints and further DNA taken from the house also revealed that only Suzie and Watkins had been in the house recently. There was no forced entry. "That seems conclusive enough" suggested Darwin.

After the forensic reports, there was a section on the follow-up calls to all of Suzie's known associates. Darwin smiled and made Stephen slow down when he came across his name. "Look" said Darwin excitedly, "…that's me, look 'Darwin Litton'. I knew some day I'd make it on to a police report."

"Cool" said Bob, and put her arm around him. After the follow-up calls, there was a copy of Watkins file, which they quickly paged through again. There was then a section on Sally, and the connection between her and Suzie, which again they flicked through relatively quickly.

Stephen seemed a bit confused as he scrolled down through the last 4 pages. Each one was blank. Darwin took control of the mouse and hovered it over an icon at the top left, then left-clicked it, and choose the 'properties' option. Stephen and Bob were impressed. Sometimes Darwin surprised them. A grey box appeared in the middle of the screen. 'This page contains classified information. Your user level does not have authority to view it. Please contact your network administrator if you require any further explanation. Error Code 3455y611qw.'

"Bastard" whispered Stephen at the Grey box.

"How can we get access to those pages?" asked Darwin.

"You can't, every page is allocated an authority level. That can be based on rank, station identification, branch, or even right down to individual names. Ewan's login probably isn't high enough authorization. We won't be able to see those pages. They could be anything, but they are probably about Harman or the American connection. They don't want every bobby to be able to see information like that."

"Let's have a look at Sally's now" suggested Bob

Stephen returned to the main menu, and entered Sally's details. Like Suzie's, hers had only been created last week. There were 5 pages. The first was all her personal and contact details and, like Suzie's, the remaining 4 pages were all blank. Darwin performed his grey box routine on each of the pages, and as before the same message was displayed.

Stephen closed her file, returned to the Main Menu, and started searching for Dick's file. He tried every combination of Richard permutations, but each time, the screen just stayed blank. "No file for Dick I'm afraid" concluded Stephen. "Anyone else?"

As they couldn't really think of anyone else involved with the case, they took turns at looking up old friends and teachers from school instead.

CHAPTER TWENTY-ONE

Tarnlough Hospital was in total darkness for just a second or so, then 2 generators sparked to life and forced energy back into the building. As it was only set up to serve essential lighting and equipment, the Hospital sat in dull contemplation, with only alternate lights functioning. What was night had appeared to change back to dusk.

Sally hardly noticed. Her monitor was connected to a separate UPS system, which kept everything powered constantly and without having to wait for the generators to kick in. The bedside light had dipped off and then back on again, but she hadn't really acknowledged it. Her eyes were focused on a point that wasn't even in the room, so it had little effect on her, but she blinked to herself in acknowledgement that something had happened.

Outside her room, there wasn't quite as much calm. "What the fuck was ..." attempted a member of the SCI's B Squad who was stationed outside Sally's room. It was a vain attempt, and as he grabbed for his gun, he dropped heavily on to the floor. A whistle of a bullet hurried through one temple, then escaped efficiently out the other. The sharp thud of a well silenced handgun was the only clue to what was happening. Already a man was standing guard over the body. Two more familiar thuds could be heard further down the corridor.

The man remained silently over the slumped body, waiting for his signal. He was wearing dark jeans, a black bomber jacket, and a black balaclava hat. Two beeps from his watch seemed to be all the permission he needed. On hearing the beeps, he stepped over the dead officer and through the doors into Sally.

Sally raised her head slowly off the pillow, and squinted slightly to see who had entered. "Sally Burton?", said an American accent. Sally nodded, or maybe she just swayed. Either way he took it as read that she was acknowledging her identification

The man fiddled with his watch, as if he was sending back a signal. Two more men ran down the corridor and entered Sally's room, each dressed as the first. One lifted Sally around to the side of the bed, then pushed her upper body straight. Sally sat up on the side of the bed. The two other men each took an arm and they raised her to her feet. A rather unassuming blue Ford Mondeo collected her from the front of the hospital. The 3 men lifted Sally into the back seat, then closed the door, and disappeared like shadows into a forest on the right hand side.

Inside the Mondeo, one man was driving, and another one sat in the back holding Sally up straight. Both were wearing balaclavas. The one in the back stabbed a short needle into Sally's left arm and within a few seconds, she relaxed her head back and closed her eyes. He declared "clear" to the driver. They both took off their balaclavas and their jackets and placed them methodically in a white plastic bag. The one in the back placed the bag under the passenger seat, then reached behind him and unclipped the split rear seat. He pulled Sally and himself to one side, while he dropped the seat, then lifted Sally over and pushed her limp body into the boot behind him with meticulous precision. He closed up the rear seat then climbed into the front passenger seat.

The 2 men didn't once look at each other. The driver had a blue checked shirt on, and was about 25 to 30 years old. He was slightly unshaven and had shoulder length mousy hair. The passenger was slightly older, early thirties and was wearing a white t-shirt. He was clean shaven and had darker, shorter hair. A few miles down the road, a white van hurtled around the corner and whizzed past the Mondeo.

Morrison was sitting on the passenger seat and was shouting down his radio mike. "What the fuck do you mean, Canless? How the fuck can she be gone, how the fuck can 4 of our men be dead. What the fuck are you doing?" Seven heads bobbed up and down in the back seats of the van.

As the van approached the front of the hospital, Morrison and the rest of the A Squad could see the first of the fallen bodies. Two of the B Squad were kneeling at either side of the body. Morrison was first out. The two B Squad members stood up and said "sir" simultaneously. "Martins?" asked Morrison quietly. "Yes sir", replied Canless. "We still don't know exactly what happened sir. "

"Martins, Crossly, Bexton, and Jones were all on early watch. Myself, Clispen, Franley, and Smith were all in the old back ward asleep. Clispen heard something and tried to get out of the ward doors, but they had been padlocked closed. We heard a car leave, then we blew off the lock, raised the alarm, and ran down to check on Sally.

"Crossly and Jones were lying dead in the ward corridor, and Bexton was slumped at Sally's door. Sally was gone, then we came out here to find Martins. I've sent Franley and Clispen around the back to see if they can see anything. Morrison knelt down beside Martins body, and touched lightly on his shoulder. Everyone stood in silent shock. Morrison tried to compose himself with several big breaths. "A Squad, I want this entire area combed. So get started … Now!" They all jumped up alert, and ran through the doors of the hospital.

He looked over to Canless and Smith. "You guys just take it easy for the moment. Keep Martins and the others company until the ambulances get here."

CHAPTER TWENTY-TWO

Darwin and Bob had had a busy and eventful day and weren't really in the mood for much more idle chit-chat. They were just happy to be alone for once. They had gone back to Flans after eventually getting bored with the police computer. Stephen had got chatting to more of the new English visitors, and decided to stay on for a few drinks. Darwin and Bob opted instead to leave Stephen on his own and went back to the hotel. As usual, there was no-one else in the hotel bar – not even Bryn, so they had poured themselves two pints of the local bitter.

"Thanks for the chat earlier", started Darwin, "...I really appreciate it. Sometimes I just need a kick up the arse to wise myself up. I just do the most stupid things. I don't seem to be able to see the consequences at the time."

Bob smiled, "It's my pleasure ... mate. I don't agree with you, but it's still my pleasure."
"You don't agree with me? ... you don't think I need a kick up the arse?"
"No, no, that bit is fine, and I'd be first in the queue with my steel toecap boots at the ready. But I don't believe that you can't see the consequences of doing stupid things ... I mean, what did you really expect the consequences to be? You were dicking about with experienced interrogators. You were inventing characters, and trying to cover up. You knew you

would be out of your depth. Even now Darwin, think about it. You are impersonating a senior police officer, you're in possession of sensitive information, you're in the middle of a very messy and dangerous murder investigation, you've accessed the police computer system, the list goes on. The consequences of that? You know what they are – you're looking at 5 to 10. And I mean years, by the way." She added after noticing Darwin looking at the clock. It was just before 10 o'clock.

"I'm just confused." Offered Darwin. "Fuck off." rejected bob in response. "This is the way I look at it …Its one of 2 things. Maybe you think you're so smart and so resourceful, that you can fight your way out of any situation. Maybe you're subconsciously satisfied that you can deal with whatever is thrown at you. Okay, so you spent 7 hours or whatever in interrogation and nearly ended up in prison, but at the end of the day, here you are – sitting drinking beer seemingly without a care in the world. You've managed to blag your way through the situation, and you've come out the other side without even a scratch. Maybe you always believe that you will survive, so therefore it really doesn't matter what the consequences could be."

"I can see where you're coming from. …or the second reason? You said it could be one of 2 things."
 "Yes, the second possibility is that you're simply in denial. You clearly know what the consequences are,

but you won't let your conscious thought processes be influenced by them."

"Again, I see where you're coming from. Its good to see that amateur psychology still has a future."

"So what about you then?" Darwin retaliated. "You're certainly no angel. Unless I'm not mistaken, you're also impersonating a police officer, and are in the middle of a dangerous murder investigation. What do you think the consequences will be?"

"It's simple for me. The absolute worst scenario is that I will just blame you. You've taken the lead on everything, and I technically haven't actually impersonated a police officer. I'll say it was your idea (which it was), I reckon I'll get away with it. I never really say much in front of anyone else, so they'll work out that it was you that instigated everything. Everyone will back me up, including Stephen and Harry. I'll walk, no problem at all."

Darwin shook his head in almost dis-belief. "I can't believe you just said that."

"Why not," said Bob, "I'm thinking about the consequences. I'm thinking - well what is the worst that could happen, and what is the best way that I could get out of it. The moment the consequences are more than I'm prepared to accept, then I'm off – simple as that. I don't expect to ever have to do that, but I've thought about it. That's what I mean about you Darwin. I just can't work out what your plan is.

The consequences are really high now. The worst that can happen is getting more and more serious every day. Everybody is warning you to get out, but you just don't want to listen."

Darwin agreed, "I know, I know. It's a bit strange isn't it? You're right the consequences are getting a bit serious now, but I've told you before Bob, for me it's a journey, in fact its 'thee' journey. I don't know why I'm doing this, but I know I've got to see it through, and whatever happens, happens. I've spent all my life working on intuition. This is no exception, so for me I don't really challenge it. When Harry or Stephen warns me to get out, I genuinely do think about it. I always stop and reflect. I even let the doubts and arguments enter my head and have a swim around and flirt with the other thoughts. But at the end of it, I'm guided to follow this journey. I can't help it. If I get sent to prison because of it, I'll just kill myself and then start all over again."

Bob was getting worried. "I hope you don't mean that?" Darwin smiled lightly. "I don't know, maybe, probably. But perhaps therein lays the answer. The consequence to everything. The ultimate and only consequence. The undefeatable power of suicide. That's why these Muslim terrorists are simply undefeatable. You can't effectively counteract an attack from someone who is prepared to die. All our defense mechanisms pre-suppose that someone values their own life, more than yours. Once you tilt that balance then every defense strategy fails. Whoever thought of it as an idea is a genius. If you've got tens of thousands of people all prepared to die, then you are pretty much undefeatable. You have the ultimate power."

"Yeah, but there's a difference between having the power and using it. That's the bottom line. I don't believe you would actually use it, so therefore it has no real value."

"It has enough value Bob - it has enough to keep me driving on this journey. That's pretty powerful. In fact it's death itself that has brought us here in the first place. Suzie, then Dick. You see death holds the power, it holds every hand in the deck."

"Yeah, but you can't use that strategy for everything Darwin can you? The stakes are too high. You can't just think 'I want a million pounds by next Tuesday, otherwise I'm going to kill myself'. It doesn't really work does it?"

"It might do, you'll have to wait until next Tuesday to see. If you get the money then it will have worked wont it?"

"But what if I don't get the money?" asked Bob.

"Simple" said Darwin, "You either top yourself or just change your strategy. You write your own rules. Nobody is going to force you to do it. Look, I'll be straight with you – if this all goes tits up and I got 10 years in prison, which is a distinct possibility I suppose, then I would probably kill myself, and that's how I feel now. When I started up my businesses at first in Dublin, I won the biggest advertising account in Ireland's history. I took a big gamble with the creative then promptly lost the biggest account in Ireland's history. Shortly afterwards I was made bankrupt and everyone lost their jobs. I took risks because I knew that if anything like that ever happened then I could just top myself and it would all be over. However, I reflected on it for a few minutes then decided to pack up and go back to Belfast and start again. Big deal, I changed my mind and it all worked out in the end."

"Its all about upping the anti isn't it Darwin? You just put all your chips on the table, and hope that lady luck is on your side."

"Nearly my friend. The only thing is that you don't have to put all your chips on the table; you just have to make it look like you have. That's what counts. The dealer or the other players don't know how much you keep in your pocket. They can only see what's on the table"
Bob liked the analogy, "I'll remember that."

"Look, here's a slightly more positive 'plan B' okay. No matter what happens Bob I would definitely get bail – I'm hardly a dangerous threat to anyone am I? I'm just an annoying little prick. Anyway, I've got loads of cash hidden away at home and offshore. I would just disappear, and pop up again somewhere else. When I've got myself sorted, I'll call you and we can live happily together in South America."

Bob smiled wryly at that thought, "I think I preferred the suicide option. So you were made bankrupt, wasn't it hard to set up business again straight away?" Darwin winced, "Well, not really Bob, you see I made that bit up – but it could have been true. It certainly helped prove the point." The cheerful couple stared quietly into their glasses in mutual disbelief.

"Guess what?", asked Darwin after 2 minutes of silence. "What" answered Bob.
"This could finally be our first night together, you know, like … together. Are you up for it?"
Bob slowly turned to meet Darwin's eyes, "Am I '*up for it*'? … God you are a romantic old fool aren't you. How could I turn down an offer like that?"

Darwin laughed lightly, "Yeah sorry about that. What I meant to say was … Would you like to retire together this evening? We'll go back to my place and I'll slowly undress you, then give you a lovely back rub, then we'll crawl into bed together and hold each other tight. We'll whisper sweet nothings to one another, kiss gently, then make slow, and delicious love all night. How's that?"
"Its better I suppose… but to be honest I'd rather have a quick shag, then get some sleep. I can't be doing with all that making love all night crap, I'm too tired."

"Shag it is then." Agreed Darwin, and he leant across and kissed her on the lips. He realized it was probably the first time they had kissed romantically. He was just about to point this out when Bob pulled him closer and kissed him back. Bob's lips were soft and warm, and exactly as Darwin had fantasized they would be. They just seemed to fit perfectly on to his lips. "This is going to be so good" she whispered into Darwin's ear as she rubbed her hand down his chest and onto his stomach. "The best", he whispered back. They kissed again, and held each other tighter.

Over the past 3 years all of Darwin's romances had followed pretty much the same pattern. He would fall in love straight away, then woo and seduce a beautiful girl. The girl would be flattered – he was good-looking, rich, and generally quite entertaining to be with. Then the girl would fall in love with him. Then suddenly, and for no good reason, he would fall out of love. He would leave himself floundering in a relationship that he didn't want to be in any more, with a girl that was obsessed and madly in love with him. Every time he would try and try to fall in love with her again, but it was gone for good, so he would meet someone else and fall in love again. As Darwin held Bob he thought that maybe this could be different – finally a girl that he could maybe spend the rest of his life with. Circumstances had forced them to become friends first, and so the usual cycle had been broken. He really liked Bob, he loved being in her company, listening to her theories and thoughts, he loved the idea of the two of them chatting and laughing in the evenings, making a lovely dinner, then relaxing in front of the TV until they both feel asleep in each others arms. For the first time he could feel himself falling in love with someone that he already knew.

Darwin and Bob started to get up together, still hugging and kissing. Just then, a rumble of footsteps poured down the stairs. They both looked up to see Harry sprinting past the bar door, and out the front of the hotel. As the front door opened, they could hear sirens squealing in the background. They sat still and quiet for just a moment, hoping that whatever was wrong would simply go away and leave them alone... even for just an hour. Maybe Harry had diarrhea and had run out of toilet paper, or perhaps he wanted to go for a jog. Probably the sirens outside weren't connected and there had been a totally unrelated car accident. That all seemed possible for just a few seconds.

Darwin's phone rang. "It's Ewan here Inspector Litton. There has been a serious incident at the Tarnlough Hospital were Sally was staying." Darwin released himself a little from Bob's grasp and held the phone between their ears so that they both could hear. "What is it Ewan?"
"The hospital came under a major attack this evening. Four of the SCI's were shot dead. Sally is missing,

assumed kidnapped. It was a very professional operation. They were in and out in a few minutes"

"I'll be right there." and he disconnected the phone. "Holy shit, did you hear that? We'll call Stephen on the way." They ran outside before they realized that they had no transport, nor even Bryn to arrange for auntie taxi to take them. At the far end of the car park, a small red hire car was turning over quietly. Through the passenger window they could see the familiar figure of Harry talking on his mobile. They sprinted across just as Harry was pulling off. Bob managed to open the rear passenger door, and Harry brought the car to a halt. Darwin moved round to the other side, and smiled at Harry through the half-closed window.

Darwin was determined to get the first word in before Harry told him where to go. "Hi Harry, off to Tarnlough?"

"No Darwin, I'm going for a pizza and a coke, now fuck off."

"C'mon Harry, we're all on the same side here. We've a direct line of communication to the SCI's – we know exactly what has just happened. 4 SCI's down, Sally missing, in fact we may even know more information than you." and he winked at Harry. "We can help each other Harry. What do you say?" Bob had already started to open the back door. "Please Harry, just give us a lift to the Tarnlough Hospital. Please?"

Harry looked to the sunroof for inspiration. None appeared, and when he returned his eyes to normal level, he noticed that Darwin and Bob were already sitting in the back seat. They were perched quietly and obediently, and promised not to ask 'are we nearly there yet?'.

"Do I have a choice?" sighed Harry. "Thank you" said Darwin. "Yes, thank you" agreed Bob with equal sincerity. Harry re-engaged the gear box, and headed off along the sea road out towards Tarnlough. Darwin didn't stay quiet for long "Actually can you do us another small favour please. Stephen is still in Port Sinton. If I give him a call, can you please swing by and pick him up?"

"No Darwin I can't."

"Well, that's a bit nasty." Replied Darwin. "No need to be like that – it would only have taken a few minutes … it's practically on the way." Harry smirked quietly to himself. Darwin picked up immediately that Harry knew something that he didn't. "Harry, is there something you need to tell us?"

"You really don't know do you?" teased Harry.

"Okay, you've messed us around enough Harry, just please tell us." Said Bob. "…Please"

"Nope" said Harry.

Darwin signaled for her not to pursue it further for the moment, so they both sat in silence in the back. Eventually a few minutes silence defeated Harry, "It's about Stephen. He's not exactly being very straight with you guys. I heard him in the dining room the other day. He phoned someone and was giving them an update on the situation here. All the details, including who said what to whom and when."

"Maybe he was just reporting back to his office, to keep the records up to date or something.", offered Bob meekly. Darwin was just about to offer his opinions, but Harry continued on quickly, "No, I reported it back to HQ and since then they've put tabs on all his lines. He has been phoning a non-geographical number that has been routed to a message service in London, which is then being picked up by an American mobile number, which we're trying to trace. He has also been emailing reports back to his office, which are then being printed and faxed to a solicitor's office in Pennsylvania. He has also been receiving calls from a different number, again American, but it's from a call box, and is normally about an hour or so before he phones in his report. Anyway, I'll not bore you with all the details, but needless to say we're 100% sure that he is an informant. If truth be told we couldn't really give a toss what he does, as so far it's all been information that we were aware of anyway, but we desperately need to try and find *who* he is informing, especially in light of tonight's events!"

"I don't fucking believe it!" spat Darwin. "Bastard", Bob joined in on the assault. Harry agreed. "Yep. Of course we would have let him continue informing as each report was getting us closer to his source. But after tonight's attack, my Serg has handed it over to the SCI's – in fact I would say that they're probably on their way to Port Sinton now to pick him up. With 4 of their mates butchered, I guess they are not feeling particularly sympathetic at the moment, so I do hope Stephen doesn't try and get all smart with them." Harry laughed. Darwin and Bob didn't.

Darwin was confused. On one hand he wanted Stephen to get the kicking of his life from the SCI's because he had been double-crossing him, but on the other hand he somehow felt responsible as he had brought Stephen into this situation, and now he was about to be lifted by the Serious Crime Squad, and probably unlikely to be released in the foreseeable future. He decided however that he would spare his sympathies until he had heard Stephen's explanation, so he favoured his first thought. "I hope they give him the kicking of his life." said Darwin. "They will." Laughed Harry again.

"So" Harry changed the subject, "I've given you all my information, so I think its time to share. You said when you got into the car that you had direct communication in the SCIs, and that you probably know more information than me. So com'n, spill the beans, how did you know so quickly about sally's kidnapping, and what more information do you know?"
Darwin was thinking and missed most of the question.

"Surely you know Darwin better than that Harry" said Bob eventually, "You know he's full of shite. Ewan called to tell him just as you were running out the door, and we know fuck all about anything that you don't know about. Well at least I think we do. It depends what you know I suppose."

Harry replied knowingly. "No, you're probably right, I've seen the transcripts Stephen sent back, so I guess I know everything you know." Bob felt guilty about always getting another one over on Harry. "What about the police computer records. Did you know that there are 4 classified pages on Sally's and Suzie's records that can't be viewed?"

"What the hell were you doing accessing the police central computer system? ... actually, forget I asked that. I really don't want to hear the answer. The classified pages are in connection with Witness Protection. That information is only available to selected individuals or departments."

"That's what we thought" agreed Bob. "I suppose you know all about Watkins, Suzie's boyfriend?" "Yep" replied Harry, "what a dark horse he turned out to be?"

"Yeah, but I suppose he got his come-up-ins in the end."

Harry forgot for a moment that he was in a huff with Bob, and talked freely. Darwin decided wisely to stay quiet. It would be quite a while before Harry would forgive Darwin enough to be involved in idle chit-chat with him.

A helicopter whirred overhead. In the distance they could see a series of beams coming through and around a small copse which was adjacent to the hospital. They made their way up the loose stone driveway. It was less then an hour since the attack, yet already 2 press photographers were snapping away, and chirping reports back down their mobiles. "At the moment we have no confirmed indication of what has happened here this evening. It is believed that a top criminal was being detained at the hospital, and that there was an attempt to break him out. It is believed that at least 2 officers were injured in what could only be described as a shoot out..."

Darwin was pleased to really be a part of the action. All his life he had stood on the periphery. Guessing at stories just like the premature reporter. It was so pleasant for once to be in the know. He was tempted to offer the reporter the gaps around his story, but instead decided to play it cool, and brushed passed them. Darwin and Bob stuck like glue to Harry. He had his identification on show, so they needed him to get through the initial taped barrier to the scene. Once through, they stopped.

"Wow, this is so cool." said Darwin. Bob didn't respond but was clearly equally impressed. They stood on a raised step just down from the front entrance. A yellow tape had been stretched around an area approximately 100 metres all the way around the hospital. Police cars and vans had all been parked strategically to shine as much light on to the car park, the hospital, and the nearby trees. Above, a helicopter beamed its powerful rays over the car park and gardens.

There were 2 ambulances parked close to the front door and a continued parade of paramedics and police moved efficiently between the ambulances and the hospital. It seemed that every minute another team would arrive at the scene. Another ambulance would roar in, another police car would screech to a halt, or another unmarked van would slip through the tape. The noise was orchestral. One moment the helicopter would totally dictate the sound, then suddenly it would bank off above the forest, and an ambulance would take over, then the helicopter again, then the sirens of a police car, then the shouting of Morrison as he passed by on his way into the hospital. Madness and confusion, yet somehow there was order. Nobody seemed out of place, except Darwin and Bob.

"You look lost" yelled Harry as he appeared behind them. Darwin was having such an amazing time that he just couldn't speak. Harry motioned for them to follow him, and they made their way around to a side entrance. They walked along a narrow and dark corridor, and with each step the blazing noise slowly subsided. "In" said Harry, angling towards an office door on the left.

Morrison was already in the room, alone, staring aggressively at the air. "We'll keep this brief Sir" said Harry, "…I just need to get my initial report back to HQ as soon as possible." Morrison stayed quiet.

"It happened about an hour ago yes?" said Harry quickly.

"Four of your men were killed, is that right? What about the others?"

Morrison finally offered some information "The team was split into two four-man watches. Four were asleep, and were locked in the rear wards while they slept, the other four were on duty guarding Sally and were all shot dead. Sally was gone."

"Cameras?" quizzed Harry.

"Yes, I've watched them a few times, but it only shows how they arrived. All the cables and power were cut when they entered the building. There were 6 of them in total. All dressed in jeans and black jackets with their faces covered. Four arrived through that forest, the other 2 arrived in a stolen Mondeo, which we're assuming was used to take sally away. We're getting copies of the tapes done, and we'll circulate them in a few hours."

"Weapons?" Morrison looked down at the table. "Not confirmed yet, but initial findings indicate that they were Grons handguns, fired at close range. None of our guys had their weapons drawn, so it was clearly a surprise attack."

"Grons?" Quized Harry.

"They are a Swedish gun strangely enough, but have been exported extensively to the Middle East and the US. They're not military guns, and are usually used by private protection agencies."

"What about the car?"

"Its lying a few miles down the road. They think the switch car was probably a four-wheel drive, maybe a Mitsubishi or something, but there are no sightings so far." Harry was jotting down the points as Morrison spoke. "Any signs that sally was injured or shot?"

"None, as far as we know at the moment. We believe she was taken unharmed and without any struggle."

"Thank you very much sir" said Harry formally. "Is there anything else you think I should know?" Morrison didn't lift his gaze "No, that's about everything. I've about 30 bodies now covering the fields around us here, but nothing yet. I'll circulate updates later."

Morrison looked at Darwin and Bob for the first time. "You probably remember being questioned by Bexton – he was the tall guy with the Scottish accent, you remember him?" Darwin and Bob both remembered him. Neither of them liked him as he shouted at them during interrogation, but he probably didn't deserve to die. Morrison continued, "…and Jones, you remember

him Litton. He was the one who threatened to lock you up." Darwin motioned sympathetically.
"Anyway, I hope there's no hard feelings? The boys were just doing their jobs." Said Morrison.

"None, whatsoever sir" replied Bob. "…but can I ask…Why was Sally not transferred to a more secure location, or even a safe house? This is hardly very secure is it? It's a secluded location, only occupied by hospital staff during the day, and without any facilities to properly treat Sally anyway?"

Morrison straightened his face up. "Orders." Darwin hadn't said anything yet as he was worried whether his rank meant that he had to call Morrison 'Sir', or whether it meant that Morrison should call him 'Sir'. Darwin decided to risk it. "From whom?". Morrison stared hard in Darwin's face. "Who knows. Not me. I was told to look after her for a few days while they got a safe house sorted in Glasgow. That's all I know. If it's any consolation, I agree with you. Knowing Harman's past and the active contracts out on his head, I can only assume that Sally was being used to tease out either Harman or whoever is after him.

"Sally has gone, I've lost 4 of my best men, and everybody else is still at large. So it wasn't a very good strategy was it?"
Morrison continued, "Suzie Marlin is shot dead, her murderer Watkins is shot dead, and now my men are dead. I'm running out of living people to help in this

case. We've got one new lead through - that the private detective McCracken is an informant … apparently he has been providing intelligence back to an American source, including telling them where and how Sally was being held – so that's how they knew. We're pulling him in now." Morrison was starting to ramble on a bit on autopilot – clearly his thoughts were on something else. "We got new intelligence reports earlier to say that both of the main contracts on Harman had been increased to 5 million dollars each. That's 10 million dollars! Every hitter and head-ball in the world is going to be after Harman."

"Where you very close to your men?" Bob could feel that there was something painful going on in Morrison's head.

"Yeah, we were a good team. Especially Bexton … he was due to marry my daughter next month. I suppose I had better tell her what has happened… so if you'll excuse me, I better get on with it."

In the corridor, Harry explained that he had to go and sit in relative quiet whilst he dictated his initial report back to HQ, so he was going back to the car. Darwin and Bob said they would 'sniff around' for any evidence and they agreed to meet up 5 minutes later at the front of the hospital. Harry went back to the car, started the engine, and took off back towards Port Sinton. He giggled quietly to himself, then started dictating his report into his mobile as he drove along.

After half an hour of sniffing around like lost sheep, Darwin and Bob finally realized that Harry had gone. "Fucker" said Darwin. They had no police ID - because they weren't in the police - so they had very little authority to order anyone to do anything, and they just avoided every eye contact in case someone challenged them. Darwin flipped open his phone. "Ewan, its Darwin here. Yeah I'm at the scene now... Yes, I just had a meeting with Morrison ... Yes, I know, he said. So are you coming to the scene? I was expecting you, ... oh right, yes, I understand. I'll tell you what to do, why don't you just come over here now, then you can run me back to the hotel, and we can have a chat on the way, okay?" Ewan arrived shortly afterwards, and one chat later Darwin and Bob pulled up outside the hotel. Harry was sitting smugly in the bar.

Darwin walked in first. "Sorry about that Harry, we just got too carried away at the scene. Totally forgot the time. I hope you weren't hanging around too long waiting for us?" Harry smiled "No problem." He had already predicted that Darwin would say that. Maybe Harry was starting to understand him.

"Any word from Stephen?" continued Harry. "Nothing at all" replied Darwin, "...but then again I haven't tried to call him. I wouldn't want to alert him to the fact that he's hopefully going to get an extremely hard time from angry Morrison and his team."

Harry agreed "You can say that again."

"Did you get your report back to HQ okay?" asked Darwin.

"Yeah, it's a great new system they use now. You just tap in a special code on the mobile, then you dictate it into the phone, then within an hour or so, it has been typed up and emailed around the circulation list."

"Seriously?" said Darwin genuinely. Harry perked up. "Yeah, it's really good, in fact you even get it emailed to you first, normally after about 30 minutes, then you get 30 minutes to check it and make any changes, otherwise it will be circulated. So my report is probably already on my laptop. But I couldn't be assed checking it, so it will be automatically sent shortly." Darwin appeared to be really interested. "Mind you, not that anyone is likely to be there reading it at 2 o'clock in the morning."

"You'd be surprised Darwin. The team is pretty much working around the clock on this, and also you've got Interpol on different time zones who are on all circulation lists for this case, plus the FBI and other American agencies – its still early evening for most of them."

"So what do you think about Stephen? What a bastard eh?".

Harry laughed lightly, "Yeah, but I wouldn't take it personally. You can guarantee someone bribed him or threatened him. That's what normally happens."

"Yeah, well I'd guess 'bribing'. The greedy bastard."

"Probably Darwin, but I just hope he's not got himself in too deep. These are not nice people we're dealing with. They would wipe Stephen out in a blink if they didn't need him any more, or found out that he had been arrested or was questioned about his activities. It's what they do, they don't like loose ends."

"So where is this all going to end Harry?"

Harry shrugged, "I suppose there's only a couple of ways. One is that Harman could just keep his head down, and eventually let all the activity settle, but of course the problem is that they probably have his daughter. How do you keep your head down when the lunatics that killed one of your daughters are holding the other one? Other option I guess is that Harman arranged for Sally to be taken, so now perhaps they have no way of getting to him. He has all the cards, so all he needs to do is keep hidden away with Sally, and eventually they'll get bored again and back off. He's done a pretty good job of hiding so far."

"The scary thing Harry is that every day this goes on there seems to be more people dead."

Bob was smiling in the background and stayed perfectly silent and invisible. It was great to hear Darwin and Harry getting on so well again. Obviously Harry had either temporarily forgot that he despised the air that Darwin breathed, or perhaps he considered that it was time to forgive and move on, or maybe Harry had now considered that his stunt of leaving Darwin and her behind at the scene earlier had evened things up, or maybe it was because he had told Darwin about Stephen being a bastard turncoat and perhaps that helped even up the honours, or maybe... Bob let herself have one long blink, just for a second. 'I'm just resting my eyes' she would say if anyone noticed. They didn't, and she drifted off to sweet sleep.

Darwin wasn't ready for sleep yet. "What gets me Harry is the way everyone is talking about Harman now, as if he was just some poor innocent father protecting his children – a man that was just in the wrong place at the wrong time. I don't believe it all. I saw the letter that he wrote to Suzie a couple of years ago – he was so fucking nasty."

"It didn't come from him. Harman couldn't make contact with any of his family. The letter was mocked by Witness Protection. They had instructions that if his 'missing' daughter should trace him to his original identity, then they were to put her off the scent, but somehow get her to meet the other sister. That letter was the plan they came up with. It was a good plan – it worked... for a while. Suzie and Sally got to be friends and sisters, and they both hated their father and never wanted to see him. From Harman's point of view, he got to keep his daughters protected and even communicating."

Darwin pretended that he had really worked that out already. "What about Stephen, would he have known at the time?" Harry shook his head, "No, Stephen was being used to communicate with Suzie, probably through you. So there you go Darwin, you were actually a part of this great adventure years ago, without even knowing it." Darwin laughed, and looked around for Bob's smile to join him. "Cant believe she's asleep."

Harry yawned, "Why not? It's bloody late."
"Well, you see Harry, tonight was going to be the night when ... well you know..."
Harry laughed, but not too loudly. He certainly didn't want to wake Bob up, and give Darwin any pleasure. "So you guys haven't 'done it' yet? What's wrong with you? She's beautiful, witty, and a heart of gold. Her ass isn't bad either." Darwin smiled awkwardly. He didn't like the ass comment, but decided that their new friendship was still in its infancy so he would let that one pass ... unless of course Harry had seen her ass, maybe she was shagging him as well!

"No, things just haven't worked out yet you know. Timing, circumstances, sleeping patterns, emergencies, adventures, deaths, interrogations, and murder hunts ... that sort of stuff. Nothing important.

"Well there's a price to pay for being an international crime investigator. Celibacy just happens to be part of the price. There's a lot worse too, but I'm sure you can handle it." They both smiled lightly. "Look about that stuff before, and the stunt we pulled on you …" started Darwin.

Harry stood up, "I don't want to know Darwin. Let's just leave it. You're a fucker, and I hate you. Simple as that, but it doesn't mean that we can't use each other to get information." Harry kept a solid face and looked deep into Darwin's eyes, then left.

Bob opened her left eye. "Don't worry Darwin, he's coming around." Then she closed it again.

"Oh, you're awake", said Darwin optimistically. Suddenly a shag seemed a real possibility again. Bob had appeared to have gone back to sleep, but at least there was a glimmer of light.

He whispered deeply in Bob's ear, "Hey sexy, would you like me to carry you up to bed. I'll even undress you, and make you all comfortable and warm." Bob smiled but still hadn't opened her eyes, so Darwin took that as a green light, and started to put his arm under her legs. Just then the loudest blast of Squeeze's 'Coffee in Bed' roared in polyphonic from Darwin's pocket, which happened to be about 2 inches from Bob's ear as he bent over to lift her. "For fuck sake!" shouted Bob as she bolted awake. "What was that?"

Darwin fumbled with his phone, trying to turn it off, but then noticed it was from a local number that he didn't recognize.

"Hi Darwin – its me, listen I'm in a bit of a pickle here…" said Stephen quietly.

"You're fucking right you are, you two-faced, yellow bellied, turn coat, back-stabbing, sheep-shagging bastard you. What's wrong, can't handle the pressure now. SCI's giving you a hard time? Well don't be expecting any sympathy or help from us any more. Fucker."

Darwin was hoping to get a response from Bob, but she had decided that she was too tired and had disappeared upstairs unnoticed. "Hello?", said Stephen's voice from the other end. "…has something happened that I should know about?"

Darwin changed his tone after realizing he didn't have an audience. "Where are you?"

"I'm somewhere in Port Sinton. Remember those guys I was drinking with at the bar? … Fred … the guy in the jumper. Anyway his wife arrived down later, and about ten minutes after that he got a call to say their house was broken into in London, so he left to go back home, and she stayed. Anyway, one thing led to another … and…well…lets just say, I'm here in their house. She's finally gone to sleep, and I desperately need to get out of here and …"

"You mean you don't know? The SCI's haven't found you yet?"

"What the fuck are you talking about Darwin?"

"Listen Stephen, I know that you've been double-crossing us."

Stephen played the silence card for a moment, "Ah, well, I can explain Darwin if you just …"

"Fuck up Stephen. Anyway, that's the least of your problems at the moment. While you've been playing with Mrs Fred, Tarnlough Hospital was hit, big time. Four SCI's dead, and Sally kidnapped."

"Holy sh…" started Stephen.

"Oh that's nothing Stephen, that's just the start of it. Following the attack, the cops in Northern Ireland decided to inform the SCI's that you had been passing information to some American source, and specifically that you had told them that Sally was being held at Tarnlough Hospital. You see, they had been monitoring all your calls and faxes."

"Oh"

"So anyway, there's a rather angry team of SCI's out there at the moment looking for you. They've just lost 4 of their colleagues, so they are kinda pissed off, and looking for someone to blame. As the attackers at Tarnlough left absolutely no evidence whatsoever, I would guess that you would make the perfect scapegoat."

"Ah" said Stephen.

"Bottom line spunk-head, is that you're fucked, and as you've been betraying us good and proper old chap, I don't really think that we will be wanting to help you very much. Anyway, remind me, why did you phone?"

"Of course you'll want to help me Darwin. I know stuff, that's why I've been working with another 'client' as well. Its not personal Darwin, they just pay a hell of a lot more than you, and they don't argue over rates or timesheets. Help me, and I'll help you."
"Harry reckons that if you get arrested for questioning, then your 'clients' will probably blow your head off."

Stephen sighed, "Yes Darwin, that's very likely indeed, thank you for pointing that out. Listen, I'm going to have to move. Enough people saw me leave from Frans with her, which means they could trace me here. I'll maybe catch up with you some time. Give my regards to Bob and Harry."
Darwin sat quietly, not even letting a breath be heard down the other end. Stephen gave one more last sigh. "Bye Darwin". Darwin sat even quieter. Stephen gave an encore sigh, "Please fucking help me Darwin. I'm in the shit here and I'm sinking bad."

"Where are you?" Darwin decided that Stephen was finally out of sighs. "I don't know Darwin; I'm within a 5 minute walk of the Port, but I can't risk walking there, the SCI's are very likely to be looking for me."
"Cant you find out where you are … you're an investigator. Go investigate an envelope with an

address or something on it. I'll get a map from reception."

"Good thinking", and he rummaged through the draw on the telephone cabinet. Barnets Road, number 4."

Darwin was scanning the map on the wall in reception. "Got it. I think I can find it. It's up the hill from Flans, then left at the traffic lights, then second left, then first left, almost back down to the sea again. I'll be there as soon as I can… be bothered.", and he hung up.

Darwin sneaked upstairs and gently pushed Harry's door open. Harry was lying naked on the bed. Bob was completely naked too, sitting astride him, facing the other way, looking straight at Darwin. Harry was grunting as he pushed himself harder and faster up inside her. Bob let out little yelps as she started to climax. Well, not really, but they could well have been if Darwin's suspicions were correct.

Instead Harry was sat up in bed still fully clothed, with his mobile to his ear, giggling hysterically down the mic. He stopped when he saw Darwin. "Listen honey, I had better go … yes I will, yes I always do, yeah you too, love you too, bye hun."

"Sorry Harry, I didn't realize that you were on the phone."

"It's okay Darwin. So, how can I help you? Looking for some tips to get Bob into bed. First piece of advice

I can give you is to try and make sure she is awake, although in your case that might not..."

"Its Stephen" interrupted Darwin "...he's just phoned. He had no idea about what happened tonight, or anything about being hunted by the SCI's. He's at a house in town, and I need to borrow your car to go and help him."

Harry chuckled. "Hmmmm, let me think...um... no."

"He needs our help Harry. Besides, he says that he's got some juicy information that we don't know about." Harry thought for a moment. "The answer is still no... to borrowing the car, but I'll take you. It will be safer. Besides, if we get caught, I'll just pretend that I was arresting him."

"Let's go!" shouted Darwin excitedly. Harry didn't share his excitement.

The second that they pulled up outside of 4 Barnett's Road, Stephen launched himself over the garden wall so quickly that Harry and Darwin jumped. Darwin had locked the doors, so Stephen's enthusiasm was short lived, as he grabbed hopelessly at the rear handle. "Open the fucking Door" he whisper screamed. Instead Darwin got out of the passenger side, and went round to the back where Stephen was ducking down, trying to force the door open. He looked up at Darwin, just in time to see a right fist land perfectly on his nose. It was harder than Stephen thought Darwin could punch, and it knocked him clean off his feet and on to ground. Darwin walked back round to the passenger side and sat back in again with Harry. "Good dig!" congratulated Harry, "I didn't realize you had it in you."

Darwin pretended not to hear, and held his right hand with his left.
"It hurts doesn't it? People don't realize how much a punch hurts your hand." Advised Harry. Darwin winced in agreement, but managed not to cry. He pushed the central locking button to release the lock on the back door. Stephen heard the click from his dazed position beside the curb, so he scrambled up and into the back seat, lying across it. Harry leant back and closed the door for him, to save him any more embarrassment.

Darwin tried not to smile. He had done it. Finally he had punched someone. For years it worried him, just in case he ever had to do it...which he never had before. He feared that he might miss or something even worse. Imagine the embarrassment if Stephen had moved out of the way and Darwin had punched the car door. Imagine if he had actually landed one right on the nose and then … just nothing happened – it didn't even hurt or make him move. Stephen would be pointing at him and pretending to cry whilst Harry would be pissing himself laughing.

The punch was a gamble, but one that paid off. He had landed it squarely, kept his eye on the target, and followed through – just like the book said. Stephen had been thrown unceremoniously to the ground like a bag of shite. There was even blood on his knuckles – Stephen's blood. Darwin considered it a resounding success in every department. Perhaps now he could start to be a real fighter, he could go to boxing school or maybe take a karate correspondence course. Now that he had defeated his demons, there would be no stopping him.

"What the fuck did you do that for?" screamed Stephen from the back. His bloody nose was dripping through his lips and made it look like he was spitting instead of shouting.

Darwin had tasted blood. He liked it and it had worked out fine. He considered jumping over the seat and into the back. Stephen was still clearly dazed, so he reckoned he could give him another good pummeling, with a few punches to his cheeks and jaw. A couple of slaps round the head, maybe even a Chinese burn or a dead arm to finish him off. However, bearing in mind his knuckles were throbbing and inflamed, Darwin decided not to follow that course of action. Besides that, Stephen was pretty angry and looked a bit mean. Chances were that he'd give Darwin a good hiding if he tried any more of the rough stuff. Darwin decided just to cut his losses. He considered himself a good decision maker. "Sorry mate, but that was from Bob and me, for double-crossing us."

Stephen came round slowly. "Okay, I suppose I deserved it. Good punch by the way. I'm impressed. I think you might have broken my nose, but nevertheless I'm impressed."

"Thanks…" smiled Darwin, and he passed him a box of tissues, "…now dry your eyes you big girl."

"So what's the plan?", asked Stephen through his face of tissue.

Harry realized they didn't have a plan so he looked to Darwin, who gallantly accepted the job, "We're taking you to Swansea. Best to get into a big city and as far away from here as possible, you'll be harder to get to. We'll find a small hotel in the centre for you, then we'll drive back before morning. Nobody will know we've gone. In the morning, you can buy yourself another mobile phone. So while we're driving, you'll have lots of time to tell us about your double-crossing deceiving antics."

Stephen tried to defend his actions, "It's really not like that Darwin. I got an email out of the blue from some solicitor's office in an off-shore Caribbean island that probably doesn't even exist. The email asked me to check my bank balance, and then call a telephone number which was at the bottom of the email. I rang my bank and there was an extra fifty grand in it! I called the number, and it was a recorded message. It said what they wanted, gave me some leads to follow up, and gave me another number to phone my report into. I also had to prepare a written report every few days by fax. It was no big deal, and every day another ten! grand! goes into my account. I'm just getting paid by a client for being a private detective.

"At least once a day, I get a call from an automated recorded message. Some days it includes new information to work on and other days it's just a message to tell me to provide an update at a specific time. I simply phone and leave the message as instructed."

Darwin sat quietly to take in the information. Was Stephen telling the truth?

"Sounds fair enough to me", said Harry. For the moment, Darwin decided to give him the benefit of the doubt. "So that's the price to sell your soul then is it Stephen?" Stephen fought back quickly, "Actually, no it's not Darwin. Truth be known, I would have done it for a fraction of what they're paying me. But you see it's different for me - this is my job and there's fuck-all wrong with earning some reasonable money for once. I haven't done anything bad – I don't earn a salary from you and you don't have me on an exclusive contract Darwin."

Darwin knew Stephen was sort of right, but now wasn't the time to agree with him, "You've been lying and cheating, and scheming around behind our backs. We trusted you, and you shafted us. And just for the record, you won't be getting any money from me." Stephen started to retaliate again, "Listen, if you think…"

"Anyway…" butted Darwin, "…you said that you had some information for us. Tell us now, or we're dropping you off back in Port Sinton."

"I was going to tell you anyway" argued Stephen.

"Yeah, whatever"

"Anyway … There's a second level of Witness Protection that is top secret. It's used whenever someone has to go seriously underground. There was a worry that Harman's pursuers had bribed or threatened a member of the Witness Protection. The scheme is called WIPE, and it's run by ex-members of the Witness Protection Scheme who report directly and exclusively to the Home Secretary. They are all anonymous, but they are paid very handsomely indeed. Harman was transferred to WIPE, and therefore as far as everyone is concerned, he has just disappeared. He didn't, and WIPE have been looking after him. It is so confidential that the WIPE operatives don't even know the identities of the people they are protecting. It's all done through email and with code-names and code-words.

"So, don't ask me how my clients know, but they have been able to confirm that Harman definitely lives in this part of Wales. They know his WIPE code-name is 'Dolphin', and that he reported in for his monthly email just last week. I would guess that there is now a WIPE operative with a very healthy bank balance."

"...or with a hole in his head" said Harry. Stephen shut up for a moment and thought about his own chance of survival. It wasn't looking good.

"So Harman could be living amongst us? He could live down the road, watching all this happening. Just watching and waiting. What is he going to do now that they have Sally? He'll have to do something." said Darwin.

"Maybe" said Harry, "but maybe Harman is responsible for Sally's disappearance. It all makes sense, and kidnap is just not their style. Also, it appears that Sally wasn't harmed in any way, which again points to someone who cares for her. Our other friends don't exactly have a reputation for caring."

Darwin didn't really get Harry's logic. Even if you were taking somebody for kidnap, you still wouldn't harm them. The point of kidnap is that you are trading someone's welfare for a higher stake. Surely if you harm someone you weaken your position. He decided however that he was a bit too new to all this investigation stuff, and decided not to challenge Harry for fear of him having some really obvious explanation that Darwin had overlooked. "What about Watkins then?...was he killed by 'them' because they were finished with him, or was he killed by Harman, for killing Suzie?".

Harry didn't know, "Not sure. My gut feeling is that 'they' done that one. I can't see Harman risking going back to Northern Ireland, although I suppose he could have simply paid someone to do it."

"Couldn't you ask your 'clients' what happened Stephen? – I'm sure they could help us out" tried Darwin. Stephen laughed "No Darwin, they don't do 'help', sorry".
"Looks like we need to find Dolphin then" concluded Darwin.
"I've got an idea Stephen" said Harry, "Why don't you ask your clients to give you the name of their WIPE contact. Tell them it's important and that you have a new lead and believe that you could locate Harman or Sally if you got to talk to their WIPE informer. Might be worth a try."

Stephen agreed unconvincingly, "I'll give it a go, but I doubt very much that they'll entertain the idea. If they wanted to give me the name of their WIPE informant, then they would have done it already." Stephen's phone beeped twice, to tell him that he had got a new message. "Talk of the devil" said Stephen in surprisingly good humour. As usual it was recorded by a female American accent. He put it on loud speaker so that the others would definitely now believe his story. "Please call 01298454332 in 1 hour's time with an update. Sally Burton has been taken from Tarnlough hospital. This was not the work of this organization or any of our direct subcontractors. You need to locate her. She is an important person to us. Our WIPE contact is reporting back this evening, and we will update you if relevant. As you'll know by now, the SCIs have a warrant out for your arrest. If you are arrested or interrogated by the SCIs regarding our relationship then we will immediately terminate … our arrangement. Your code word for the next report is 'Town Planner'. End of message."

They all pretended not to have heard the word "terminate" in the message. "So, it definitely wasn't 'them' that took Sally – that almost certainly means it was Harman, doesn't it?" confirmed Harry. Darwin still didn't agree, "Not necessarily – there are a couple of contracts out on him. Just because it wasn't Stephen's '*clients*' doesn't mean it was Harman. But it certainly makes it a possibility."

Stephen was staring blankly out the window. He was desperately trying to think of some exit from this situation. He knew he couldn't keep running, but he also knew he couldn't stand still. The SCIs were going to get to him somehow. Maybe he should just give up now – put his hands up and walk down the middle of Port Sinton Main Street. However, just for the moment, he felt safe with Harry and Darwin in their tiny red hire car on the motorway to Swansea, and he hoped and preyed the journey would last forever.

"Don't worry Stephen" continued Darwin, "we'll get you safely to Swansea. You'll be fine there."

"I'm of no use to them any more" he mumbled quietly. "If I'm in hiding, I can hardly be effective at finding out information can I? Cant do much 'investigating' from a hotel room can I? The moment I stop giving them information, then ..."

"Stop being so miserable Stephen" encouraged Darwin, "Look on the bright side."
He quickly realized that there was no bright side, so he continued on before anyone could challenge him, "We're all in this together Stephen. What we'll do is this; when you need to update them, you give us a call. You can give us any information that they give you, and we'll feed you some information to give to them. Harry's a real cop, and I'm a very senior ranking pretend cop. Between us, we'll come up with some juicy intelligence to pass through to them. If not, we'll make something up. We'll work it out, wont we Harry?"

Harry certainly would not be passing any information over to Stephen but he smiled gently anyway, "Don't worry it will be fine"
"Exactly" agreed Darwin, "don't worry Stephen". Stephen was now even more worried, but he agreed with them anyway "Don't worry, I'll not worry"

CHAPTER TWENTY-THREE

Bob was fast asleep on the bed – she hadn't even bothered to get undressed she was so tired. She awoke to shouts from down the corridor. "Safe!"

She looked at her door which sat patiently on its hinges. In a split second the hinges ripped out from the frame and the lock flew across the room, smashing a vase on the sideboard. The door slipped perpendicular across the floor at first, then flipped over and landed flat. Five black bodies stood at the door. Two had guns pointed at Bob, one was holding a hand ballard which had so effectively removed the door. The other two had their guns pointed outwards down both directions of the corridor.

"Safe!", screamed one of the black figures. "Body here sir" screamed another. They all pulled back from the door, and in a few seconds Morrison marched up to the bed. "Where the fuck is he?" Bob was genuinely confused. "Where, who, what?" she just about managed to mumble.

Morrison launched himself across the bed "don't fuck with me you stupid little bitch. Where is he? Where is he?" and he grabbed Bob's jaw hard. Stephen McCracken! Where is he?" he yelled even harder into her face. "I don't…" started Bob. Morrison spat at her "Fucking bitch" and he threw her head back off the headboard. "Tell me where McCracken is or I'll fucking finish you off, here and now..." he engulfed her throat with his big right hand.

"Sir!" a strong voice stated from the door. Morrison composed himself briefly. "Isn't she one of us sir?" Morrison stood up, "There is no big 'us' any more ... the only fucking 'us' is our squad ... the rest of the fuckers are all 'them'. It's 'us' and 'them' now. It's only 'us' that has just wiped up 4 of our dead bodies. They weren't your dead bodies were they?" he screamed at Bob.

"No sir" admitted Bob. She was happy to say anything at the moment as long as it didn't mean Morrison attacking her again. She really thought he was going to kill her. For a split second, she thought he was going to run her head harder and harder into the headboard, then trail her across the floor and punch her to death. That was the look he had on his face. Bob suddenly started shaking. She didn't know why, then she started crying. She didn't know why either. She had lost control of her body. She was trying to be strong, but her body simply wasn't listening any more. It was in a world of its own, and it decided that it wanted to shake and cry.

Morrison stared down at her with a mysterious look on his face, "I'm sorry, I ..." He stopped and looked over at the black figure in the doorway for some help. "She said she didn't know sir" said the figure. He returned to Bob, calmly this time "I don't want to see you or any of your friends again – make sure you're on the first plane out of here."

A few more doors were being kicked open down the hall. Bob could hear a rumble of steps, then a large thud, then "Safe", then more steps. Eventually the steps kept going and she heard them rumble down the stairs and out of the main entrance.

Bob buried her face in the pillows and sobbed sorely. Why was Darwin not there to protect her? She knew of course that he would be away on some other adventure. Somewhere that he could be so absorbed in himself and his journey that he wouldn't be capable of thinking about her. If only Brian was here, things would be so different – he would be beside her in the bed, ready to fend off Morrison. He wouldn't be able to, but nevertheless at least he would be there with her. She hadn't considered getting attacked as being one of the consequences – she had overlooked that one. Bob was pretty sure that Darwin wasn't being attacked or threatened. No doubt he would be skirting around the edges of attacks and murders as usual, never actually getting drawn in to action, but always close enough to benefit from the excitement.

CHAPTER TWENTY-FOUR

It was just starting to get light, when Darwin and Harry returned back to Port Sinton. They had only intended to drive past the port on their way back to the hotel, but as they approached, they could feel the port was acting differently. It felt as if it was bustling quietly, whispering in the background. Above the outline of the rooftops, a long pole sat high in the air. Down at the quayside, almost every car park space was taken. There was not much movement, but the potential was definitely there for an explosion of activity.

As they rounded the Main Street, they could see that the large pole was connected to a 'Sky TV OB Unit'. On further examination, most of the vehicles in the car park appeared to either be TV broadcasting units, or plain white vans, presumably hired as backup. Amongst the quietness, 1 van was alight and revving hard. It was the 'Good Morning Satellite Unit'.

"Looks like the case is attracting quite a bit of attention now Darwin?" said Harry in apparent shock of the situation. They pulled up within earshot of the Good Morning van. A reporter was practicing his lines…

"Yes, thank you John. I am reporting live this morning from the normally quiet and remote village of Port Sinton. Unbelievably, it was here that the drama surrounding last night's massacre at a nearby hospital started. The missing patient, Sally Burton, lived just here" he pointed over to his left "...and another resident who was found shot dead a few days ago lived just here" and he pointed in the other direction. "It's also believed that one of the dead Police Officers lived just at the top of the hill behind me. Currently the area around Turnberry is sealed off until..." A young producer raised her hand to shut the reporter up. "Turnberry?" she asked, "Don't you mean Tarnlough?"

"Yes, thank you John. I am reporting live this morning from..."

The producer was intrigued when she saw Harry and Darwin sitting with their windows open. "Hi, how are you?" she shouted over. She was obviously employed to schmooze. She was lovely, she was young, she was beautiful, she was blonde, she had nice teeth, she was polite, she was professional. "Hi, fine thanks" said Darwin.
"Hmmm, no local accent, so I suppose you're either cops, reporters, or holiday makers down for an early nosey. If you're not reporters (and I suspect your not) then can we interview you? It will only take a moment or two and we can pre-record it. You'll be famous. So, which one... cops or holidaymakers."

"We're Co…" started Darwin. Before Harry stepped in with a short dig to Darwin's ribs, "I'm a Police Officer, and this gentleman is helping me with my enquiries. And no, sorry, we cant do an interview." he put the car into gear and headed back out of the Port. "Spoilsport" snapped Darwin. "I'm media trained you know, I could have given a great interview." Harry ignored him, and they maintained silence until they approached the Hotel gates. They noticed firstly that the car park was much fuller than usual. A few old small cars and a few small vans. The front door of the hotel was lying crooked on its hinges.

They peered into the bar to see 5 men sleeping on the chairs, and another 2 on the floor. They all looked kind of semi-respectable. Wearing mostly suits and ties, although the suits were clearly very cheap and probably bought on a 2-for-1 offer, the ties were mostly mock-silk and hanging loosely, and their hair styles were seriously out of date. At a guess, Darwin reckoned they looked like a pool of reporters.

Bryn was still brushing up pieces of glass which used to form a part of the dining room door. They were leaded stained glass, so he was collecting them carefully in case they could be used to reconstruct the door. "What happened here?" called Darwin.
"Hi Darwin, Good morning Harold. Bit of a mess here. Police decided to enter every room to look for someone. They also decided that using the keys just wouldn't be dramatic enough. Don't think they found

whoever they were looking for. Probably something to do with all that shit in Tarnlough last night."

"Who are the guys in the bar?"

Bryn shrugged with his usual apathy "Not really sure. They all arrived at various stages throughout the night apparently. They were looking for rooms but Barney told them that all the locks were broken and that they would have to wait until this afternoon. He charged them ten pounds each to sleep in the bar for the night. Miserable shit."

"Well I suppose they didn't really have much of an alternative did they?" Darwin motioned Harry out into the hall, "Do you think it was Stephen they were after?" he whispered. "Yeah" Harry whispered back. "We had better check upstairs."

All the doors had been dumped to the ground in exactly the same fashion. At Bob's door, Darwin stopped and looked around the room. It didn't really seem any different than the others at first, but for some reason he felt he needed to investigate further. Where was Bob? The Bed had no quilts or blankets or pillows. They had all been squashed together and wedged down in between the bed and the wall to the side. "Bob?" he called out gently to the pile of material. He heard a sniff, then a tired weeping sound. "Bob?" and he yanked out the top quilt to reveal Bob curled up with the pillows, wrapped in blankets, half under the bed, and half in the gap. "Bob, what's wrong?" said Darwin. Bob lifted her head up to reveal the effects of several hours of crying. Her eyes bulged around the room, making sure that only Darwin and Harry were there. Her cheeks were red, almost raw, and every vein had been scraped up to the surface. Every piece of makeup had been pushed and rubbed across her face in every direction.

Darwin started to lift her up from under her arms, but as he connected, she grabbed him hard, and started crying again, sobbing with all her heart. "I don't want to play any more Darwin", she spurted in between sobs. "It'll be okay pet, I promise" Darwin repeated warmly into her ear.

Harry realized that he was surplus to requirements, so he came to the side of the bed, and reached across to touch Bob's hair. "We'll look after you" he said sincerely, "I'll go for a walk, and I'll see you downstairs later." Darwin returned his attentions to Bob. If there had of been a door, then Harry would have closed it gently. Instead he tapped the door frame to let them know that he had left.

Bob slowly released her hold on Darwin, and let him pull her up on to the bed. "I bet I look lovely" she joked on an outward sob. "Well, I would still give you one" said Darwin, trying to keep the mood as positive as possible. "Whatever has happened Bob, it is all over now. I'm here to look after you. We'll sit here quietly until you're ready to talk. There's no rush." Bob smiled with a slobber-filled mouth. Saliva was now running out of one side of her lips, her tears were still dragging her eye makeup down her cheeks, and snot traced its way persistently down to her top lips. Darwin pretended not to notice and smiled into her red, tiny eyes.

"It was Morrison and his squad. He had totally lost the plot Darwin. Completely flipped – I thought he was going to kill me. His eyes were evil – he wanted me to be dead. He said he was looking for Stephen. Seemed to think that I knew where he was." Darwin dropped his head, "I'm sorry Bob, it's my fault – I shouldn't have left you on your own, but you were tired and I just didn't think. Stephen called, and myself and Harry went and picked him up, then we took him to …" Bob raised her hand to stop him, "Shhhhhh. Please Darwin, I don't want to know. I don't give a toss where Stephen is, and if I don't know, then I don't have to be involved anymore. I don't care, and I'm going home. It's all over for me. Morrison has warned us all to leave Darwin. He was serious. "

Darwin was being outwardly sympathetic and caring, but really he was thinking about why Morrison would think that Stephen would be in Bob's bedroom, or that Bob would know where Stephen was. Perhaps the SCI's had been following Stephen and discovered that he and Bob were lovers. That was the only thing that made sense to Darwin, and he made a note to ask Morrison next time he saw him. He held her tighter, "Don't do anything while you're feeling like this Bob. Tell you what we'll do. You throw some water over your face – freshen yourself up. I'll nip down to the kitchen, and see if we can't get you some breakfast. How does that sound?"

"Can I have sausages?" slobbered Bob. "Of course you can my babe." Darwin was halfway down the stairs before he noticed Harry sitting at the bottom steps. "Is she okay?"

"Yeah, she'll be fine Harry – just a bit knocked back. It's awful seeing her like that. It was Morrison – she said she thought he was going to kill her – he came to her room looking for Stephen last night. It's really affected her. She says she is going home."

"If you really care for her Darwin, you should send her home. It's not safe any more."

"Not up to me" said Darwin defensively, "If she wants to go home, then that's up to her – I'll not stop her." Darwin of course knew that he couldn't survive without Bob. If she went, then he would go too. He would have no choice. Harry was his friend again, but at the end of the day Harry was a cop first and foremost, and he had a job to do. Stephen was now in hiding in Swansea and was probably not the safest person to associate himself with. He couldn't continue on his own, and he never realized that until now. He felt like a wimp. Why wasn't he strong enough to drive himself forward now? He normally was, and he rarely needed the support or company of anyone else – let alone a girl. He didn't like that thought, so he replaced it with an image of Bob and Stephen shagging – it worked, and now he didn't need her any more.

"Maybe we'll both go home." He offered Harry. "or … maybe we'll both stay."
He skipped down the last few steps. "Bryn!" he sung across the dining room. "How would you like to earn yourself a crisp £20?" Bryn shouted back. "Breakfast?"
"I'm impressed" Darwin said, "I need a couple of breakfasts. Just whatever you can rustle up will be fine, but make sure you cook the sausages – although preferably not in the microwave this time!"

Darwin turned back to Harry, "Breakfast my friend?"
"Sounds good" agreed Harry.
"That'll be another tenner then Harry?" butted in Bryn. "No it won't" said Harry quickly, "I'm not in a good mood at the moment Bryn, so just get my breakfast please. If you're quick and I like it, then I might not kill you. That's the best deal you're going to get." Bryn smiled sarcastically, "I was only joking"

"So was I" replied Harry, "…even if you're quick and even if I like it, I still might kill you, just for a laugh."
Bryn never looked back, but repeated "yeah, yeah, yeah, whatever"
"So what do you think about Morrison – why is he so pissed off with us? … well, with Bob anyway."
"I suppose you would feel the same if you had just lost 4 colleagues, including a future son-in-law. He

was just told that Stephen had passed information about Sally's whereabouts to an American source. You can understand why he is feeling a bit pissed of, cant you?"

Darwin clearly didn't agree. "Yeah, but you should see the state that Bob is in. He really scared her. I think there's something else in it."

"Who knows, who cares?" said Harry quietly, "I'm too tired to care at the moment. I just need some food, and then I need some sleep." Darwin slapped him firmly on the back, "Com'n then, let's go and wait for our fabulous breakfast".

Darwin turned on the television, and switched immediately to Good Morning TV.

"… and we can reveal exclusively here live! on Good Morning that there may be some truth in the speculation that there is a link between the multiple murders here in Wales, and the 2 murders last week in Northern Ireland. Earlier on, one of our producers spoke informally to undercover police officers from Northern Ireland just here" and he pointed to where Harry and Darwin had pulled up earlier. He continued, "Although the officers failed to confirm the connection directly, it was hardly coincidental that Northern Ireland plain clothes police officers happened to be at the scene immediately following …"

"Ooops" said Darwin, and he turned off the TV. "What?" said Harry as he fiddled around with his mobile. "Didn't you hear the news?" asked Darwin. Harry didn't reply and was desperately trying to recover some messages from his phone. Darwin realized that Harry hadn't heard the news and decided it was best not to discuss it for the moment.

"News?" mumbled Harry, as he tried relentlessly to enter a pin code to pick up an international message. "Yeah, nothing important. Arsenal lost at home to Spurs." Darwin decided to change the subject quickly "I'm going to see Bob. Make sure she's okay." When Darwin came out to the main hall, 2 men had already started repairing and re-instating the front door. They had blue t-shirts on with "Lough Locks ... Covering all your Loughs and Locks" written across the back in yellow. Darwin decided immediately that he hated them.

"So, you decided to come back, did you?" Darwin spun around to face the voice. Morrison had positioned himself behind reception and was looking very angry and tired. The 2 lock-fixers were within hearing distance, plus some of the reporters in the bar had started to wake up. He was also within screaming distance of Harry and of course he could also now do punching. All this led him to decide that he could be brave without jeopardizing his life. Even if Morrison grabbed him quickly, he could scream and cry loud enough to attract sufficient attention to break up the situation.

"I've just found Bob hiding under the bed" said Darwin sternly, staring Morrison hard in the eyes. "I only wanted McCracken, I've no problem with Bob" replied Morrison calmly.

"So, why the fuck did you have to scare her like that, you tosser. I don't suppose you fancy being as brave now do you? Come on over here, and try to scare me as much. I'll tell you what, I'll make it easier for you – I'll come over to you."

Darwin remembered that Morrison thought he was an undercover cop; this made him even more courageous. Morrison knew nothing about his imaginary career so Darwin could have been an undercover drugs investigator – fighting off dangerous gangs with regular shoot-outs and bare-fisted brawls to the death. "Don't play the big-boy with me Litton, or I'll tear your frigg'n head off." Morrison leaned forward. Darwin moved closer to his face. "Tear away, tosser. Assume I'm playing the big-boy. Or I'll tell you what I'll do, I'll play big-girl instead, that way you can play even rougher. You obviously get a big kick out of slapping girls instead of boys. Maybe I should put on a girls voice shall I? … that should get you going."

Morrison was chewing his lips, and his eyes had started to open wider and wider. He stayed silent, and kept his gaze on Darwin. Suddenly Morrison relaxed his pose and smiled "As I said, I have no problem with Bob – she was just in the wrong place at the wrong time. I was looking for McCracken. So maybe you just tell me where he is and I'll leave you lovely people from Northern Ireland alone."

"Why don't you just fuck off out of here now, and maybe I'll not give you a good smack. You're lucky there's a few too many people around this time, but you might not be so lucky next time. So if I was you, I would take the opportunity to get out of my sight, while you can still walk." Darwin lifted his right hand up to wipe his nose – a double strategy - to try and look cool, and at the same time let Morrison see his bloody knuckles and swollen fingers. Just to let him know that he was now an experienced puncher and that he meant business.

Morrison didn't do fear, which was starting to worry Darwin a little, but he certainly couldn't back down now. "We'll chat again" Morrison said, and came out from behind the reception. Bob was standing nearly at the bottom of the stairs, and had heard most of the conversation. She timed her walk down the remaining stairs to arrive in the main corridor just after Morrison. With a single swipe of her right foot, she skillfully clipped Morrison's ankle with a slicing blow. Morrison screamed "what the…" before his foot crossed across the back of his other leg, and he twisted and fell towards a table in the hall. He grabbed for it, and both the table and Morrison hit the tiled floor of the porch with a painful combination of cracks and bumps. The locksmiths tried to avoid any contact, and 2 of the men sleeping in the bar came to see what all the commotion was.

Darwin and Bob turned quickly into the dining room before anyone associated them with what was happening. As they walked across the room, Bob grabbed Darwin's bum hard. "Thanks for that Darwin". Harry finally gave up on his mobile, and held his arms out for Bob to walk in. She smiled, and welcomed the embrace. Harry closed his arms around her. "Are you okay love?" he said. Bob said nothing, but let out a small sniffle, and sobbed a little, but re-assured him nevertheless. She was so annoyed with herself again. She was feeling fine, yet the slightest excuse and she had started crying. She was trying so hard not to, but again had no influence whatsoever. They held quietly for a few minutes, each listening to Morrison swearing uncontrollably out in the hall.

Darwin decided to phone Stephen – just to check up on things and keep him up-to-date. "Yes Darwin" the phone speaker said. "Hi Stephen, how are you?... good .... Yes, about half an hour ago...Yeah, they were here okay – every door kicked in, every room searched. I just had a run-in with Morrison myself there ... yeah he is ... he gave Bob a really hard time last night when he was looking for you ... yeah I did ... haha .... He sure is ... haha ... yes, I will. Yeah, you too. Bye."

"Stephen sends his love Bob" Darwin shouted from across the room, then wished he hadn't said it. What was he doing passing on Stephens love to Bob? Harry lifted a clean handkerchief from his inside pocket, and gently wiped the wet away from Bob's eyes. "Its okay love, trust me, we'll look after you" and he gave her a gentle kiss on the forehead. "Thanks Harry, and I'm sorry about all the blubbing … I just can't seem to stop."

"Food's up!" Bryn was balancing three plates and walking gingerly towards their table. The food was fine, although the sausages had of course been microwaved, but Bryn appeared to have given them a blast of something, one of those chef-blow-torch things to take away the anemic look of them. It more or less worked, and they tasted better than last time.

After breakfast, Darwin offered the Loughs Locks an extra 50 pound if they could fix his bedroom door first. They accepted and within half an hour Darwin, Harry, and bob were all lying across the bed. There was a mass of banging and shouting outside the bedroom as the hotel was put back together again. Despite this, all three of them slept like babies, side by side. Bob was in the middle, and held on to Darwin's and Harry's hand on each side. She felt safe

CHAPTER TWENTY-FIVE

A gentle knock on the door hardly disturbed the room. The knock got louder, but it had such competition that it really had no chance of wakening them. It was almost 1 o'clock. They had been asleep for hours, yet not one of them had moved an inch from their original sleeping position. Their 3 phones buzzed aggressively one by one on the sideboard, all turned to vibrate. The hotel room phone sat motionless – it was unplugged but you could tell by looking at it that it would be ringing madly had it been connected.

The futile knocking started again, then kicking, and then swearing. Nothing worked. It all stopped, then a few minutes later the door opened slightly.

"Thanks Bryn, I appreciate it" whispered a voice outside the door, followed by the noise of money changing hands. Bryn took the key from the door, and tiptoed downstairs with his pieces of silver. The tall male figure entered the room and gently closed the door behind him. He made his way over to the bed and sat down on a small gap beside Darwin's legs. The man took his hand close to Darwin's neck, then retracted his index finger behind his thumb, flicking his nail precisely on the end of Darwin's earlobe. It was a classic flick, solid enough to make the lobe move, but yet fine enough to cause that sting that really hurts other schoolboys. It had taken many years of practice to perfect such a technique.

"Fuck", and Darwin bolted upright. Stephen smiled inanely in total satisfaction. If it wasn't for the fact that he had the start of few black eyes, then he may even have looked triumphant.

"Good Afternoon gentlemen"
"What are you doing here?" asked Darwin, "Don't you know you're a wanted man. Morrison is after your balls!" At the sound of Morrison's name, Bob bolted upright too, immediately breaking into a scream. Harry turned and held her tightly. "Its okay Bob, it's just me, Darwin, and Stephen. You've had a bad dream. It's all okay now."

"I'm not worried about Morrison any more", smiled Stephen. Darwin stretched his arms and legs to a chorus of clicking and cracking. "What are you talking about Stephen? I saw Morrison a few hours ago and believe me, you should be worried – he's not a happy bunny! He wants you badly. As far as he's concerned you are responsible for killing his team."

"Tough" said Stephen, and he reached into his inside pocket and pulled out a printed sheet. "It's Morrison's CV … very interesting reading. I think my American clients sent it to me. I asked them who their contact was in WIPE. First they told me that they couldn't give me the information directly, but then 2 minutes later I received an email with this attached."

"I'll begin…" started Stephen, annoyingly.
1966 Joined RAF, blah blah
1969 Graduated from Harten RAF College
1973 Joined RAF Teaching school, blah blah
1978 Appointed to Accelerated Officer Program in the Met
1985 Promoted to Sergeant in Met, blah blah
1990 Transferred to Special Services and seconded to Witness Protection
1995 Appointed to position of UK head of the Witness Protection Program
2002 Left Witness Protection Program to join Manchester Serious Crime Squad, blah blah
2005 Appointed head of Swansea Serious Crime Squad"

Bob was confused. What was the relevant bit? She stayed quiet.

"Morrison is ex Witness Protection Program. He's the WIPE operative, I'll put money on it!. What's more I'll put money on him being the WIPE informer to my American clients." Smiled Stephen. "Why else would they have sent me this?"
"I think you're right" admitted Darwin.

"Let's go visit him then" suggested Harry, and they all bumbled down the stairs. "Stephen, you had better stay here. The chances of getting to Tarnlough without being noticed are pretty slim. We'll call you as soon as we know anything." Stephen started to protest, but it was too late, and he was left standing in the reception. He wanted to go too, but he knew that they were right, and besides he hadn't slept at all last night, and could really do with a rest.

Darwin called ahead to Tarnlough station. "Litton here. Get me Morrison please, it's urgent."

"Morrison? ... what? ...I don't give a toss what your rank is...Listen, that's not important now ... we know where McCracken is and we're coming in to see you now, okay? ... no I will not! ... are you serious? ... what? ... yeah, whatever, I'll see you shortly" and he flipped his phone closed. "Can you believe it? He only wants us to bring him a pint of semi-skimmed milk. They've run out and nobody there has had a cup of tea all day. Tossers." concluded Darwin.

"I'll stop at the garage up on the main road" agreed Harry. "It will only take a few minutes. I'll get some biscuits as well." Darwin sat cross-armed in complete disapproval. Clearly all real cops stick together when it comes to important things like tea and biscuits.

CHAPTER TWENTY-SIX

Morrison was sitting to the side of his desk, replacing some files into a small cabinet. "Sit down" he ordered.

The office was previously a stationery store, so lacked any sense of grandeur or authority. Instead of strategic planning instructions on the whiteboard, there were re-ordering procedures for A4 paper and printer cartridges, and instead of arms sign-out forms, there was a list of pen types and note books with initials and dates beside each one. Despite this, Morrison's presence made it feel like the White House Oval Room.

"We'll stand thanks" replied Darwin as he paced across Morrison's room and defiantly slammed the semi-skimmed milk and Jammy Dodgers on to the table. But it was too late. Harry and Bob were already both sitting down. They thought about getting back up again, but they considered it to be even more embarrassing than watching Darwin standing up on his own. Darwin looked over at them in disgust – *where was their loyalty?* ...he refused to sit down as well. Instead, he covered up the lack of solidarity by going straight for the kill. "You used to work for the Witness Protection Program, didn't you Morrison?"

"I used to head it up Litton. Its no secret, in fact I even got a CBE for my services there." He threw Darwin a card across the table, and true enough he was a CBE, "It's hardly confidential, in fact I would guess that if you asked anyone in this station, they would all know, and I'm not even from here. It's not something that I've tried to …"

Darwin realized he had started on the wrong track, so changed strategy, "I was only stating a fact … don't get so defensive." It was a master stroke, and knocked Morrison off guard for a moment or two. By way of retaliation Morrison tried an offensive "Oh, and by the way Litton, its 'Sir' to you". Darwin had already been trying to work out what CBE stood for so Morrison had set him up nicely with that comment. Darwin responded in a split second "Really? … Is that Knight with a silent 'C' then?" It went so far over Morrison's head that Darwin decided to just keep on the attack.

"Have you ever heard of 'WIPE' ?" jabbed Darwin. Morrison sighed again. "Of course I have Litton … off the record of course, but I'm afraid I can't comment further. It's extremely classified and this conversation is over."

"Sit down", and Darwin launched forward landing 2 palms hard on Morrison's chest. Thankfully it was just enough to knock him off balance and tipple him back into the chair. Another risky move. Imagine the embarrassment if Morrison had just stayed exactly where he was, and didn't move an inch – he was a big man and it could easily happen. Darwin was half the weight of Morrison, and if he hadn't of landed squarely and with an element of surprise, he was sure Morrison would still be standing now. Darwin realized he had now probably really pissed Morrison off, and guessed that Morrison's next move would be to jump back up and beat the living daylights out of him. This was in fact completely correct, and Morrison scowled at Darwin and started to jump up.

"Dolphin" he said screamed urgently to Morrison, stopping him in his tracks. Morrison sighed again into his seat, "Litton, you're way out of your depth here."
Harry intervened, "Okay, let's cut the crap and bravado here shall we? Look Morrison, you work for, or probably even head up, WIPE. It's an unofficial protection program that looks after Witnesses who need to go seriously underground. The operatives never meet the people they are protecting, and its all done with email and codenames. You were either Harman's WIPE contact, or you know who was. Harman's code-name was 'Dolphin'. We're also pretty sure that you're getting paid very handsomely indeed by some American agent for being an informant. Stephen is as well … and it's the same people as you. You're bollocks'd, and so is Stephen. The only chance that either of you have of getting out of this alive is for us all to work together."

Morrison maintained his 'I-can-neither-deny-nor-confirm-that' look and motioned for Harry to continue. "The bottom line is that we know enough about you to have you locked up for a long time Morrison, but that doesn't particularly benefit us. On the other hand, we need your help to find Harman and Sally, and we need your help to get the SCI's off Stephen's back. If we work together then we'll all benefit, okay?" and he held his hand out to Morrison.

Morrison held his gaze for a moment "I guess your right. Neither of us has much choice do we" and he held his hand out towards him, but Harry pulled his hand back before they touched, "Just one thing Morrison. Perhaps you could explain to Bob why you acted the way you did the other night. If she's happy with your explanation, then we can move on."

Morrison looked over towards Bob, "I have a daughter not much younger than you. If any man threatened her the way I did to you, I would kill him. Simple as that. I can't give you an explanation – I just panicked. I lost 4 of my men a few hours earlier, I lost a son-in-law, then I was told McCracken was the informer that gave over the details of where Sally was being held. I still haven't faced my daughter. I can't look at her; I might have killed her fiancée. I really didn't mean to hurt you Bob. The truth is I was guessing that McCracken and myself were informing the same client, so that's why I needed to get to him first. I was looking after myself as usual."

Bob stayed looking at the floor "Okay" she said to Harry calmly. There was absolutely no emotion in her voice. Inside, the only thought she had was to stop herself from crying. It took 100% concentration to say the word "Okay" without letting out a yelp or a high squeak. She hardly heard Morrison's words. It didn't really matter to her. It was just important that she didn't cry for now. She could work on the rest later. Morrison and Harry eventually shook hands. "Okay, lets get started Morrison. What do you know about our elusive Dolphin?"

"More than most. You're right about some of the things you say about WIPE. I can't discuss anything with you that you don't know already, but you've done well. What makes my situation different, is that I met Harman not so long ago. It is a very unusual situation for a WIPE operative to meet anyone on the program, but we were facing an unusual problem at the time, and the bottom line is that Harman and I met briefly in Cardiff. He passed over some documents that MI6 wanted urgently. It had to be done on a manned swap, so they decided that I would be the one to meet him. To be honest it wasn't really a big deal at the time – no-one knew that this was going to happen back then."

Harry was starting to piece things together "So that's what makes you so valuable to the American group. You're probably the only person who has seen Harman in a long time – probably the only person in the world who is able to recognize him."

Morrison agreed, "Yep, that's about the height of it. There is an old photo that we keep on file and drag out every now and then, but it's absolutely nothing like him now." He paused, "I don't really provide much information to the Americans. That's not why they want me, but they pay me a lot of money for pretty low level information. I only ever tell them stuff that's either widely known, or is just about to break in the press. I would never betray my team." He looked around the room for acknowledgement, "...Never!" he repeated.

"Where is Harman?" Darwin got straight to the point. "I wish I knew" replied Morrison quickly, "Then this whole nightmare could be over. I'm sure he's around somewhere. He used to live close to here. We were able to trace his computer IP Address back to an internet Café about 5 miles out of Tarnlough, so he must have lived within striking distance. Right now, I suppose he'll be trying to find Sally – which is of course exactly what they'll be expecting. They'll be sitting with her now, watching and waiting for Harman to try and find her."

Darwin pursued, "Yes, but the Americans said that they didn't take her, so who did? Maybe Harman himself – to keep her safe."
Morrison laughed, "No, no, no. Trust me; it was another group that took Sally. Probably the Centro Family, who operate mostly from South America these days. Don't forget there's a lot at stake for

getting Harman. Apart from all the pride, and families with damaged reputations, and the hatred, and the betrayal...apart from all that, there's also at least $10 million on offer, probably more by now. That sort of money raises the interests of a lot of resourceful people.

"Sally is all that Harman has left – he'll be searching for her now, and they'll be waiting for him. Either way, it's unlikely to end very nicely."

Darwin interrupted "So what do you do if you find Harman? You can't force him to go into hiding if he doesn't want to, and he'll be killed if you pass him over to the Americans.

"We would just pull him for his own safety. WIPE will hold him for as long as they deem necessary. In the meantime I'll retire due to ill health, and then the Americans will have to find some other WIPE contact to do their dirty work for them."

"You seem to have it all worked out" confirmed Darwin.

Morrison smirked "Not really Litton, but I live in hope. There's still a chance I could get out of this alive and maybe even with my pension, my family, and reputation intact. Whilst there is that chance, I'll hang on to it. If we can work together and manage the situation, then I'm sure it will be good for all our careers."

Darwin laughed at that thought, "It won't be good for my career no matter what happens!"

Morrison looked puzzled, but Darwin and Bob had a quiet inward giggle. Sometimes they even forgot themselves that they weren't really undercover cops.

"So what new information have you got Morrison?" said Harry quickly to try and deflect Morrison from watching Darwin and Bob exchange knowing glances. Morrison lifted a folder. "Okay, intelligence reports indicate that at least 3 contract firms have already successfully infiltrated the area. One is almost certainly the Centros – that's the ones I think took Sally. They have a private 'army' of about 8 to 10 men, all ex Special Forces. They live and train in South America mostly nowadays, and rarely go after contracts worth less than 10 million dollars.

"There is a North American team operating from Washington called the 'Stigs'. We have a camera grab from a Dover ferry which we believe shows Marco Valero arriving here … he's the top guy in the Stigs firm. They are mostly ex US Marines, and again tend to deal in top-end stuff, at least in the millions.

"The third group, you'll be delighted to know, come from your neck of the woods. Things are a bit too quiet back home in Belfast, and apparently there isn't as much money in drugs and extortion as there used to be, so a combination of loyalists and republicans have bizarrely formed together to chase big contracts. They are all pretty well trained, they have plenty of weapons and contacts, and what they lack in army experience, they make up for in sheer ruthlessness. These are nasty bastards. They would blow your knees off for a fiver, so you can only guess what they'd do for a few million quid. Two of their top guys were spotted in Swansea a few days ago, so they're almost certainly after Harman as well."

Darwin and Bob listened intensely. This was great stuff and they were all totally absorbed.

Morrison continued, "So those are the 3 main groups that we believe are on the contracts for Harman's head. There are of course dozens of independent contractors. In fact, MI6 lifted 2 probable hitters this morning from Heathrow. Although they are known to Interpol and the FBI, there's very little that we can hold them on unless they've got outstanding warrants, so they'll just get sent back home to America." Morrison was reading the details of this from a printed email.

"May I?" asked Darwin, holding his open hand out towards the email. "Sure, of course"

Darwin scanned across the details as Morrison moved on and continued with another incident of a suspected 'hitter' being apprehended the previous week. On the email there were 2 photographs of the men, each trying not to look suspicious, as the secret closed circuit camera watched them. FBI agents were working with the UK Special Forces at Heathrow and had recognized them from the pictures. Within minutes, a team of 4 heavily armed 'police officers' had swooped and trailed the 2 men back into secure areas for questioning. Both denied any knowledge, and claimed to be on a sight-seeing trip in London. Neither of the men had any record of how they had arrived at Heathrow, and intelligence sources were trying to match their details to incoming flights from America, but without any success. They concluded that they must have arrived on a short-haul flight under a different identity, having flown from the US to another city first, then on to Heathrow. They would then have destroyed their flight tickets (which were always one-ways and always bought on the day of departure at the airport) along with their false identification. This was a common tactic, and didn't really raise any eyebrows at Heathrow.

Darwin's eyebrows on the other hand were well and truly raised. He didn't realize that this was the normal tactic of traveling for 'covert operatives', as the email referred to them, so he was very confused why the intelligence services couldn't work out where they had come from. Darwin wandered slowly across the room and took a photocopy of the 2-page email. He felt sure there was something in it that they were missing.

"That's everything for the moment guys" concluded Morrison, "and if I get any more information, I'll let you know immediately. For now, I have a daughter who probably needs me more than you lot." It was difficult to argue with that, so they all agreed to end the meeting for now.

"Don't forget to call your guys off from hunting Stephen" Reminded Harry.

"Shit, good point" replied Morrison "hopefully they haven't found him yet" and he smiled wryly around the room. "I'll call them off straight away. He'll be safe now."

CHAPTER TWENTY-SEVEN

Stephen had retired to his room only five minutes earlier. His bedroom door was still smarting from its previous damage, but this didn't stop it sliding and dropping exactly as before to the familiar thump of the SCI's making their entrance.

Within a second, he was pinned to the bed by 3 large black bodies. The fourth had started pummeling his face. Stephen was already unconscious, and his head moved softly side to side in time with several more hard and precise blows. The silence was broken by a persistent beeping. They all stopped and stood up, each checking their pockets for the source of the beeps. Stephen lay perfectly still, totally unaware of what was happening.

Eventually one of the SCI's pulled out his phone from an inside pocket. "Yes Sir…I understand…Yes…well it's a bit late actually…Yes Sir…Yes." He turned to the rest of the team "Um, apparently they made a mistake. This poor bastard wasn't involved. I think we need to try and help him, he doesn't look very well."

Darwin, Stephen, Harry, and Bob all sat in a circle in the hotel bar. Stephen, unsurprisingly, looked the worst. The SCI's had managed to get a doctor to the hotel within 20 minutes, by which time they had more or less brought him back to life, with the help of several glasses of cold water over his head and some persistent talking.

The doctor had patched him up pretty well. He had a very large plaster above his right eye, which was cleverly concealing 5 stitches that Stephen didn't even realize he had yet. His nose was red and ever so lightly pushed to one side. His eyes were just moderately bruised, but it was inevitable that they would soon be shining black and yellow like a porcelain banana. He had a few other cuts and scrapes around his cheek, but nothing too serious. Some hair on the right hand side, above his ear, was matted and coloured reddy-black, so clearly there was at least one cut in his head somewhere. Fortunately, with the power of morphine and a few cosmetics, the doctor had turned these potentially serious injuries into 'some minor superficial markings' on Morrison's instructions. Stephen didn't really know what day it was, so he signed the doctor's medical report to that effect.

Although Stephen seemed happy sitting around the table in his state of blissful ignorance, it was simply a matter of time before the pain and reality started to kick in. Darwin was looking fine – he had no cuts or bruises. In fact he was clean shaven, well dressed, and neatly presented as usual. "I still don't understand how Special Forces can't seem to work out how these guys arrived at Heathrow" He was still staring hard at the photocopy of the email from earlier.

"Don't worry about it Darwin" offered Harry, "...there will be a logical explanation. These hitters travel around the world incognito. It's their job – they're probably quite good at it. For all you know, they could have arrived in on a flight from Amsterdam an hour earlier dressed as women." Bob picked up on Darwin's clear disbelief in Harry's explanation, and examined the photograph. "Why Heathrow, I mean surely it would be the one airport you would avoid. Why fly into Heathrow, then get a flight to Cardiff?" Bob tried to join Darwin's argument.

"They weren't" replied Harry. "They will have arrived in Heathrow because it is the busiest airport in the world, and statistically the easiest to travel under a false identity. They would not have risked traveling to another airport – especially since they weren't in their disguise any more."

Stephen was smiling politely at each explanation, not really understanding one word of it.
"Well, where were they traveling to then?" said Bob persistently.

Harry was confused "I don't know, probably to the railway station or bus station to get here - or maybe Cardiff first." Bob disagreed, "No, no, no – they were flying somewhere. Look, the sign to the right of WH Smith's … you see it?"

Harry and Darwin focused, "Yeah, I see it" said Harry. "Shit, I knew it!" trumped Darwin, "I said there was something funny didn't I?" Harry eventually caught on to what Bob and Darwin had noticed. The 2 men were clearly walking in the direction of 'International Departures' according to the sign. Bob confirmed their thoughts "My guess is that they were departing, not arriving. If it wasn't Cardiff or anywhere in the UK, then where was it? Maybe Harman has made a run for it – he could be anywhere in the world. Is there no way of finding out where these guys were heading to?"

Harry shook his head slowly, "They travel discretely, probably hadn't even bought their tickets yet."
"What about Morrison. Could he help?"
"I'll give him a ring." Said Harry, and he grabbed his mobile and marched out into the hall.
"Well spotted Bob!" said Darwin brightly.

Stephen was still smiling, but he didn't know why. He could see people and hear conversations perfectly but had slipped into goldfish mode. Look, there's Darwin, and Harry's here too. Oh, they were at Heathrow? International Departures. Nice to see you Darwin.

Hey, Bob, you're here as well. He mouthed Bob to complete the goldfish cliché.

Darwin tried to ignore him and continued, "If we could just find out where Harman has run to. With Morrison now on our side, we could get there first and intercept him before everyone else catches up. We're the only ones that can identify him, so we have a distinct advantage. Maybe we should head to Heathrow now, and wait there until we find out where they were going to."

"Maybe" said Bob in dull agreement. She scanned the photograph again. Stephen's pocket had been beeping every 5 minutes or so, and this was really starting to annoy Darwin. "For fuck sake Stephen, can't you hear your phone beeping?" Stephen reached inside his jacket pocket and passed the phone to Darwin. It was the closest he could get to responding effectively to Darwin's comments.

Darwin was greeted by 1 new voice message, and 8 reminders that the voice message hadn't been listened to yet. He was unimpressed with Stephen's uselessness, and played the message on loud speaker to save Stephen the trouble of having to hold his phone near to his ear … "Your contract with my clients has been terminated. You will not receive any further updates, and today's money transfer has been cancelled. My clients would like to thank you for your assistance. End of message."

Even Stephen managed to respond. There is nothing quite like shock to dilute the effects of morphine. "Ah well – it was good while it lasted." Sighed Stephen "but I'm sure I'll survive. Darwin, that means that you are paying me again!" and he laughed heartily, alone.

CHAPTER TWENTY-EIGHT

Things weren't going well for Morrison at his large Georgian Mansion second home, on the edge of a pretty forest and overlooking a river where several boats belonging to the house bobbed gracefully in the breeze. The plaque outside the impressive house didn't quite say '*Welcome to Grace and Favour*', but it may as well have.

His daughter, Leyla, was sitting on the edge of the coffee table. Her mousy hair was tangled with sweat and tears. She had been crying for more than 30 minutes now, so she had started to dry up a little, and her whimpering had developed slowly into gasping sniffles. Morrison was little comfort and was perched on the edge of the settee, head in hands.

Leyla held her Mum's hand tight as the 2 of them sniffed in time together. "Why?" snorted Leyla at her father, "Why?" Morrison dropped his head further into his hands. He pretended he didn't know why. "I should have protected him, but I wasn't there. I know it's my fault, babe." He reassured, "I know it's my fault" The 3 of them then sat in pensive silence.

Secretly Morrison was pleased when his phone rang, even though he cursed at it and screamed about being left alone. He took his phone out into the kitchen and composed himself surprisingly quickly. "Thompson, this better be important" he started off the conversation. "Yes sir, I think it is. Bob here has picked up on something from the Closed Circuit pictures of the 2 hitters from Heathrow. If you look at the photo carefully, you can actually see a directional sign in the background. From that, you can tell that they were walking towards International Departures – it's very clear." Said Harry quickly, he could sense Morrison was not in any mood for prolonged conversations or small-talk today.

"I'll have to take your word for that, but okay, so what does that tell us then?" replied Morrison impatiently. "Well sir, neither the Special Forces nor FBI could trace where the hitters had come from. I know these hitters use sophisticated covers and disguises, but nevertheless there is a possibility that perhaps they didn't just arrive at Heathrow. Maybe they had been here in the UK from last week, but were now heading off to another location. They were clearly not just arriving. Maybe Harman has taken off somewhere, and those guys know where."

"Its possible" agreed Morrison, "but what can I do about it now?" Harry spoke louder into the phone. "Can't you speak to whoever is holding them, and see if you can get access to their interrogation? You could maybe get to interrogate them directly, then drop in the conversation that we know they were leaving the country. See if we can get them to tell us where they were going. After all its not as if they can still continue to pursue Harman now is it?"

Morrison agreed apathetically, "Um, yeah sure, I'll give it a go. I'll let you know how I get on. Listen, I've got to go." As Morrison was considering what to do next, he noticed a missed voice message on his phone. *"Your contract with my clients has been terminated. You will not…"* He hung up quickly.

"I have to nip out for a bit", he mumbled. When he got outside, he flipped open his phone again.

"Mark? … yeah, its Morrison here…yeah I know…I will and thank you…she's fine thanks…yes there is actually. The 2 guys you picked up at Heathrow…yes, them…I need you to do me a favour. I have reason to believe that they were departing Heathrow, and not arriving. I need to know where they were going to. Look, they're not much use to you any more – so do whatever deal you can with them to tell you where they were going, yeah…I know…thanks, I appreciate it. Listen, when you find out, can you give DC Harry Thompson a call. His number is 0766875414. Cheers."

He listened to the voice message again, this time all the way through. He approached his car, and started a new call. "It's Morrison here. I need the Home Secretary, it's urgent…what!…I don't give a fuck if he's in a meeting with the Pope, tell him it's me and that it's urgent. No, now … I'll wait."

Morrison was tapping his steering wheel. One-two-three, One-two-three, One-two-three…"Yes, thanks…hello Martin – listen I'm sorry to spring this on you but we're in serious shit. Anyway, I have probably got minutes, maybe hours at the most before an attempt is made to take me out. I need you to get my family into protective custody urgently. I'm going to try and get myself as far away from them as I can at the moment. I'll head for the WIPE safe house in Liverpool. Can you get a chopper here as quickly as possible? …I'll let them know now that you're on your way. Thanks, I'll call you later."

Morrison drove outside the gate, and pulled up at the side of the road, he called 'home' on his phone. "Beth, it's me love. I'm sorry about having to leave like that, but there's a really serious problem, and our lives are in extreme danger. I need you to listen carefully to me. I want you all to pack a small bag, and make sure you have all your passports and cards. Then I need you to go down to the shed and stay hidden in there until a helicopter lands in the garden…. I know Beth, but you're going to have to trust me on this one. I Love you, and I'll see you in a few days."

CHAPTER TWENTY-NINE

Harry re-joined the group in the bar. He immediately picked up on the atmosphere. Stephen appeared to be in great form, and was mumbling about what type of car he was going to buy with all his new fortunes. Darwin and Bob had really given up humouring him by now, and were instead resigned to simply ignoring his mumblings. Harry looked at Darwin, "What is it?" Darwin lifted Stephen's phone, and motioned for Harry to follow him out to the hall. Darwin selected the last message, and gave Harry the phone.

"His contract is over. Is that not what you expected?" said Harry, "They had all but said that in their last message to him. Stephen had become a liability – he was attracting too much attention, and the police had traced him to the American connection. I'm not exactly surprised that they terminated … it."

"I suppose so Harry, I didn't really think about it like that. I just assumed it was all over for him. You know, that they didn't need him any more, so they were going to waste him."

Harry disagreed "We've got Morrison on our side now, all that stuff will be sorted, and Stephen will be fine."

Bob had resumed slight smiles at Stephen. He was on to Boats now – stuck between whether to buy a power boat or a sailing yacht. She was looking at his face,

278

but cleverly avoiding the words. Stephen's eyes were grey. They were smaller than usual, and looked as if they should have been red. The morphine must have caused them to close a little, without the usual alcohol-induced redness that normally accompanies partly closed eyes. His whole face seemed much more relaxed, again no doubt a side-effect of the cocktail of pain numbing drugs.

Bob was watching his face carefully, and musing over these subtle differences. His smile seemed to be different too – the sort of smile that came through total inhibition. A big generous smile that held nothing back, and seemed to show off every tooth, and every gum – much wider and carefree than usual. His head bobbed from side to side as he spoke. She had never noticed that before, so she smiled gently. On spotting the real smile, Stephen of course assumed that he was entertaining Bob with his boat stories, and so this unfortunately encouraged him to talk and smile even more. Bob was praying for Darwin and Harry to come back. She wasn't sure how much longer she could take Stephen's inane rambling.

His nose didn't seem to have changed much, or maybe it had. She noticed a mark above his nose, one she had never spotted before. It's strange how you could miss something so obvious on someone else's face. What was even stranger was that the mark seemed to be getting bigger. Darker and bigger. What was happening? In a fraction of a second, what could have been described as a small pimple, had turned into something the size of a one pound coin.

Stephen was starting to slow down – perhaps he had felt the mark appearing as well. Bob was going to lean forward to investigate further, but it was too late. The mark had turned into a precise hole. Just as she got to focus on the hole, it erupted, spraying her eyes with dark warm juices. She couldn't see any more. She brought her hands up to her eyes to protect them further.

Bob heard a crash of a glass window behind, followed by a deadening thump in front. She still couldn't open her eyes. She could feel Stephen lying against her legs, but she had no idea what he was doing down there.

"What the fuck...", she heard Darwin shout.

She could hear to 2 sets of footsteps running quickly across the bar. Someone moved Stephen off her legs, which was good because his weight was starting to hurt her left knee. Damn, if only she could get this bloody liquid out of her eyes, then she could see what was happening. Darwin was holding her tight and promising that everything was going to be okay, so that made her feel a bit better.

"Ambulance!, Ambulance!, Police!, Ambulance!" she could hear Harry shouting frantically in the background.

Bob couldn't explain everything that had happened in the last few seconds – it all started and ended too quickly, but she was now realizing that it certainly wasn't anything good or positive. Stinging eyes, bangs, smashes, screams, and shouts. All pointed to something bad. The sticky juices ran down her face, and just as she started to open her mouth to yell or cry, the liquid darted in under her top lip and on to her tongue. It took another full second for her to truly recognize the taste. A taste that took her back to her childhood, when she frequently had to soothe her cut fingers and arms in her mouth.

CHAPTER THIRTY

A blue Toyota Landcruiser trundled slowly along the dark country road. It looked intimidating. Its lights were brighter than other cars, and the fallen leaves and dirt seemed to scarper to the sides of the road in fear. It slowly came to a stop, and the driver waited for a few minutes to make sure that no-one was nearby, and then he made his way around to the back to open the tailgate. A female's wincing body lay crumpled in the corner, each limb bound tightly.

The driver was dressed in dark jeans, a black bomber jacket, and a black balaclava hat. He lifted a can of petrol and tipped it over the back of the jeep, then threw the can on the ground, spilling most of the liquid around the back and under the vehicle.

Two female eyes peered out from between the mess in the back of the jeep. Her feet and arms were tied tightly and she had coiled herself up against the back of the rear seats. The dark figure dropped a lit match on to the puddle of petrol, then ran into the safety of the bushes, and off into the blackness. The whooshing of the excited fire was her only queue. She closed her eyes and pushed her legs hard against the rear of the seats, with just enough power to get her to the edge of the tailgate. She made two rolls, then fell hard unto the ground. The fire was everywhere – it seemed that it was following her. She knew she only had seconds, so she rolled and rolled again on the ground, each roll taking her another few feet away from the main blaze. Flames were still lapping around her, burning off the remaining petrol. She knew her only chance was to keep rolling, just keep rolling and rolling and rolling.

Eventually she could feel the soothing coolness of wet grass, and she angled her rolls into the edge of the road. Just a few rolls later, and she was lying on her back in a roadside ditch - wet, burnt, cold, and alive.

The car had started blazing wildly behind her, but she didn't really care any more. She knew she had done enough to escape death for the moment. The driver watched the blaze from an adjoining field, partly hidden behind a straw bail. When he was satisfied that the jeep and the body were well and truly destroyed, he beeped twice on his watch.

Endangered Species

CHAPTER THIRTY-ONE

Stephen had been dragged to the middle of the room. Two ambulance men sat on the floor beside the body. There was a tube down Stephen's throat and a mask sitting at the side of his face. The ambulance men had been making a few futile attempts to put some life back into Stephen. The doctor stopped them immediately when he arrived, and was now shaking his head at Stephen's body. An hour ago, he had stuck a plaster on that very same head to cover up a few stitches. Stephen's eyes were wide open.

Darwin and Bob had avoided his glances at all costs. Harry was standing at the bar door, arms spread wide. "Can you please stay back!!" he was screaming at a group of 4 hotel residents, who were pushing and vying for position. There were also reporters who would normally be throwing questions at a crime situation, but on this occasion they fought only to triumph against one another. The view inside the room told them everything they needed to know.

Ewan was standing at the entrance behind the bar, fielding off the attempts from 3 other reporters to get into the room. "This hotel is now a crime scene" shouted Ewan, and he pushed the reporters through the back of the bar, and into the corridor at the rear. Harry followed suit and moved forward with his arms out wide, escorting the reporters towards the front door. The bar door closed, and a little decorum returned to the situation.

The doctor checked his watch and noted the time. Stephen's head was propped up on a bar cushion and he was now looking straight at Darwin and Bob. It was however an unrequited look, which somehow seemed appropriate. God only knows what Stephen was thinking. Was he cursing Darwin for getting him into this situation? Was he thinking of his estranged wife and weekend son? Perhaps he was thinking about his late parents, or maybe he had slipped into a utopian state of suspension waiting for St Peter to greet him. Or maybe he was still deciding on a power boat or a sailing yacht. Perhaps he had been whisked away into another body to start a new adventure. Whatever it was, his eyes were determined not to give any clue.

Ewan returned via the bar. "Scene's of Crime Officers will be here shortly." He informed the assembled group. The doctor closed Stephen's eyes shut and moved slowly away from the body, retreating to another bar stool to continue filling in his forms. It seemed like just another day at the office.

Darwin and Bob released their grip on one another. It was as if they could tell that Stephen wasn't looking at them any more. The coast was clear. They both opened their eyes, and slowly sat up. Darwin stroked her forehead. He wanted Bob to feel as if it was a gesture of emotion, although secretly he was disbursing some thick globules of blood which looked as if they might gain enough momentum then dribble into her eyes.

Bob liked Stephen, maybe even fancied him a little. Although mostly she only pretended to fancy him in order to annoy Darwin. Stephen had one of those full personalities. Alive, he always filled a room. She dropped her eyes to his body on the floor. Somehow in death he was still managing to fill the room. Every cubic centimeter of atmosphere was being occupied by Stephen. Every fraction of thought belonged to him now. This was his moment.

"I'm sorry Stephen" whimpered Darwin, but it was useless, there was no more space in this room for anyone else's emotions, let alone Darwin's pathetic self-pity. At least Stephen was managing to maintain his dignity. Even in death the air - Stephen's air - was filled with strong and vibrant energy. So strong that no-one even heard Darwin's weak attempt at solace.

.

CHAPTER THIRTY-TWO

The reality of their situation was finally starting to penetrate into their deeper subconscious. They had all been driven by adventure and impetus, but suddenly their adrenaline pipeline had been severed, and their veins filled with liquidized remorse. Stephen was dead, along with probably 6 or 7 others. They had lost count. What had they all done?

"When are they sending Stephen's body home?" Darwin broke the prolonged silence of Fran's Bar.
"Depends who will be doing the autopsy I guess, I'll see if I can get it done in Belfast, so we can get him moved there as quickly as possible" said Harry.

Bob was staring at the TV trying to pick out winners at the Lincoln meeting which was flickering away in full colour in the background. Obviously she didn't really care who won, it was just something to look at while her brain was digesting the awful memories of feeling Stephen's body fall against her, and tasting his warm blood. She took a large gulp of beer and swished it around her mouth. She was sure she could still taste the last of Stephen's life behind her teeth. The usual regulars were speckled throughout the lounge and 3 journalists propped up the bar, whispering and looking over at Bob every few minutes. Even they knew that it wasn't the right time to get an interview or find out more information.

Ewan approached the table apprehensively. "Hello Sir, Sir, Mam" he looked at each one individually. "I just wanted to pass on my condolences, and tell you how sorry I am to hear about Stephen. I think he was a great ..." Ewan stopped, recognizing that he was about to talk too much and loose his lamenting audience. "Anyway, I'll not go on, and you know where I am if you need anything." Darwin and Harry smiled politely to him. Bob didn't move as the race was nearly finished and she had probably picked the winner. "Thank you Ewan" offered Darwin.

"Oh, just one thing ... DC Thompson, I have had your sergeant on the phone a few times. He has been trying to reach you and can't get through on your mobile. Can you call him please?" said Ewan formally.

"Yes, I'll call him now thanks."

Ewan started to leave again, then Darwin suddenly called his name, and Ewan returned to the table, "Sir" he approached Darwin's side. "Ewan, I know this isn't probably the most important thing at the moment, but there are a few loose ends I need to clear up. Did you confirm whether there was a letter at the scene of Dick's death?"

Ewan confirmed his suspicions, "Yes, Inspector Litton I spoke ..." Darwin interrupted "Ewan, please call me Darwin, we're actually.... off duty now." For one moment, Darwin was tempted to confess that he wasn't really an undercover officer, but that split second was enough for him to reconsider. He knew that the moment he would have said it, then the adventure would all be over. Even in this darkest of times, he still couldn't bring himself to let it all end.

"Ok sir" he continued awkwardly "Yes … Darwin… I spoke with old Mrs Canning and you were right, she found the note and then confirmed that she gave it directly to Sally. I've told her that she had in fact committed an offence and has tampered with a crime scene and potentially perverted the course of justice. I was going to charge her Sir and have her locked up, but my Sergeant said that I should just let her off with a warning as she thought she was doing the right thing at the time."

"That's probably the right decision Ewan, anyway what about the forensic report on his death … murder, suicide, anything else we should know?"

"I'm sorry Sir, but despite numerous phone calls and internal mail, I have been informed that the report and all information pertaining to Dick's death are now 'Classified'. I even tried to call my cousin who works at the forensic lab in Swansea but he says that the files are now empty and the computer access codes won't even let him view Dick's records. It simply says 'Classified' and then throws him out of the system."

Darwin was contemplating the answers carefully – piecing together the information about the letter and the forensic report. He knew he shouldn't have been. Stephen was dead, and Darwin was thinking about something else. He tried hard to forget about Ewan's answers and even regretted for a moment having asked the questions. He tried to think only about Stephen, and the night they met Bob and her friend 'Barbie'. It was no use, the thoughts went from there to forensics in a split second, and without even a look back.

"Thanks Ewan" said Harry in an attempt to end the conversation and let Ewan go on his way.
"Did you hear that Bob?" whispered Darwin excitedly.
Bob smirked sarcastically and stood up. "You are such a cock Darwin. When are you going to learn? Stephen's dead for fuck sake. It's all over!" she screamed.

Darwin tried to "Shhhhh" her, but she had already finished what she wanted to say and was leaving the bar. The journalists all watched as Bob passed them with tears dripping down her face.
"I'll go …" started Darwin.
"Just leave her alone and sit down. You'll only make matters worse. She probably just needs a bit of time on her own right now." Harry said sternly. Darwin dropped his eyes and his ass, and returned to his slouch in the chair.

Secretly of course, Darwin was just happy that Bob wouldn't be running off into the arms of Stephen, so he was actually quite prepared to let her go for once.

Harry was fiddling with his bloody phone again, trying to work out how many missed calls he had. He punched a few buttons and finally made a connection. "Hello Serg, its Morrison, I'm sorry I didn't answer earlier … Yes … Yes … I know Sir, I was there when it happened… Yes sir … I did yes, he was a friend of mine … no, not yet, it looks like it was a marksman shot from outside the hotel … Yes … Are they? That's strange Sir. Ok, I will Sir… you too … Speak later."

"What's strange?" perked Darwin. Harry stopped chewing his lips for a second "The Belfast hit squads were spotted boarding a ferry last night from Wales to Ireland. On their way home it seems. Strange." Darwin chewed his lips too. He so wanted to be a real detective.

Harry poked at a few more buttons and connected again. "Hello, my name's Detective Harry Thompson. I have several missed calls from this number. Yes, that's fine, I'll hold." Harry held his hand over the mic and addressed Darwin "It's the Central Intelligence unit in London." He whispered, then returned back to his call. "Yes, hello DC Thompson here, oh yes … yes … that's right … really … today … yes … yeah

… I understand yes … ok, thanks for that. Thanks, Bye

"They had been given my number from Morrison, to update me on the 2 hitters lifted at Heathrow. They confirmed that they were indeed heading to International departures, and when they let them go earlier, they headed straight back to Heathrow and to international Departures again. On their way home they think."

"Maybe all this death and misery is getting too much even for the contract killers." Said Darwin.
Harry raised his eyebrows " …or maybe…" Ewan burst through the doors and interrupted. "Sir, sir sir …" he bellowed excitedly. I have some great news." He stared at the reporters almost leaning backwards to hear at the bar.
"Outside" he ordered. Harry and Darwin quickly followed Ewan outside. Bob was sitting on the windowsill near to them, but avoided any eye contact.

"What is it Ewan?" prompted Darwin.
"Its great news sir…Tarnlough police found a burnt out Toyota along the N675 earlier and they were conducting a routine search in the surrounding area and then …" he took a deep breath "…and then they discovered someone tied up and unconscious lying near to it in a ditch. They rushed her to hospital and she is going to be okay! She has bad burns and a few cuts and bruises, but she is going to be ok!"

Bob had stood up by now and joined them to find out what all the commotion was. Ewan was so excited, he grabbed Bob and started hugging her "She's going to be okay" he repeated, consoling himself on Bobs head.

"Ewan!" bellowed Darwin.
"Ewan, calm down" said Harry as he removed Ewan's arms from Bobs back. "Ewan … WHO is going to be okay?"
"Sally!"
They all smiled. They looked confused and bemused, but smiled never the less. They patted and hugged each other in a surreal moment of temporary relief. They didn't even know Sally, but somehow it made them happy, made them forget about Stephen for a few seconds. Maybe it was just knowing that someone … anyone … was still alive in this whole investigation. They didn't care much about why… it just seemed appropriate and Ewan's enthusiasm was pure and infectious.
"I have to go to the hospital!" and Ewan skipped up the road towards the police station.

Darwin, Harry and Bob slowly reverted to their previous demeanor. "It's all over" said Darwin slowly. Bob looked from Harry to Darwin and back again a few times. "Oh, you finally accept that it's over now do you? … You had to wait until one of us died …" started Bob, about to launch into a speech which she had been rehearsing on her window sill earlier.

"No, Bob ... you don't understand" interrupted Harry "It really is all over. The hit squads and contractors have all gone home. Sally is freed. Its all over ... they must have got Harman." Darwin confirmed Harry's summing up. "It's all over" he repeated.
"Let's go home."

CHAPTER THIRTY-THREE

Sally lay partly sedated again in a hospital bed. This time however it was in a secure ward in the main Swansea hospital. "How are you feeling?" said Ewan from the doorway of her room. Two armed guards stood either side of him inside the room and several more lined the corridor and the exit from the lift. Sally peered over her blankets with tired, dreamy eyes. "Hi Ewan, I'm good thanks, how are you?" she said surprisingly positive. She was delighted to see him.

Sally's right arm was heavily bandaged and the right side of her face was red and blistered. But apart from that she actually looked good. Her hair was swept straight back, but that was normal for Sally. Even through the effects of sedation and pain killers, her bloodshot eyes still shone of hope and genuine love. Ewan bent over and kissed her on the forehead, and smiled warmly into her welcoming eyes. "I'm so glad you're okay Sally, I really thought we had lost you" Sally squeezed his hand tight "I'm quite glad I'm alive too Ewan, even after all that's happened. When you're faced with death, even in the moment of greatest despair and hopelessness, you only remember the reasons you want to live, and I've still got a few good reasons."

"Sally, I'm not here on official business, even though I'm still in this ridiculous uniform but ..." Sally interrupted "Hey, I like the uniform handsome!" Ewan smirked uncomfortably. He was obsessed and deeply in love with Sally, but he never thought in his wildest dreams that she had felt anything in return for him. Sally giggled inwardly at Ewan's reaction. She had always known that Ewan wanted her but had never given him any hope in the past. Now she didn't care about the consequences of anything. "Sorry Ewan ... you were saying?" Ewan let his mind wander for a few seconds about being with Sally then quickly recovered his professionalism, remembering he was still his Her Majesty's uniform "Ahem, yes I was just saying that I'm not here on official business, I'm just here to make sure you're okay and ... well ... to see if you need anything. But if you want to talk or tell me anything, or ask about what's been happening, then I'm here for that too."

Sally stopped smiling. Her reality had come back. "I don't know how I got out of that car alive Ewan, I just kicked and struggled and rolled with every bit of energy in my body. I didn't even have a plan, I could smell the petrol and all I knew was that I had to get away quickly. They tried to kill me ... they tried to burn me alive. They had been quite nice to me up until then, they didn't hurt me and they gave me food and drink. I was sedated most of the time, and had no idea how long I was there, and ..."

"You've been so brave Sally" reassured Ewan. "... and I don't know how much you understand about what you've been through, but it's a long and complicated story about your real father. About a man you've never even met. It's difficult to understand Sally but…"

Sally silenced him. "I know more than you think Ewan". She pointed over to the side table. Under her watch and some coins Ewan could see a slightly burnt envelope with 'Sally' written across the front. "They caught me reading the letter, and snatched it from me, read it, faxed it somewhere, then threw it back at me, bundled me up and tossed me into the car, then it was all over. I guess they got what they wanted."

Sally could see that Ewan was somewhat confused. "Read it"
Ewan carefully moved the watch and coins to one side and opened the envelope.

Sally closed her eyes and lay flat on the bed "Read it out loud please Ewan, I can't really see at the moment, my eyes are burning and everything is cloudy. I just want to read it again and again, but I can't." Sally listened and tried to recall every moment she could remember about her father.

Dear sally

I hoped I would never have to write this letter to you, but unfortunately I now have no alternative.

I have just found out this evening that your sister Suzie was murdered yesterday. I made a few calls after I heard the recorded message from that Irish guy Darwin. She was shot by an old adversary of mine. I don't know how they found out about her, but they did, which means that they'll almost certainly trace you now.

There's no easy way to say this Sally, other than to just come out with it straight. You know me as Dick, but there is more to me than you realize - I am your father, also known as Rod Harman.

I got into a bit of a stupid situation a long time ago, and as a result I've spent most of my life in hiding. The enemies I made back then killed your mother, my dearest love Rebecca, because they couldn't get to me. They even tried to kill my father, but he escaped, although he died a few weeks later from a heart attack.

I know I have their blood on my hands, and probably quite a few more by now, but I promise you I never meant it to happen. I agreed to testify against two gangland families in America as part of a plea bargain. They threatened to kill me. The police held me at a secure location and told me not to worry about it, and then within 3 days your mother was shot dead. I had no time to think or change things. There was nothing I could do and I had to stay in hiding.

The Witness Protection Program took over the legal guardianship of you and your sister. Your names were changed and you were separated and shipped off to various homes. It was the only way that your safety could be guaranteed.

I could only watch from afar, never daring to contact you directly until I was sure that you were safe and that my identity was protected. It was the greatest day of my life when you and Suzie made contact with each other. I have never been as happy as when I saw the 2 of you together here, walking along the beach. It was a moment I feared I would never see, and one which I'll cherish to the grave. When I told you that I was going to see my sister in Glasgow, I was actually going to Belfast, just to look at Suzie. I would follow her around for days on end, and a couple of times I even said hello to her as a passing stranger. She smiled and said hello back once or twice. She was so beautiful.

Yet here I am now telling you that your sister is dead because of me. Cold-blooded murder because she happened to have the misfortune of being lumbered with me as her biological father.

It turns out that Watkins, the guy she was seeing, was working for a family that I upset all those years ago. Ironically I even saw him, and nodded to him a few months ago when I was over in Belfast but I was just another stranger in the street to him. He was obviously trying to use Suzie to find me. I always worked on the principle that if you didn't know about me, then you would always be safe. Well, that didn't work this time and Watkins decided to kill Suzie anyway. He'll be dead by tomorrow though, that's for sure.

I have no words that could apologise enough for this nightmare situation, and every day I pray for hours that things could be different, and that I could wind back the clocks. I love you and Suzie so much Sally and I hope that this last act of mine will at last keep you alive. By taking my own life now, I pray that they will finally stop, and that your life may be spared.

Please don't ever forget me, and some day maybe even find it in your heart to forgive me.

I must go now.
With All my love

Dad

Ewan dropped the letter down by his side. His eyes and eyebrows tensed as he thought through what had happened the last few days. He tried to piece together everything he could remember. Then he stopped. "Sally, I'm so sorry". He just couldn't understand how she must be feeling now. Everyone in her life was dead, everything was such a mess. The only thing she had left was her own life.

Sally lay still on the bed. Only a tear running down her cheek gave any indication of life. Ewan watched her intently and vowed to himself to look after her and love her for the rest of her life. After a few minutes a nurse informed Ewan that Sally needed some rest. Ewan agreed, and gave Sally a peck on the cheek. She smiled but she was deep in dreams, lovely vivid dreams about her beloved father. A man who had given up everything to keep her and her sister safe.

CHAPTER THIRTY-FOUR

At Cardiff airport, Darwin and Bob stood in silent memory of Stephen. Darwin had stopped apologizing now, as Bob had told him to shut up otherwise she was going to kick him in the balls so hard that he would be spitting pubes.

"Gin and Tonic" said Bob to the barman. "Pint of lager" said Darwin quietly. He was worried that Bob might constitute that as talking and fulfill her threat of kicking him. Harry had gone to get a newspaper but had arrived back paperless and grey beside them. "Pint of Guinness" he muttered.

"You ok?" fished Bob. Harry sat silently until his Guinness finally arrived "We need to sit down, I have something to tell you." They all made their way to the nearest table and Harry faced them sternly "I've just spoken to my Serg who got an update report from Swansea CID. He has just seen a copy of the letter that Dick wrote to Sally. It was a suicide note."

Bob and Darwin acknowledged his revelation. They thought so. Which of course they didn't because they were the ones that started the rumour that it was murder. They didn't really care that much. Nothing really made sense, but they pretended it was relevant as Harry obviously found it interesting. "That's amazing, a turn up for the books eh?" said Darwin instinctively. "Well, maybe since that's the last piece of the jigsaw completed, we can now forget this whole damn thing, and never speak about it again." Bob for once agreed with him.

"No, listen" said Harry abruptly "That's not the important bit, well it is important but not thee most important bit. It was also a confession letter from Dick as to his real identity. HE was Harman, Dick was Rod-fucking-Harman!"

Bob and Darwin re-engaged "Fuck" said Bob. They both sat in shock, going over the last week bit by bit. Harry kept going "It explained in the letter that he found out about Suzie's death then decided the only way to keep Sally safe was to kill himself. Unfortunately he didn't count on Mrs Canning taking the letter from the scene before the police arrived.
"Holy shit" Darwin sat in disbelief. "That must have fucked Sally's head up a bit. But…hey guys…at least we've solved the case."

Harry and Bob now considered a joint ball-kicking exercise on Darwin, but they were rudely interrupted. "Last Call for flight BD455 to Belfast George Best Airport…" bellowed in the background. They walked silently and separately to Gate 12. There were no more questions to ask, except perhaps … why would anyone name their airport after a drunken ex-footballer who would be pretty much frowned upon by most other countries in the world.

Bob thought of another question just as they were climbing the steps of the plane. "When is Stephen's funeral?"

"It will be another week but we managed to get him flown to Belfast today so they are going to do the autopsy tomorrow probably." They all knew that there was only one flight to Belfast each day, so they stopped at the top of the stairs and looked down to the right where the ground staff were loading the luggage and other freight.

No-one acknowledged whether or not they saw a coffin being carried on, but they all knew that Stephen was definitely there with them. They had famously arrived together and now they were all leaving together. It was little consolation to be honest, but even a little consolation was better than none at all.

They had all checked-in for the flight late and the plane was full, so they didn't get seats together. All 4 of them sat quietly alone as Wales disappeared into the background.

The adventure was finally over.

CHAPTER THIRTY-FIVE

Thailand is actually quite a big country.

Sam Samola is a small island about 30 kms from the mainland. Its total population is 120,000 spread across 4 main towns. The second largest town is called Mi Mi Toland. It was on the sea, as where all the others, and it pretty much had everything that a town needed... 2 long rows of Shops, a dozen bars, and a full beachfront of restaurants, post offices, banks, whore houses and massage parlours.

The outskirts of the town spread about 5 kms back into the island, up mount Simona and across the most fabulous sub tropical forest and lakes. A wooden house on stilts stretched gracefully into Lake Amin Hon, the largest and most beautiful lake of them all. It was a superb house – Imposing and opulent.

Morrison talked calmly on the phone in the Merecedes as it rounded the last few corners towards the house. At the front door the remaining Morrisons waited impatiently for him to arrive. They had prayed for this time to arrive almost every minute they had been separated.

Morrison was talking to the Home Secretary on the phone, and was keen to end the conversation as he suspected he was nearing the house where he would finally get to meet his beautiful family again. The driver kept pointing "Over there, sir" each time they passed a gap in the trees, but Morrison hadn't managed to catch a glimpse yet. Besides, he was busy on the phone and pretended that he had seen the house by raising up his left thumb every now and then to the driver.

"Yes, I know but its all over now ... I don't know what happened Martin, I put the letter for Sally there myself - right beside his body, it's a mystery – I heard that a neighbour took it and gave it to Sally, but I'm not sure ... yes, I know, sometimes even the best laid plans go astray ... yes, of course and thank you for everything ... Dolphin?, yeah he's fine, I spoke to him earlier. He's just happy that Sally is still alive. We're moving him to Brazil later today after he's been to Suzie's funeral ... yes, Martin, I understand... okay, well love to Brenda and we'll speak soon. Take care... bye."

The car stopped outside the house and Morrison jumped out to the warm embraces of the temperature and his family. They hugged silently for a few moments, and then walked slowly into the house arm in arm.. "So, how was your trip daddy?"

CHAPTER THIRTY-SIX

On arrival in Belfast, unfortunately George Best couldn't be there to great them personally. Bob stopped suddenly as she walked through baggage control and out into the real world again.

"Brian?" she shouted. A tall, older man in his late forties, tanned and grey - but looking great, walked quickly towards her and they embraced each other with the hardest of hugs, which seemed to last for ever and get stronger every second. Darwin consoled himself by concluding that it must be her father, but he knew deep down in his heart that it wasn't.

"How did you know I was …" Bob was almost crying again as she spurted out the first words she had spoken to Brian in 3 weeks. "I met your mum at Tesco's earlier and she said you were coming back today from Cardiff – there's only one flight."

"Brian, I want you to meet some friends of mine, this is Harry…"

"Hi Harry how are you?"

Harry admitted that he had had better days, but was fine anyway.

"…and this is Darwin…"

She turned to the place were Darwin was standing only 20 seconds earlier.

Darwin walked around the car park in confusion. He couldn't believe that he hadn't taken a note of where he had left his car. Stephen would know where it was, but then again Stephen was probably being carried off the plane and put into an ambulance, the lazy bastard. Or maybe not. There was nothing that an ambulance could do for him now, so maybe a special car would be picking him up, or maybe a 'coffin truck' from the autopsy department that moved bodies from planes. He didn't really know the answer, but he was sure that someone else would know and that it was all sorted. Stephen was an only child, his parents were dead, and his ex-wife hated him, so Darwin thought momentarily that there would be no-one to great him, and that perhaps he should make some enquiries, and ensure Stephen was not alone. That thought didn't last long.

"Fuck you" he shouted aggressively at the rows of empty silver cars, "I'll just buy a new one"
He walked back to the taxi rank, in time to see Bob and Brian getting into their taxi; arm in arm, kissing and hugging like a pair of fucking teenagers.

Harry however was standing under the exit sign on the phone as usual "Yes sir … yes … I understand sir … yes … that's right sir …"

Darwin waited until Harry had finished, then pretended to have just arrived. "Hey fancy a beer?" he said in an almost jolly tone. "I'd Love one Darwin, but I have to get to Crawfordsburn in 15 minutes. There's been a break-in at the Old Inn, and one of the

night porters was shot in the arm. The Serg decided that …" Darwin stopped him excitedly
"You need any help Harry? I could come along and maybe we could work out who …"

Harry almost smiled "No, it will only take 20 minutes. Joan, my wife, is meeting me there, we haven't seen each other in a while and I was hoping to ..."

Darwin retreated, "I didn't know you had a wife. Anyway, another time eh?"

Harry gave a thumbs-up but had already started to take his luggage in the opposite direction.

"Another time!" re-confirmed Darwin over his shoulder and he made his way back to the taxi rank alone.

The End

Stuart Anderson
Stuart@CapongaBeach.com

www.ingramcontent.com/pod-product-compliance
Lightning Source LLC
Chambersburg PA
CBHW060550030726
47498CB00005B/1342